I0789619

THESE GENTLE WOLVES

BOUND BY A FAE BARGAIN
BOOK TWO

CLARE SAGER

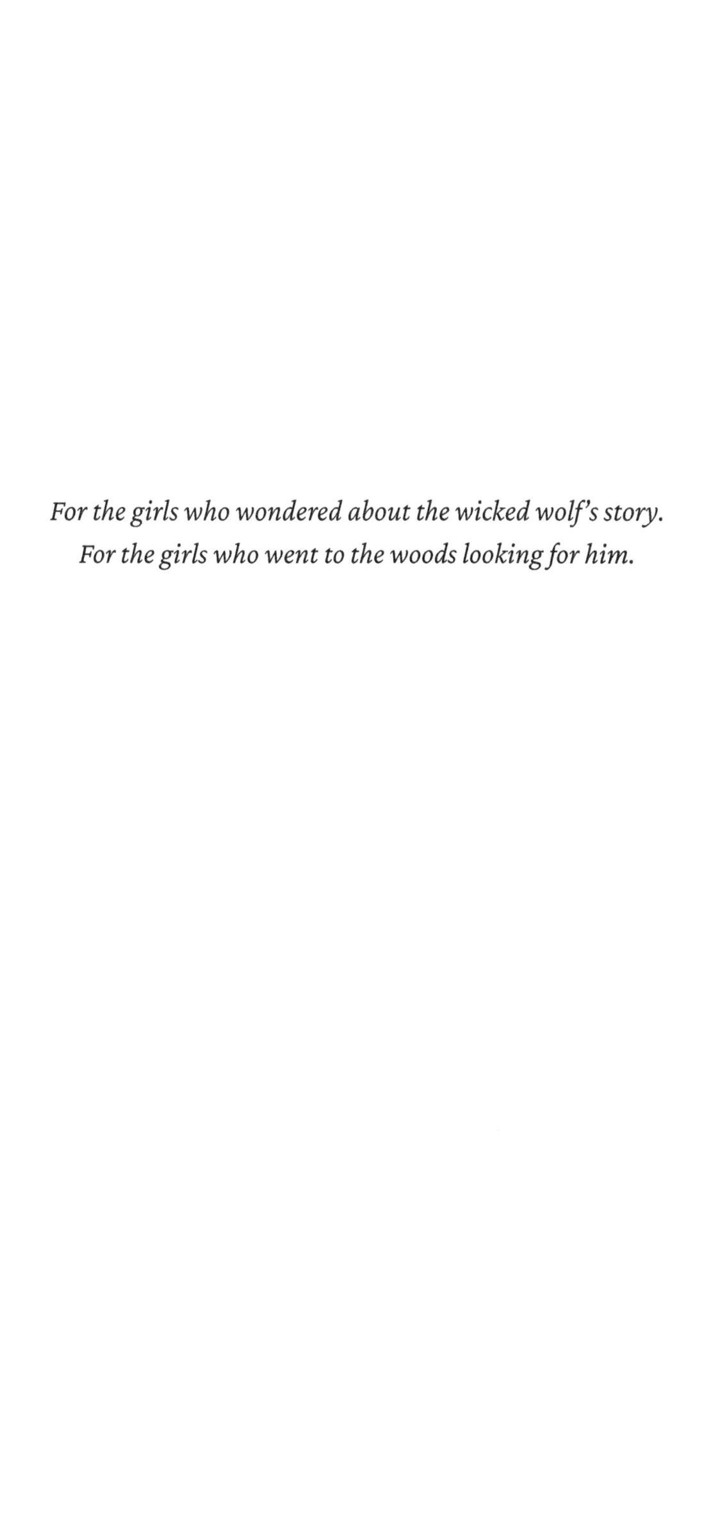

For the girls who wondered about the wicked wolf's story.
For the girls who went to the woods looking for him.

CONTENT WARNINGS

Please note this book contains themes of an adult nature, including the following content:

- Violence and injury—on the page, detailed.
- Suicide—two mentions, weapon shown, little detail.
- Threat of gendered violence—suggestion of sexual assault.
- Death.
- Explicit sexual scenes.

Across the Wall

When I reached the wall, I wondered if maybe—*probably*—this was a terrible idea. I squeezed the knife tucked into my belt. It wasn't a dagger—it was far too crude for that, but it was iron.

In a country where iron was illegal, and for a woman about to cross the wall into faerie, it was worth more than all the gold in the kingdom.

The wall itself didn't look like much, just craggy hewn rock some seven feet tall, grey and blotched with yellow and white lichen. The stories Ari's papa used to tell us said it was infused with iron to keep the fae from crossing over.

Bullshit.

It hadn't stopped that fae lord from coming and taking her, had it?

Last night, as he'd stood over us, ready to take her,

she'd looked up at me tears in her eyes together with desperation.

I knew she saw tall, strong Rose, her protector and friend. But I couldn't save her. All I'd had were words. I only hoped they weren't empty ones.

"I'll find you." I'd whispered it to her, and now I said it out loud.

This time the wall was the only audience to my promise.

I had the iron knife, a steel dagger, and food. On a whim, I'd grabbed a small sack of flour. Stories spoke of invisible creatures beyond the wall, and I figured a handful of flour would reveal any such beasts. I'd managed to scrounge an old tent from one of the market-sellers, and I'd pulled out the little pouch of coins that I was saving towards a second dagger.

Saving Ari was more important.

She had no one else. She needed me.

That thought circling, I squared my shoulders and placed my hands on the wall.

Cold. Hard. Rough grain under my fingers. It felt like any other stone wall. I wasn't sure exactly what I'd been expecting—a magical barrier pushing me back perhaps —but not *normality*.

This adventure was getting off to a good start.

Grinning, I dug my fingers into craggy handholds and climbed up. The wall was so old and the stones so rough with no mortar in between, I scaled it in moments and lifted my head for my first glimpse of faerie.

The sky over Alba—or Elfhame as the fae called it—

continued clear and blue, the sun edging towards noon. Scrubby grassland rolled away across the hills, and dark woodland pooled in a valley ahead, creeping up the slope beyond.

It didn't look so different from Albion. Maybe the stories were all exaggeration.

Admittedly, the fae lord who'd taken Ari had made her disappear in a puff of darkness, and I'd never heard of a human doing such a thing.

But I had iron.

I got the blade from the wise woman who lived on the edge of Briarbridge, the one whose house we always ran past as kids. I went to her at first light, and she understood why I wanted protection from the fae and didn't want to leave my friend at their mercy. She pulled up a wonky old floorboard and gave me the blade with the words, "Iron cuts through flesh. Iron cuts through fae. Iron cuts through lies."

Good luck to the fae who came between me and Ari.

Iron was hard, but my determination was harder. I wouldn't give up until she was safe.

Left and right, I cracked my neck, then patted the iron blade. "Here goes." I swung my leg over the top of the wall and jumped down.

I landed in Elfhame.

Sun overhead. Grass and mud underfoot. It didn't feel any different to home.

As I adjusted my pack and started north, no vines tried to grab my feet, no fae monsters leapt out to attack; there was only me and the spring day.

With each step, clouds gathered overhead. By twenty yards, snow began to fall, thick and white.

I pulled my cloak closer, fingering the oak leaves embroidered down the front. Ari had sewn it, whispering magic into the stitches. And as I walked on, huge flakes of snow flecking the green wool and melting in my strawberry blond hair, I didn't feel the cold. She'd spelled it with warmth.

"Bad luck, Elfhame. You're going to have to do better than a bit of snow to keep me out."

Honestly? I wasn't sure anything could keep me away. Not when Ari needed me.

I pulled up my hood, smiled into the breeze, and pretended the white dusting on the ground was flour, just like at home.

Ma and Pa would've realised I was gone hours ago, when I didn't show up to help finish the morning's loaves and cakes and open the shop. They'd struggle wrangling my twelve brothers and sisters without me; it left a bitter taste in my mouth as I crunched through the fresh snow.

But I'd let that fae bastard take Ari, and that was a far, far worse flavour on my tongue. Sour and acidic like bile, burning even when I took a sip of water from my canteen.

I was the strong one: I looked after *her*. But at the stone circle, she'd looked up at me, and I'd been the one crying while she'd held back, jaw tight as her eyes gleamed with unshed tears. She'd protected me, even as she'd been stolen from us.

And I'd let her down.

I squared my shoulders and lengthened my stride.

"I'm coming for you, Ari. Just hold on."

I walked.

And walked.

And walked.

I hummed and sang little songs to myself as the afternoon sun passed overhead. Truth be told, Elfhame didn't seem as frightening as the stories made out. Great trees stretched high above, and I used the moss on them to keep myself on track, always aiming north. No paths or roads cut through the land, so I was grateful for nature pointing the way.

Admittedly, "the way" suggested a more concrete plan than the one I actually had.

And maybe "plan" was overstating it.

Quickest would be finding Ari and the fae lord who'd taken her. He'd magicked her away, but for all I knew, he'd only taken her just the other side of the wall. But I hadn't found any tracks in the snow. Though the fresh fall would've covered any tracks anyway. Great.

Which left plan *B*. If I could find a town, I'd be able to ask the locals. There couldn't be *that* many humans in Elfhame nor fae lords who were bound to take the Tithe from one of our towns. Even if they didn't know, they'd be able to point me to their capital city somewhere in the north. The fae had said he'd come by order of the Night Queen, so they would know of him there.

Not much of a plan, but it was the only one I had.

Sunset splayed across the sky in such a glorious display of gold and pink, I almost forgot what it meant.

Night.

Although Elfhame in the daytime seemed pleasant enough, I wasn't fool enough to think it would be safe at night. Even the woods around Briarbridge were off limits after dark, with wolves and bears and, on the new moon, the Wild Hunt haunting the game trails.

I also wasn't fool enough to think a tent and fire would keep me safe from whatever dangers came out here after sunset. Most likely a fire would attract more attention that it scared off. So, I climbed a tree and fastened the tent between its branches to keep off any rain that might come in the night—or more snow. Nestled at an intersection of several boughs, I found a cosy spot and tied myself in place using one of the tent's lines. On the edge of a copse, my tree's position at the top of a hill gave me a view down into the valley, but its leaves shielded me from sight.

That was when I heard the howls.

Three, long and low and eerie against the rising moon and evening blackbird song.

Every hair on my body stood on end as goosebumps crept across my skin.

Although wolves never ventured into Briarbridge, they roamed the land around. When I was five, a little girl had been helping her ma and pa round up sheep, and she'd disappeared. The wolves had taken her. That night, Ari's pa had told us the story of Little Red Riding Hood.

What big teeth you have.

I shivered and pulled my cloak closer.

I was safe up here and warm. It would all be fine.

In fact, this warmth? It was that gorgeous carpenter who travelled through town each spring and always found his way to the tavern and to my table. I closed my eyes and hugged myself. These were his arms around me. I would say something funny and throw him a grin and a wink. We always found somewhere quiet for a bit of fun.

Something shrieked.

The cold trickling through me was nothing to do with the weather. It wasn't the kind of cold this cloak could save me from.

That sound.

Fuck. *That sound.*

It was like nothing in Briarbridge *or* the woods. It didn't sound human *or* animal. It was…

I screwed my eyes shut. They had sprung open at the noise without any instruction from me. I was up a tree: no animal could reach me. For anything less mundane, I had cold iron.

I squeezed the worn leather hilt.

But another shrill cry pierced the night, different from the earlier shriek. This one was sharp and brief. Not close, but still…

My heart pounded, and as much as I tried to keep my breaths quiet, they came that bit too fast and much too ragged, steaming before my face in the moonlight.

I abandoned all ideas of sleep.

A low keening drifted up from the valley. It was a sad sound that made my eyes sting.

Or maybe it was a realisation that made my eyes prickle. A stupid, useless realisation to have up a tree, but here I was.

For all the stories I'd heard from Ari's pa, I knew nothing about Elfhame and its dangers. All I had was an iron dagger and a pack full of supplies.

And it was not enough.

INTO THE FOREST

I must've eventually fallen asleep, because I woke with a start to dawn sun flooding the sky. No howls. No prowling shapes in the valley or the copse below. Only birdsong, trees, and the snowy hillside.

I huffed a sigh that I felt down to my bones and descended the gnarled oak. Considering I'd slept in a tree, I wasn't too stiff. That had to be thanks to my morning runs.

They were the only times I had quiet. No Peony demanding to be picked up or Rory complaining he was hungry. No child on my hip while I fed another. I loved my brothers and sisters dearly, all twelve of them, but they were a whirlwind of chaos and endless work.

Running was my only break, even if it brought a twinge of guilt. Between that and dagger training, I only needed a quick stretch before I felt ready for another day of walking. I'd known the exercise would come in handy, even if they would never let me join the town guard.

Stupid old men and their stupid ideas about what women could do.

With a *hmph*, I dug the loaf from my bag. It was two days old now, so it took some effort to tear off a hunk, but it was edible.

Checking the moss on the trees, I started north again and ate as I went. What had looked like a copse of oaks huddled on the top of this hill actually trailed down the far side, joining the woods crowding a rocky valley.

Where was Ari now? Was she in the wilds or had that fae taken her to a town? Were there even towns like—?

A low howl crept through the trees to my left.

The iron knife was in my hand before I even thought about it. My breaths stilled as I searched from tree to tree, shadow to shadow. No movement. Or was that—?

Another ghostly howl, this time from the right.

I spun, breaths starting again, quick now where they'd been steady before.

Craggy brown bark. Green ferns. The occasional patch of snow that had broken through the canopy.

More howls came, this time joined by yips and something that sounded suspiciously like a laugh.

Blade before me, hand shaking, I turned. My eyes strained, my ears, too, but my thundering heart was so loud, I'd be lucky to hear any soft noises over it.

A silent shadow split from the shade of a thick tree trunk. Over six feet tall, it walked on two legs, but it was *not* human—not with that long, shaggy head, the large ears, the bent, clawed fingers. It had arms, yes, but they were coated in dark fur. It didn't even bother to hide as it drew closer, yellow eyes on me all the while.

My lungs twitched as I backed away. I worked my tongue around my mouth, longing to tell the creature to fuck off, but the stories Ari's papa had told us were clear: don't offend the fae. If there was one thing they loved more than a bargain, it was a rule, and if there was one set of rules they loved most of all, it was *good manners*.

"Good... good morning." I tried to smile. "I don't mean you any harm." My smile threatened to turn into a hysterical laugh. My little knife, the blade no more than six inches long, against this beast with a muzzle full of sharp teeth. Sure, he was *really* scared I might hurt him.

Tittering laughter and yips echoed from all sides. Clearly they found it just as ridiculous.

"Is that why you bring iron into our forest?" Behind me.

I gasped, whirled, and found a man less than two yards away, though there had been no rustle of leaves or crunch of twig.

Yellow eyes, a toothy smile, more claws. He didn't have the first one's wolf head, but his fingers were long and bent. Brown fur tipped his pointed ears, and more fur peeked over the collar of his shirt and darkened his bare forearms.

Beyond him, three more shapes slipped from the shadows. Bent and shaggy, they ranged from wolf to man and all the twisted forms between.

Throat tight, I blinked and it was as though that

brief, blank moment let my brain catch up with reality and serve up the word.

Werewolves.

As clever as people; as strong and vicious as beasts. I'd never found the wolf in *Little Red Riding Hood* that frightening—not when wolves were very much *out there*, beyond Driarbridge, while people could walk our streets and taverns and be far more cruel to each other.

But these wolfmen?

They had my heart in my throat, cold sweat trickling down my neck, stomach churning around the couple of mouthfuls of bread I'd eaten. At five foot ten, I was tall for a woman, but they were all over six foot and thick with muscle.

My mind coughed up another detail from the stories: they could only be hurt by poison, silver, or iron.

I kept my blade between myself and the one who'd spoken.

He'd asked a question, hadn't he? And I was only gaping in response.

Backing off a step, I swallowed down the tightness in my throat. "It's for defence, not attack."

His smile widened to a grin that showed off long, sharp canines. "You're going to need it, girl."

Screw politeness.

He took a step closer, but I was already gone, bolting into the trees.

"We only want to play," they called after me.

But I crashed through the undergrowth, bread forgotten somewhere in my flight, one hand shoving away branches, the other gripped around the iron knife.

My legs pumped. My lungs heaved like the bellows I used to stoke the fire for baking. My heart roared.

Not a single footstep sounded behind me, but their yipping laughs and snarls said they followed, some much too close.

From somewhere behind and to my right: "We need a new plaything, pretty girl."

"Girl touched by fire." A whisper so close, it made my hair stand on end.

Movement, even closer, then snapping jaws, inches from my right arm.

Squeal lodged in my throat, I slashed and darted left, around a huge old tree, fingertips grazing its rough bark. My blade only found thin air, but it was enough to make the beast back off.

No sooner had I huffed my relief than long fingers reached from the undergrowth. As I twisted away, claws scraped my arm.

Wherever I turned, another appeared. They leered and grinned and laughed like this was all a game.

Despite Ari's magic in my cloak, a cold weight dragged on my chest.

They were toying with me. This was easy for them.

Meanwhile, my legs burned as I sprinted as fast as I possibly could—so fast, I barely had time to register the ground until it was a step away.

Mud, snow, an iced puddle. Ferns whose tips swayed overhead. Fallen logs and crooked branches.

I passed between the ferns, trying not to shake their leaves. If I could just get out of sight and take a winding path, I might lose them.

Then, a step away, there was no ground.

I leapt, barely. For a second there was only air and a brook burbling below, cutting through the soil, winding around roots.

Then, with a jolt, I landed, half-stumbled, and dropped into a roll. My body knew what to do. It was like fighting, and I'd practised for that. A moment later, I swept to my feet and resumed my pounding sprint.

The howls and laughs came from behind and either side, almost level with me. Still on my tail. Shit.

Breaths sawing through my chest, I turned downhill and used gravity to lend me speed. I jumped as much as I ran—over logs and down banks.

But their calls overtook me. They were too fast. My stomach was a solid ball, weighing me down even as my muscles burned with adrenaline.

Somewhere ahead and to the left, a howl broke into a sharp yelp, then an ear-splitting squeal. My blood ran cold—that sound was pure pain. I veered away. Had one of them fallen and injured themselves? Or...?

I kept up my breakneck speed, chest about ready to explode.

A rustle in the bushes, a whine, and one of the beasts stumbled from the undergrowth, blocking my path. I skidded to a stop, barely two yards away, fighting for breath.

My eyes burned as I stared at it for long seconds

before truly registering what I was seeing. It clutched its arm. Or the bloody remains of one—there wasn't much attached to its shoulder other than torn flesh.

What the hells had done that?

Despite being so close, the wolfman barely gave me a glance. Its wide, yellow eyes flicked in all direction as crimson blood spilled between its bent fingers.

From the undergrowth came a low snarl.

With a yelp, it turned. Behind it, the ferns shook and I caught a glimpse of a dark shape.

What was bigger than a werewolf and bad enough to frighten one?

Did I even want to know?

My legs knew the answer before my head and sent me hurtling off to the right, downhill.

Another squealing shriek pierced the air.

What the fuck was that thing? Tears gathered in the corners of my eyes as I sprinted, pushing, pushing, pushing. Moments later, there was another yelp, answered by uncertain whines. But their pursuit continued.

Ahead, through the brown trees and green ferns, a different texture snagged my gaze—large, grey, worn smooth by time. Boulders and huge stones—maybe an old rockfall. They turned the valley's bottom into a maze, and I charged into its winding pathways.

No greenery here, only dirt and shade. Yipping cries bounced off the rock, sounding like they were coming from everywhere at once, but this place would also echo my steps and heaving breaths, making me harder to track. It was my best chance.

If these monsters killed me, Ari really would be on her own.

There were no more yelps of pain. Maybe that shape had just been a bigger member of the pack and it was all part of their brutal game to tear each other apart in order to be the first to reach me.

"Come play with us." The call echoed from all directions. "We promise not to be gentle."

Fuck you. Left, right, ahead, I moved as quickly as I could through the tight passages. Gods knew if I was heading north, south, east, or west—even the narrow glimpse of cloud-veiled sky above was no help.

It didn't matter what way I went, as long as I got away from—

Something clamped over my mouth.

CAPTURED

I'd barely registered it was a hand when a thick arm fastened around my waist and the ground wasn't under my feet anymore. Something—some*one*—whirled me through the air into the narrow gap between two rocks.

My heart thundered. They'd caught me. Fuck. Fuck.

And this one was huge, his chest against my back solid like the granite around us. The muscular arm around my waist held me off the floor as though I weighed nothing. If I'd known who he was, if this had been another day and different circumstances, I might've enjoyed being pressed against someone with a body like his.

But he was a werewolf who wanted nothing more than to "play" with me.

I went rigid, muscles burning, groaning as I tried to free myself—or at least my right hand. If I could land a slash, it would burn the fae bastard.

But his grip was as hard as my iron blade.

Kicking backwards, I bellowed against the rough, salty skin and a mouthful of my own hair, but barely a squeak escaped. My heels connected with something, but the form at my back didn't even grunt.

Instead, he squeezed my forearm and my fingers twitched. The knife clanged to the floor.

I was dead.

A scrape of metal on stone, like he'd kicked the blade away.

I was really fucking dead.

Thrashing, I screamed into his palm. I tried to bite, but he curled his hand, keeping his flesh from my teeth.

"Shut up, unless you want them to hear you." A soft, growling voice hot in my ear, rumbling against my spine.

I huffed through my nose, breathless. *Them?* That meant he wasn't one of the wolfmen—or at least wanted me to think he wasn't. Still, he'd grabbed me and I had no idea who the hells he was or what he wanted. And this was Elfhame—he was fae. They were *all* dangerous. I'd been stupid to think a bit of iron was enough to keep me safe.

But I couldn't let Ari down. I couldn't—

"Are you going to keep quiet or do I need to keep this here?" His fingers flexed, making his nails dig into my cheek.

If I was going to save Ari, I needed to survive and get out of this—this... whatever it was. *Mess* didn't seem a strong enough word. Playing along might win me time and a chance to escape. I sagged in his hold as if defeated and nodded.

"Good."

The hand fell away, and I gulped down greedy breaths, tossing my head to get the hair out of my mouth. I caught a glimpse of his arm—not furry like the werewolves'.

But in that case what *was* he? Something else… something *worse*?

And was that dark, wet mark on his sleeve blood?

That shape in the ferns. A monster *had* hunted the wolfmen—something large and violent enough to rip the arm off one.

And I'd found it.

My throat closed and I didn't even pull away when he pushed my hair back. What was the use? This thing had made that werewolf screech in terror. If I tried to fight him or just pissed him off, he would tear me apart without a second thought.

"A human." His hold on my waist tightened. "What the fuck are you doing here?"

Had he really not realised what I was before now? Or was this a ploy to win my trust?

Turning my head brought my cheek against his, against the tickle of a shaggy beard. It revealed the edge of a bumped nose and, right on the edge of my vision, a low brow spattered with crimson blood.

I stared at the craggy rock opposite, since I couldn't look him in the eye. "My friend was stolen," I whispered, barely above a breath. "I need to save her."

"By them?"

"No. A fae lord. If I can find him—"

"The only thing you need to worry about right now is that pack."

The howls and searching yips filled the silence he left, some loud, some distant, all echoing through the rocky passages.

"And *you*." I huffed.

"I'm the least of your worries." His head lifted and cocked as the pack's calls grew quieter. Fingers crossed, they'd given up. "You're trespassing on their land. By law, you're theirs to do with as they see fit."

Even though that idea made my skin crawl, I shifted, testing his grip. It was as tight as ever. "*You're* trespassing too. What will they do to you when they find you?" If he also needed to escape, maybe I could persuade him to help me.

"I work for the Night Queen. I can go wherever I want in Elfhame."

That meant he had some degree of power beyond sheer brute strength. "Then tell them to leave me alone."

He scoffed, a hot breath on my skin that made me shiver. "It doesn't work like that. *I* am under Her Majesty's protection; *you* are not."

"Then distract them while I run."

He grunted what might've been a chuckle. "You stink of fear, but you don't give up easily, do you?"

He could *smell* it? Good gods, what *was* he? Still, I shook my head. "Never."

His sigh came out edged with a long-suffering groan,

as though he'd been arguing with me for hours rather than only moments. "Why do I get the feeling it's going to be a waste of breath to try and persuade you to go home?"

"Waste of breath, time, energy—*everything*. I can't leave Ari with that thing." Despite the fear he'd rightly noted in me, my throat ached for her, threatening to break my voice on those last words. Where was she? Had he made her marry him yet?

My captor made a low sound and turned his head. I couldn't see him properly over my shoulder, even pressing my face against his, but I could *feel* his eyes on me, and my heart stuttered as I realised what I'd just said.

"Sorry, I didn't mean—I'm not saying you're a *thing*—"

He gave another grunt. "I've been called worse." Exhaling, he loosened his grip just a touch. "Problem is, if I let you go, you'll be dead by sunset. You're lucky to have survived this long."

"Girl-toy." A voice snaked between the rocks, suddenly close. "We know you're in there, hiding. The longer you make us wait, the longer we'll play with you."

A promise, not a threat. Skin crawling, I shrank into my captor's hold, taking some foolish comfort in how large his arms were.

He smelled of peppermint leaves, damp earth, and a long time on the road. The last part was like many of my conquests when they first reached Briarbridge—the actor from the theatre troupe, the huntsman with his wolfskin cloak, the mercenary who claimed he'd killed a fae. They always carried that same smell of travel and a dozen fanciful stories that were meant to impress me, as though they didn't understand all I wanted from them was a good time, a pleasant distraction. A glimpse of fun before I got back to work.

More important than my captor's scent, though, was the fact his chest was a solid wall at my back, and his shoulders curled around mine, dwarfing me. He still showed no sign of tiring from carrying my full weight. Yes, they outnumbered him, but...

"You're bigger than those beasts. Surely there's something you can do." I turned and tried to catch his eye but still failed to get a proper look at him. "Please?"

A beat of quiet from him as the wolf cries grew louder, then he groaned. "There's only one way I can keep you safe." His voice lowered. "Marry me."

TRUE ROMANCE

"**W**hat?" I spluttered out the word, trying not to burst into a laugh that would draw the wolfmen straight to us. "You want me to—"

"I don't *want* you to marry me, but it will bring you under the Queen's protection. It's not forever—we can make the vows for a year and a day."

A short marriage for the sake of convenience. Quite a big convenience if it meant the pack wouldn't get to "play" with me. Still... "What do you get out of this?"

Another humourless grunt. "You're in no position to ask questions, human. Unless you want to ask them about the games they have planned for you. Though you'll have to get your questions in *before* they tear you limb from limb."

Their clawed fingers ripping into my flesh. Muzzles stained with blood—*my* blood. Would they leave scraps for the crows or eat everything, even the bones?

My heart thudded, painful. It was nothing compared

to the pain they'd inflict on me. As soon as they'd mentioned "play" I'd known they meant something terrible, but hearing it put in such blunt terms brought a horrible edge of reality to the barks and shouts coming closer still. They bounced off the rocks, reverberating through the air, setting my hair on end.

The pack was nearly upon us

"Be quick with your answer," my captor murmured. "If it's 'no,' I'm leaving. Call me old-fashioned, but I'd rather not ruin my day by listening to your death screams."

"You don't have to sit back and listen." My voice wavered. "You could stop them hurting me."

"I can't." A snarl edged his words, and I didn't doubt it bared his teeth, too. "Don't you understand? These are ancient laws. Breaking them would get me *and* my boss in the shit with Her Majesty, and you *do not* want to piss off the Night Queen. Trust me on that."

"Girl kissed by fire." A round of laughing yips.

"Come play. Come play!"

His arm tightened around my waist. It felt more like a noose around my neck.

I was running out of time. "Just tell them we're married," I blurted.

"This is the only offer I can make: marry me and I'll protect you. Or play with your new friends. Your choice."

Then a pair of yellow eyes peered around the corner. The wolfman who'd asked me about iron.

"Ah-ha." He stepped into view but didn't enter our passageway.

Within seconds, half a dozen of his wolfish friends appeared behind him. He had to be their leader.

"What do we have here?" If it was possible, his grin went even wider than earlier.

So many teeth. So sharp. The fact he was so nearly human and yet so far from it made my mind twist away, even as my gaze remained trapped on him.

Those claws. Each one was as long as my forefinger. He could tear me limb from limb on his own, never mind with his companions.

The wolf-headed one loomed beside him, tongue lolling as he panted. His gaze skimmed over me like he was deciding which part to eat first. No sign of the one missing an arm. Had my captor killed him?

"Faolán"—the leader nodded to my captor, a stiffness in his movements that hadn't been there earlier—"you've helped catch our little trespasser."

"Hmm." He—*Faolán*, apparently—squeezed me, fingers digging into my hip.

My choice.

Marry him or take my chances with this pack of wolves.

It wasn't much of a choice, but better than no option at all, like Ari. That fae lord had taken her without even asking. I had to survive so I could find her. So...

I bowed my head. "Yes."

The leader's grin grew much too wide as though I was confirming Faolán's help.

At my ear, Faolán exhaled a breath so soft, I doubted the pack caught it. But I did and it sounded something like relief. He cleared his throat. "This is my betrothed."

Now I'd said yes, I supposed that was accurate. Fae couldn't lie, so the stories said, but that didn't mean they always told the full truth. Interesting.

The leader's dark eyebrows shot up, and behind him, the others cocked their heads.

Faolán set me down on my feet but kept his hand on my hip, something possessive in the gesture.

Still, I was no longer held in place. I could run. The passage he'd scooped me into continued away from the werewolves. But they'd only chase me, and I'd be back at square one—sprinting through an unknown land with deadly beasts on my tail.

No option at all.

"Your betrothed?" The leader lifted his head. His nostrils flared as he sniffed the air, looking past me to Faolán. A challenge sparked in his eyes. "She didn't smell of you before."

Another of his pack stepped forward, mousy hair dull in the shade of the rocks as he bowed his head. "Or we'd never have dared—"

"Shut up." The leader snapped his teeth together at his fawning packmate before turning back to me and Faolán. His grin had turned into a sneer, baring his canines. That spark of challenge flared. "I *said*, she didn't smell of you."

The hand on my hip twitched, then dropped away.

"And *I* said, she's my betrothed." Faolán's voice was quiet, not even echoing along the passage, but it contained a promise of something as utterly hard and unyielding as the stones around us.

He brushed past me, one stride, two, and stopped before the pack leader. Standing in profile, he towered over the werewolf. "We are going to the skyshrine to get married."

The mousy-haired one whined and withdrew into the pack.

Because Faolán wasn't just bigger than them—he was a fucking giant. Seven foot tall, maybe more, and thick with muscle. No fur covered his bare forearms or neck or tufted his ears, but they *were* pointed ears. He wasn't a werewolf. He was something *else*.

All he carried was a pack on his back and two blades at his hips. In my hands, they'd probably have been shortswords, but against him, they were more like large daggers. He didn't make any move to draw them.

Dark, steel-grey hair fell loose from a knot at the back of his head and brushed in his eyes as he glared down at the leader. He'd stopped a generous pace away, but at that size, he didn't need to stand close to make a space feel crowded.

The leader took half a step away.

I didn't blame him.

Not sure I'd have said yes if I'd seen him first. It wasn't only that he was huge: with that scruffy hair and the strong brow shadowing his eyes, the mud-spattered clothes, the bump in his nose that suggested it had been broken at least once, and the...

Oh, gods.

His hands.

They weren't nails I'd felt digging into my cheek as he'd held me silent, but *claws*. His fingers weren't bent like the werewolves'; in fact, his hands looked relatively normal, albeit massive. But...

Short and the same colour as the tip of a fingernail, a claw peeked over the tip of each finger, rather like a dog's.

Sure, they weren't long, dark talons like the pack leader's, but they were still claws.

My heart hammered as hard as it had when I'd been sprinting.

He was almost as beastly as the werewolves.

"Will you stand in our way?" Through the overgrown beard, there were no lines by his mouth—this wasn't a beast who smiled often, if ever. In fact, despite his dark grey hair, there were no lines on his face at all. He *looked* around thirty, though fae didn't age as we did. So the stories said.

Fuck knew how much of that was true.

As Faolán stared down the pack leader, the wolf-headed one stepped between them. "She's ours," he said in a snarling voice, ivory teeth pale against the dark fur of his muzzle. "We saw her first." He was taller than the leader but had to crane his neck to meet Faolán's gaze. That didn't stop him squaring his shoulders and baring his canines.

In the time it took me to blink, Faolán got his hand around the werewolf's neck, and now the creature's paw-like feet lifted from the floor.

None of the pack made a sound, just watched as Faolán turned his wrist. It took me long moments to realise the crunch that came with the movement was the werewolf's neck breaking. That wolf head lolled to one side, then Faolán released his grip, and the creature slumped to the floor.

Clutching my chest, heart drumming against my palm, I stared at the body. Just a heap of flesh and bone with unseeing yellow eyes. Dead. So quickly.

Faolán's chest rose and fell in the same calm rhythm it had before. He didn't look at the dead werewolf. His face hadn't even tensed like it was any effort for him. He looked so... *casual* about the whole thing.

Something shifted in the air, pressing on my ears, so discomforting, I shuddered. It was like the feeling in the air before a storm, but a thousand times more intense. This had to be a warning—they were going to attack him for what he'd done.

Yet he didn't look concerned.

"She is mine." Faolán lifted his chin. "I ask one more time: will you stand in our way?"

The pack leader held his gaze.

Faolán was all stillness, the only movement those calm breaths.

At last, the leader lowered his head. "No." His voice came out louder than Faolán's, but it carried something his hadn't: defeat.

The pack whined and shrunk away.

"Then I'll accept your well-wishes for our marriage" —Faolán's eyes narrowed as he nodded—"and bid you farewell." He didn't move, just stood there. This was their land, but in the spaces between his words, he'd just told *them* to leave.

I swallowed, caught between fear and admiration, because the leader backed off, not taking his yellow eyes off Faolán. With his pack, they took their fallen comrade's body and melted away into the rocky shade without a sound.

Once they were gone, Faolán turned to face me at last, and his sheer size, the breadth of his shoulders, the width of his chest, the massive fucking height of the man had me backing away until I hit sheer rock. Then the image of what he'd just done had me pressing into that rock, like I could seep into it and disappear.

I didn't need to wonder what he was. I knew enough. He was a creature of casual brutality. A creature for whom violence was normal. A monster.

And I'd agreed to marry him.

He eyed me. It wasn't a cruel look: his wasn't a cruel face. Hard and strong, yes, but not cruel. Not as the pack leader's had been, with his sharp yellow eyes and sneering lips. Then again, I couldn't see much of his face under the scruffy beard, just that his skin was tanned like a farmer's. Whatever he did for the Night Queen, it was physical work.

He remained silent, though his head cocked briefly as though he was listening to something.

I shifted from one foot to the other, the silence pressing on my ears. "What now?"

"Come." He nodded down one of the stone passages

and started in that direction. His hulking shoulders brushed the rocks on either side.

Run.

I could.

I wouldn't.

It would be stupid. The pack was still out there in the woods. He'd suggested there were even worse things in Elfhame.

Worse than the pack.

Worse than him.

I wasn't sure that was possible. Because he'd just broken a werewolf's neck like it was nothing more than swatting a fly.

And I was at his mercy.

A Bad Name

"You need to keep that hidden." It was the first thing he'd said to me in the half hour since we'd exited the stone valley.

We'd reached the top of the hill and now strode through heathland, purple and white heather poking through the snow. His pace ate up the ground, leaving me trotting to keep up. The sun came out, warming my back, but Ari's magic in my cloak kept me a comfortable temperature.

"Keep what hidden, exactly?"

"The knife."

I'd grabbed it before hurrying after him and now it sat at my hip.

His gaze swept the rolling hills ahead as it seemed to constantly do. A braided leather cuff peeked out from his sleeve, with a silver hoop caught at its centre. He tapped it, paused, looking expectant, then scowled and continued. "Iron marks you as dangerous. Makes you a target."

"Me? Dangerous?" I laughed, but his brows only drew lower, pooling his eyes in shadow. "You're... serious?"

"As a fucking heart attack, little flower."

I'd told him my name was Rose as we'd left the rocky maze. He'd only acknowledged it with a grunt.

"Little flower?" I raised an eyebrow. "A nickname from the gruff giant? Who'd've thought!"

He gave me a sidelong look, no hint of a smile. "The knife."

So much for my joke. I huffed and took the iron knife and its scabbard off my belt before tucking it into my boot. "How's that?"

"Hmm." Whatever that meant. But he didn't tell me to hide it better, so I took it as approval. Or at least *not* disapproval.

"Say what you like about those beasts," I muttered, rolling my shoulders, "at least with them I might've had a bit of conversation."

He grunted, mouth flattening into a scowl. "They give us all a bad name."

"Ha! I've heard the stories. I know what fae are like." They made it quite clear fae creatures were as dangerous as they were beautiful. So far I wasn't sure about the beautiful part. It wasn't that Faolán was ugly, more that I couldn't bring myself to look at him too long in case he'd take it as a challenge. "They couldn't make your reputation any worse. Were they werewolves?"

"Mm-hmm. Shapechanging fae create such beings when they bite fae, humans, or other creatures."

Great, so there were fae who could turn themselves into wolves. The two most dangerous things that I'd been warned about all my life combined in one neat package. Really great.

Still, right now, my curiosity was more immediate than any danger. "Or other creatures." I cocked my head and circled a clump of heather that he stepped over without effort. "So did some of them start off as wolves?"

"Most likely."

"Huh. A wolf who turns into a human... or human-ish *thing*. I'd never thought of it that way before."

He said nothing more, just walked on. Judging by the sun's position to our right, we seemed to be heading north, so my plan wasn't completely ruined.

"So, after we marry, are you going to let me look for my friend?"

"I have work to do."

I opened my mouth to object, but he silenced me with a look.

"You can ask about your friend as we travel."

I huffed out the breath I'd taken to argue, shoulders sagging. If we didn't get anywhere from just asking, I could always sneak away in the night. "Fine."

He glowered at me, sending my course veering away. "Just don't run off and get yourself killed like an idiot."

I laughed at the fact he'd echoed my thoughts. His almost-insult didn't even smart: to use his earlier phrase, I'd been called worse. "Wow, you already know me so well. Bodes well for a future husband."

His gaze flicked away. "Hmm."

"And here I thought you might humour me to get me to go through with the wedding."

He said nothing, which seemed his standard response unless I asked a direct question. Gods, he was hard work.

"But then, I suppose for all I know, you could just use your fae charm to make me marry you, right?"

It wasn't as though I knew what fae charm felt like. Maybe that was the real reason I'd first gone to Ariadne with her fae-touched magic all those years ago and stopped the other kids from beating her. Maybe it was why I felt protective of her. But... no, that wasn't magic, it was just that she was alone and small, and unlike my brothers and sisters, she had no big sister keeping an eye out for her. And I couldn't let that bullying stand.

Faolán made a soft grumbling sound in his throat. "Charm is not my forte."

I snorted and muttered under my breath, "I'm not arguing with that."

We walked on down the side of yet another hill. Although running every morning gave me some quiet time alone, I wasn't used to being around people and having silence. Sure, there was the creak of snow underfoot and birdsong came from overhead as we walked through a wooded valley, but he said nothing. It made my back itch.

"So, is it really true that fae can't lie?"

"There's a geas on all fae to not tell a direct lie." He pushed back a fern frond and let me go first.

A geas. Those magical obligations placed upon people in the faerie tales, some a curse, some a blessing. *You must do this; you must never do that.* In some stories the hero's specific geas was impossible to break. In others, it could be broken, but with deadly consequences.

"But you told the pack we were engaged."

He stared up at the leafy canopy as though bored. "We were when I said it."

I winced. "So you can't lie, but that doesn't mean you always tell the truth."

"The truth is slippery."

Great. So their inability to lie was no guarantee of anything. I couldn't trust anything he said.

We continued in silence for a few minutes until the path branched, one way continuing through the forest, the other winding up a steep hill.

He took the latter, long legs eating up the slope as quickly as they had covered the flat. "The skyshrine's up here."

"And what is a skyshrine exactly?"

He huffed a sigh and muttered, "So many questions." He gestured above. "It's a shrine in the open air." He widened his eyes at me like it should've been obvious.

I trudged up the path after him, breaths coming quicker, legs complaining by halfway. He'd said marriage would keep me safe. It wouldn't *mean* anything, just like my tavern conquests never meant anything more than fun, but…

But human entanglements with fae always ended in tragedy. That was one area all the stories agreed on. It was why I needed to find Ari before it was too late.

And even without that, marriage was different from a tumble in the stables with someone travelling through town, even if it was only marriage for a bargain.

I'd always pictured that when Peony and Rory—the littles, as I called them—were a bit older and Ma and Pa didn't need my help so much, *then* I'd think about settling down. A man from Briarbridge with a profession, so we would have a way of making money. A sensible option. My flings were with wilder men—the ones who'd never settle down, who lived for adventure. But flings were different from marriages...

And here I was back at the start.

Even if it was only for a year and a day, marriage meant something. It was a partnership. Settling down. It was meant to be a special day that marked a turning point in my life. Ari had promised to sew me a dress for it. We'd spoken about pilfering a rose from the Hawthornes' front gardens so I could wear it in my hair.

We reached the crest of the hill. Ahead—well, I didn't need to ask if we'd arrived.

A granite altar stood under the open air, flanked by two trees, an oak and a yew. The oak's young leaves, newly unfurled, were a light sap green against the clear sky, while the yew's needles contrasted in a dark, cool shade of green.

The hairs at the back of my neck prickled, and I realised I'd come to a halt at the sight.

This was where we'd be married.
This was where he'd make me his.

"Can't we just *say* we're married?"

Halfway between me and the altar, he stopped. He didn't turn, only angled his head so I caught a glimpse of his beard and strong brow. "I can't lie."

I groaned, shoulders sinking. Bloody fae. Lies were so useful sometimes. "We could say we're engaged. I agreed to marry you, so that isn't a lie."

His head fell back, and I was sure he rolled his eyes before he turned to face me. "A wedding contract is stronger than an engagement. We're lucky—the pack yielded. The next danger we encounter might not be so easily beaten."

"'We?'" I raised my eyebrows at him. "There's a 'we' now?"

He turned, the lines of his neck cording as he advanced upon me. I backed away until my heels hit the slope of the path and teetered, nearly sending me tumbling down it.

He stopped, toes almost touching mine. Fierce lines scored between his eyebrows as he glared down at me. "When will you get it through your thick skull? Without me, you will die. Understand?"

The werewolves in the woods, their yipping barks. I hadn't even made it two days in Elfhame without getting myself in danger. He was right.

I gritted my teeth and nodded.

"You agreed to marry me, and that is what you will do."

I blinked up at him. There was an odd note of triumph in his tone.

Was he pleased because I'd walked right into his trap? This was exactly the sort of thing that happened at the beginning of stories about the fae. Ignorant human makes deal with fae creature, not understanding exactly what she's signing up for. Fae turns out to be some sort of monster that eats his brides. The—very bloody—end for her.

I narrowed my eyes at him. "Why help me, Faolán?" It wasn't his True Name, of course, but maybe using it would have *some* effect. I was surprised to find something pleasing about saying it. The sounds were so different from the names I was used to: *Fwey-lan,* with a soft *l* that poured over my tongue on a breath.

"Hmm." It was little more than a grunt before he turned and continued towards the altar.

I hurried after him. "How do I know you're not trying

to trick me with all this? For all I know, you could've staged that whole thing with the werewolves to make me marry you."

He made another sound that might've been a laugh. "An interesting story you tell yourself."

The way he twisted out of answering made my scalp prickle. Fuck. Was I on the right track with my accusations? I tugged on his sleeve, desperation to know driving me beyond fear. "Did you? Is this a trick—a trap?"

He stopped and looked at my grip on his clothing, a cold anger in his gaze.

I swallowed and dropped my hand.

"You think I planned this?" He bared his teeth. It was more snarl than grin, but his eyes glinted in amusement so I supposed it was meant to be the latter. "This was no plan of mine, little flower. This has completely destroyed all my plans, in fact, but..." He threw his hands up. "Fuck it. I'm sure this wasn't how you thought today would go, either. Fine, if you're worried, let's seal our marriage with a bargain. What is it you want?"

The question lurched through me. What did I want? I sucked in a breath.

Shit. What *did* I want? When was the last time anyone had asked me that?

It didn't matter what I wanted. This was about rescuing Ari. Well, finding her first, then rescue.

I raised my chin. "Help me find my friend." He could twist that, though, better to specify. "Help me find my friend Ariadne and ensure she's safe. What do you ask for in return?" I squared my shoulders. No price would be too steep.

He cocked his head, eyebrows twitching together. "That's it? That's all you want?"

"That's what I came for."

"Hmm." He glanced out over the valley and lifted one shoulder. "We're to be married; you have nothing more that I want." His cool smile chilled my bones.

He wanted to marry me? What did he stand to gain from that? Why wouldn't he tell me? But if I asked again now, I risked losing the bargain before it was made. And if he agreed to this, I'd have help finding Ari.

He shrugged. "I'll call in the bargain when you have something I need."

Vague. The stories agreed that vague was bad, and yet... No price too steep. "Deal." I held out my hand for him to shake.

"No, we'll include it in the marriage vows. Come." He led the way to the granite altar.

It was huge—big enough that he could lie on it spread eagled and not touch the edges. A lantern and a few little dishes clustered on its surface. Someone had left a shiny black stone in one of the offering bowls.

He wandered off towards the trees while I brushed down my muddy trousers and tugged out a burr. Not exactly a wedding dress and definitely not one made by Ari, but if it meant I could save her, it didn't matter. Throat burning, I squared my shoulders again.

"Not how you pictured your wedding, hmm?" He'd

appeared at my side, but I couldn't look away from the offering bowls.

I would pour myself into them, a willing sacrifice, if it meant Ari was all right. "It doesn't matter. After—what? —a year and a day, I can have another one." Not sure what the men of Briarbridge would think of that. Maybe I'd have to tell them I was a widow.

He cleared his throat and held out a small bunch of bluebells, the stems wrapped in a broad leaf. "I got these for your hair."

I blinked from the flowers to him, back again. They were tiny in his grip—comical against his large hands. Although his fingers were thick and blunt and tipped with those claws, he held the bunch lightly, rather than clenched in his fist. The blue heads nodded in the breeze.

Caught between laughter and confusion, I canted my head at him.

"It's your wedding day, and this was the best I could do to give you something..." He shrugged, making the flowers bob in his hand. "Something nice."

I scoffed, more surprised than amused. After marching me across Elfhame and probably tricking me into engagement, now he wanted to be *nice*. Still, good manners and all, so I thanked him and fiddled with my hair, trying to make a space to slide the stems into.

"Here." He stepped into my space, blotting out the sky. I barely reached his shoulders, even though I towered over every woman in Briarbridge and most of the men.

My heart rate kicked up as his clawed fingers came

closer to my face. Although they weren't as sharp as the werewolves' claws, I was sure he could use them to scratch out my eyes.

Good gods, why did I let that idea come to mind? Especially as they came closer, closer, closer and his knuckle grazed my cheek. I fought the flinch that jerked through me, though I couldn't stop my gasp.

He didn't seem to notice, brow fixed in a frown of concentration. Through his beard, I caught a glimpse of pursed lips.

Despite his huge size, his touch was gentle, adjusting my hair and sliding the flowers in behind my ear. With a light stroke of his fingertips, he smoothed a lock from my face, then nodded. "There. Now..." He turned to the altar and offered his arm.

If he was about to become my husband, I didn't want to complicate things by letting anything physical happen —a couple of my tavern conquests had grown attached after a few too many nights together. It was messy and took up time I didn't have. But this small gesture seemed safe enough, so I slipped my hand into the crook of his elbow.

I flashed him a bright smile, like this really was the wedding I'd always wanted. "Let's get married."

WEDDING NIGHT

The ceremony was simple and short, no witness or druid required. I take thee, Faolán, as my husband, etcetera, etcetera, for a year and a day.

It didn't mean anything—it was just a bargain, after all. A matter of convenience. Of survival.

But there was one moment when he looked at me—scruffy, gruff Faolán, who never smiled, who looked more beast than man—and the sun came out from behind a cloud and finally—*finally* I saw his eyes properly.

Soft green flecked with gold, edged with a ring of dark brown, they held me as he nodded once, sure. "For a year and a day, Rose, I am yours. I will help you find your friend, Ariadne, and ensure she's safe. And as long as you are in Elfhame, I will defend your life with mine; I will protect you to my last breath."

It all sounded so pretty, and yet...

Fae couldn't be trusted.

I'd heard the stories. I knew that fae plus human equalled tragedy. Inevitably more tragic for the mortal involved. And hadn't he himself admitted that being unable to lie didn't stop his kind from twisting truth into deceit?

Specifically, *he* couldn't be trusted. He'd torn a were-wolf's arm off, killed another with a casual flick of his wrist, and he wouldn't tell me why he helped me.

With that in mind, I spoke my side of our bargain—being his wife for a year and a day, owing him a favour. Why had I agreed to that? It seemed so stupid now.

But then my fingertips found the stitched oak leaves running down the front of my cloak.

Ariadne. That was the *why* for all of this.

"And now we seal our bargain." He nodded, expression solemn. "It is so."

I'd heard those words in stories, in druid rituals, and when Ari sewed her spells. Words of power. Words of binding. Words that would tie me to him.

"It is so."

With a long exhale, his shoulders sank. "There. It's done. You're safe."

Was that *relief* on his face? But just as I squinted up at him, he turned and circled the altar.

"Come. We still have ground to make before setting up camp."

I hurried after him—after *my husband*. That wasn't going to feel normal any time soon. "Where are we going?"

He scratched his beard, nose wrinkling as his fingers dug into its thickness. "I said I'd help you find your friend."

"That isn't an answer."

"It's the only answer you're getting. Save your breath for walking." With that, his pace sped, and I had to lengthen my stride to keep up.

He wasn't the most talkative person, but this caginess now we were bound by a bargain made the back of my neck prickle.

A bargain where I owed him an undetermined favour, no less. Had the flowers been a glimpse of a thoughtful man beneath the coarse exterior or just a ploy to lull me into compliance?

With sodding bluebells in my hair, had I just made a terrible mistake?

As we trudged on into the afternoon, I turned over his every word, looking for untruths and loopholes. We ate as we walked—I shared my bread and he produced cheese and cured ham from his bag. He continued his punishing pace, swallowing up ground. Just as he'd said, I had no breath for talking.

After lunch, he chewed mint leaves and offered me some from a pouch. That explained the smell on his breath. They looked freshly picked, even though I hadn't seen a single mint plant on our journey. I accepted and nibbled on one as we went, the flavour exploding across my tongue, making me jolt upright. It was as though it zinged through my muscles, but mint didn't *do* that.

As the sun sank and the sky blazed, he took us to a spot in the shade of a huge boulder and untied a canvas roll from the side of his backpack.

My shoulders sagged and my legs burned, but I tried to find some strength to help pitch a tent.

Except when he unrolled the canvas onto a bed of heather, it sprang up with a *pop*, a perfectly formed, albeit small tent with a pitched roof.

"Get in before darkness comes." With that, he ducked inside.

Was that it? No campfire? My stomach growled its annoyance. And no dinner?

I ate the last of my bread before following.

A pair of dim fae lights floated near the ceiling, casting the interior in a silvery glow. Already on his back, eyes closed, hands pillowed under his head, Faolán took up most of the tent. Clearly it was only designed for one person, but he'd crowded against the wall, leaving me space and a neatly folded blanket with a pillow stacked on top.

Crawling into that spot, I found a thick, slate grey rug formed a springy floor over the heather—better than the hard ground. Even as I jostled across it, making him bounce, he didn't stir.

Was he already asleep?

His chest rose and fell, long and slow. His brows weren't pulled low over his eyes for a change. There was no glint that said he peeked out through his dark lashes.

Instant sleep. Was that a fae trick or did he just fall asleep that quickly? Then again, walking all day had to tire him out the same as it did a human. Right?

Or could he just keep going? Did fae even *get* tired?

I should've asked these things and other, more important things before marrying him. I knew he worked for the queen. He said he couldn't lie. He'd promised to protect me. But did that include protecting me from *him*?

I kicked off my boots and the iron knife fell out.

Its leather-wrapped handle gleamed in the silvery light.

That was my only protection.

Because he wasn't helping me just for my sake. I'd been the only one to help Ari when the other kids had bullied her. I'd been the only one to take her food and water when she and her family had the creeping death. I was the only one who'd tried to step between her and the fae lord who'd appeared in the market square.

The people of Briarbridge had seen her in need and they hadn't helped. They knew my family struggled to keep all my brothers and sisters fed and clothed, and yet they still haggled over every loaf and cake they bought at our bakery. They'd watched their neighbours catch the creeping death and instead of helping, they'd painted warnings and wards on their doors, protecting themselves.

People didn't go out of their way to help others unless there was some benefit to them. It was as simple as that.

Yes, I'd helped Ari with no benefit, but that was

different—that was who I was. I helped. With a dozen siblings, I *had* to. If I didn't, who else would?

Briarbridge had answered: no one.

Why would fae be any different?

What did Faolán want with me?

My heart thudded against my ribcage, its echo at my throat and temple, pounding, pounding, pounding.

He worked for the Night Queen. He could be taking me to her. The fae lord who'd taken Ariadne had said he was acting under her orders. As I'd walked back to town from the stone circle, numb with shock at the fact Ari was no longer at my side, I'd heard others talking about the Night Queen. *She bathes in blood, that's how she stays beautiful. I heard she eats human hearts—lets them watch in their final moments.*

The fae capital was to the north, and we were heading that way.

My fingers closed around the knife's hilt.

It was my only weapon against him. Convenient that he'd made me hide it out of easy reach.

Fae can't be trusted. Ari's ma had said it a million times, and now Ari had been stolen by one of them.

Hadn't he gone even quieter after binding me to him in marriage? What trap had I fallen into?

A stupid nursery rhyme, one we'd sung as children, jumping out from behind corners to grab each other, but echoed in my head, setting every hair on end.

Don't go down to the woods today, woods today, woods today.

Don't go down to the woods today,
All day long.
They'll tie you up with silver chains, silver chains, silver
chains.
Tie you up with silver chains,
All day long.
And when night comes the wicked fae, the wicked fae,
the wicked fae,
They'll tie you up and steal you away,
All night long.
When morning comes, you'll be long gone,
With nothing left, nothing left,
Your mama will cry,
Your papa will howl,
But the fae will laugh, fae will laugh,
Gods, they'll laugh
All day long.

I fought to keep my breaths even, but they fought back, heaving through me, shaky.

I'd come here to help Ari, and I would. But I shouldn't have allied with a creature like the one who'd taken her.

The knife shook in my hand, glinting in the silver light.

It was a way out.

He lay there, so serene, trusting.

"Iron cuts through fae." The old woman who'd given me the blade had said it with her eyes hard, crooked teeth bared—a look of pure hatred that had chilled me to the bone. "Monsters live beyond the wall, girl. Don't become their prey."

But Faolán had saved me from the pack. Even if he had his own motives, that was a fact. And going to sleep first was an act of trust. He'd left himself vulnerable to me, even knowing I had an iron blade.

Even if they had claws, did monsters really gather a bunch of bluebells and slide them into your hair that gently?

And maybe I was wrong about him, but I wasn't wrong about myself.

I wasn't a killer—a *murderer*.

I couldn't have his blood on my hands.

Good gods, what was I *thinking*? How could I entertain, even for a second—?

"I told you to keep that hidden, little flower."

I jolted at his movement, my arm lashing out without me consciously telling it to move.

But his fingers closed around my hand, and before I'd even blinked, I was on my back against the springy floor, his solid weight upon me.

"If you're going to draw it," he snarled, teeth an inch away, "you'd better be prepared to use it." He slammed my other wrist into the thick carpet above my head and held it pinned.

My heart was no longer separate beats, but a continuous roar in my ears. I could barely draw little snatches of breath. "I didn't... I didn't mean... I..."

But his wrinkled nose, the eyebrows drawn together,

fierce and low, the long, sharp canines—he was just like those werewolves, every bit the beast I'd feared.

And I needed to defend myself.

Energy flooded me, searing my veins, lighting up my muscles. I fought against his hold, biceps burning, shoulders and elbows creaking. But it was useless; his grip tightened, making my bones groan.

But he didn't push the blade away, he *pulled* it towards him.

Its gleaming edge inched closer to his flesh.

I tried to let go, but he kept my fingers around the hilt. "No! What are you doing?" Was he possessed? Did he have a death wish? I wriggled—or tried to, but the hard planes of his body held me still. "No, no, I don't want to hurt you! I don't—"

He laughed. It was cold and utterly humourless. Practically another snarl. "'I don't want to hurt you!' Says the girl with a fucking iron blade in her hand in *my* tent. I told you..." He ground the words out, then raised his chin, baring his throat, and pulled the knife against his skin.

It sizzled.

He tensed against me, every muscle taut, as solid as the granite altar where we'd made our vows. His teeth gritted, his throat corded, and his eyes squeezed shut in such obvious agony, it seized my heart.

But he made no sound.

I gaped as an angry red burn etched into his flesh. Sweat beaded his brow.

"Stop." It came out on a breath. "Stop!" I shrieked it the second time.

With a trembling exhale that blew across my face, he pulled the knife away. He shifted his grip and at last I could drop the damn thing. It thudded into the rug beside my head.

I sagged, not even fighting as he pinned that hand to the floor. But his clasp gentled as though he felt all the fight leave me. The earlier energy had evaporated, and now my body was even more heavy and aching than it had been from the day's hard walk.

"I told you I would protect you to my last breath, Rose." His words came out ragged, as though scoured by the pain. "Do you understand now? We are married. I will not hurt you."

His chest heaved into mine as he searched my gaze. The lines on his face faded, replacing that animalistic rage with something still hard, but... But it was hard in the same way certainty was hard. "I would sooner die," he went on, voice so soft in contrast, it rumbled into my body as much as its sound reached my ears, "or endure iron's cruel kiss than harm my own wife."

I stared up at him, catching my breath. His hazel eyes glinted with that same hard certainty.

This was no lie. Not even a half truth designed to hide one.

It was a promise. A vow.

It was the truth—or at least as close as fae got to it.

Suddenly I was all too aware of that hard body

covering mine, the way his grip on my wrists had grown loose enough that I could pull free if I wished

If.

And the fact his mouth was only inches from mine.

His breath caught, so perhaps he realised the same thing. Yes, the way his gaze skipped to my lips, trailed over them, making me shiver—he'd definitely realised it. Did he *want* to kiss me? And what would I do if he tried?

Earlier, he'd picked those flowers and bound their stem before sliding them into my hair, so there was something gentle in him, despite the fact he could so effortlessly kill with one hand. And his broken nose suggested that violence wasn't an isolated incident.

But... maybe they were fights that had protected someone else. Fights in service of queen and country, rather than brawls to satisfy his own aggression. Protection, rather than violence.

It was possible.

Beastly, perhaps, but maybe, *maybe* not a monster.

The knot of his throat bobbed before he pulled back a fraction of an inch. His fingertip trailed the soft inside of my wrist, followed by the light scrape of a claw. "Do you understand?"

I gave the barest nod. "I do."

"Then don't insult me again." With that, his weight shifted like he was going to pull away.

"Faolán," I blurted, stopping him.

The hard look he gave me almost kept the words in my throat. But he'd shown me something of himself, a different angle, and maybe asking now would encourage him to show a little more.

I swallowed and took a breath that brought my chest against his. "Why are you helping me?"

At these close quarters, I could see his lips thin, despite the thick beard. His body tightened, echoing the clench of his eyebrows as they drew together. Irritated and ready to give me no answer again.

I slipped my wrists from his grasp and clutched the front of his shirt, giving it a shake. "Why save me from the werewolves? Why marry me? *Why*? I need to know."

He huffed through his nose, one corner of his mouth rising in a smirk. "It's no great mystery." The tip of one sharp canine showed as his smirk widened. He shifted, bringing that hard, muscled body of his flush against me, and bent down until his lips were barely an inch from mine.

My mouth went dry and my stupid heart didn't understand the difference between this now and the way he'd grabbed me earlier, hammering just as heavily, making my skin all hot and tight.

He arched an eyebrow. "Why *wouldn't* I want a pretty human bound to me by a bargain?" With a last flash of that damned smirk, he was gone, and I could take a full breath again. He lay on his side of the tent, back to me.

And now his earlier words echoed in my mind, taking on a whole new meaning. *We're to be married; you have nothing more that I want.* He didn't want to be married to me, as I'd assumed, but by being my husband, he owned me, a pretty piece of meat. That's what the law said in Albion—was it the same here?

I stayed there, head spinning, for a long while before sliding my knife back into its sheath and collapsing against the rug, blanket around my shoulders. I couldn't even summon the energy to pull the pillow under my head—every part of me was too heavy, too fucking tired.

My first day in faerie and I'd faced werewolves and the biggest man I'd ever seen... And now I was married to him and owed him something of his choosing in a bargain. Things were going great.

Just. Fucking. Great.

CEDARS & MIST

The next day, we walked in silence. Well, *he* did. I tried to start conversation a couple of times, but he only replied with that noncommittal "Hmm" sound he so enjoyed.

I peered at his neck, trying to catch a glimpse of the red burn. How bad was it? But his eyes flicked to mine and narrowed. He pulled up his collar and picked up the pace.

As the morning wore on, the sun soon disappeared behind thick, flat, grey cloud and more snow fell. I pulled up my hood and marched on, warm and dry. Faolán grumbled and yanked on the hood from his coat, but as the wind built, his chin tucked deeper into his collar and the wool of his hood flapped more and more heavily as it grew sodden.

By the time the heather gave way to forest, he was muttering curses under his breath every five minutes.

Not exactly the kind of talkative I was hoping for, but if it was the closest he got, I'd take it.

Rather than oaks like I'd encountered yesterday, we passed under cedars, their boughs arcing high overhead, threaded with mist. With no low branches, I would've had a tough time sleeping up one of these. Maybe, whatever his motives, there was something to be said for my husband-protector.

"Husband." I scoffed to myself, shaking my head.

"Hmm?" The dark opening of his hood half-turned towards me. It was the first time he'd acknowledged my existence in hours.

"Nothing." I shrugged. "But I need to, uh, relieve myself."

He grunted and gestured towards the forest.

As I picked through the gloomy undergrowth, his words reached me: "Don't go too far."

"Aw, it's almost like you care," I called back with a laugh.

A couple of minutes off the path, I found a suitable spot, out of sight. Once I'd peed and pulled up my trousers, I looked back the way I'd come.

Except...

I squinted at the cedars, their dark trunks pointing straight to the sky, their even darker needles blotting out the snow clouds. Trunk after trunk, fern after fern—it all looked the same.

Was that the way I'd come? Or—I turned left—was *that* the way?

I searched the mud for footprints, the moss-covered roots for places I'd scuffed as I'd stepped over them. Nothing.

I couldn't be too far from Faolán—I'd only walked for a couple of minutes. If I picked a direction and walked, I'd soon hit the path or realise I'd gone the wrong way, then I could try again. If all else failed, I would call for him.

A minute in and nothing looked familiar. Or, rather, all of it looked familiar, because it all looked the bloody same, but there was no sign of the path. I counted out another thirty seconds and kept going. Still nothing.

Shouting might attract the wrong attention, so I just said softly, "Faolán?"

Nothing.

Fine, next direction. I turned around, retraced my steps—or what *seemed* like my steps—and tried again.

After a minute, I spotted something through the trees, but it wasn't a hulking great fae, it was… Greyer than the mist, more solid too…

A wall.

Not craggy and ancient like the Queen's Wall that I'd crossed… Gods, had that only been the day before yesterday?

This wall was so smooth, it almost looked freshly built. Around ten feet high, it stretched away, left and right, disappearing into the distance. I was about to turn around, because there certainly hadn't been a wall on my original route, when a flash of colour caught my eye.

Shiny, crimson red glared against the subdued tones of the forest, hanging over the wall a few yards away.

An apple.

And just within reach.

Faolán's cuisine consisted of cheese, cured meat, and chutney. Admittedly, it was the best cheese I'd ever tasted in my life, and the chutney was incredible, but still... I'd been brought up in a bakery. For all that we were poor, I'd always managed to sneak a sweet treat from the batch, having it to myself at first, but later sharing with my brothers and sisters as they'd come along.

The promise of a sweet, juicy apple had my mouth watering.

I plucked it from the branch and slipped it in my pocket. It only seemed fair to share it with Faolán—after lunch, maybe.

Just needed to find him first.

With the wall at my back, I set off again. This had to be the right way. That was what I told my heart as its rate sped, just a little.

What if it wasn't the right way?

What if I was lost?

What if...?

But the trees ahead opened up, and that—yes, that fallen log, splintered in the middle—that really *was* familiar.

And as I stepped out onto the path, I spotted something else familiar: arms folded, leaning against a thick trunk a few yards away, Faolán scowled into the forest. "Got lost, huh?"

I picked my way across the needle carpet to him—he actually waited for me this time rather than stomping off as soon as I was in sight. "Only a little bit."

"Mm. Well done for finding your way back."

I was still blinking in shock at the praise when we set off.

"So, where *are* we going?"

It was hours since I'd found the apple, and he hadn't pulled out any food for lunch yet.

He sighed, and I thought he was going to brush me off again, but... "To the nearest town. Bastian isn't responding, so I need to try a scryer."

From nothing to throwing *all* the information at me at once. "Bastian? Responding? Scryer?"

"Bastian's my boss. Responding to me." He straightened his arm, revealing the braided cord around his wrist, and tapped the silver ring. "That's how I tell him I need to speak to him. He's..." His gaze slid to mine, then his eyes narrowed. "He'll know who has your friend. Your description could match dozens of Dusk Court lords, but he knows their business better than I do."

My mind juddered to shift from Faolán's reticence to his sudden outpouring of information. "And why couldn't you tell me this before?"

He shrugged, steps silent where mine creaked on the needles.

And that was when my stomach decided to growl.

A huffed breath out through his nose might've been a laugh—the closest I'd seen him get, other than that humourless snarl last night. Shaking his head, he pulled the water canteen from his belt. It didn't seem to ever get empty. "What's the point in you knowing? You can't get us there quicker, and I'm sure it isn't exciting information."

"No, but..." I spread my arms. "It would've been nice to know you weren't... I don't know, taking me to the Night Queen so she can bathe in my blood."

He spat out the water he'd just taken. "You... What?" he spluttered and wiped his mouth.

"You heard me." I grinned. Getting that reaction from him of all people—it felt like an achievement. "These are the stories we hear about your kind."

"Stars above, no wonder you pulled a knife on me."

"I didn't—that wasn't..." I shook my head. "I was just thinking."

"Aye. I get my blades out to think *all* the time." He rolled his eyes.

That was practically a joke. I really was getting him to lighten up. Arguing about last night wasn't going to help with that, though, so it was time for my favourite tactic. It had worked on dozens of tavern conquests, and it was beautifully simple: a question. Preferably about himself, but he seemed the suspicious type, so a question about his world would do.

"This 'scryer'—will that let you contact Bastian?"

"Unless he's blocked all contact." In the shade of his beard, Faolán's lips pursed, and I thought he might stop there, but then he shrugged. "If he's on the Queen's business, or holed up with her making plans."

A pang in my stomach had me pulling the apple from my pocket. "Plans?"

"He's her…" Faolán's eyes narrowed as they raked the path ahead, and he made a soft, rumbling sound. "Her closest advisor. When Her Majesty needs something, she calls for her right hand."

That pause. There was something he wasn't saying. A secret. Was that a secret from everyone or just me? If the latter, was that just because I was human or me specifically?

I buffed the apple on my trousers and frowned as I took a bite.

Its flesh was so crisp, it made a loud *crack*, and the sweetest juice flooded my mouth, tasting like summer and autumn, fizzing with freshness. Good gods, it was… fuck… It was the best thing I'd ever tasted. I managed a breathless moan, and sucked juice from my lower lip as it threatened to dribble down my chin.

"Where did you get that?" Faolán's voice was suddenly low and growly, and his presence at my side had gone tense where moments ago it had started to loosen.

I chewed, swallowed, shrugged. "Found it growing back—"

Snap.

It was like a god had clapped. Just once. Just ahead.

The air shifted. The hairs on my arms lifted. Something in my ears hummed.

And a figure appeared on the path.

An Invitation

She stood three yards away, black gown and white hair streaming behind her, though there was no wind.

Faolán stepped between us, shoulders square, hands at his sides near his twin blades. He half turned over his shoulder, so I could see his cheek and the edge of his nose, but kept his eyes on the old woman. "Where did you say you got that apple? Was it in a garden?"

"No." In my hand, the shiny, crimson skin, the white flesh—suddenly they reminded me too much of blood and bone. I swallowed. "I mean... not *technically*."

Beyond him, the woman's wrinkled face broke into a broad smile, deepening the lines that bracketed her mouth. "A new friend, *at last*." Her rheumy eyes glistened in the dim light as she clutched her arthritic hands over her chest.

She didn't look like a threat... then again, this *was* faerie.

"'Not technically?'" His voice was low and dark. "You... Fuck, Rose, what did you do?"

"Now, now, youngling, don't be cruel to the dear girl. And you know you can't stand in my way once fruit's been taken and eaten." With a gesture and a raised eyebrow, she fixed Faolán with a look.

After long seconds, he edged to one side, a growl in his throat.

The woman drifted closer, feet an inch above the floor.

As well as the floating, there was something off about her, a flickering at her edges like dark flame, and something else I couldn't place.

"Rose." Her voice was a croon, so much like my grandmother's, it tugged on my heart. "What a lovely name for my lovely new guest. I'm so glad you accepted my invitation. It's been *such* a long time."

"Guest? Invitation? I..." Shaking my head, I didn't have the heart to tell her I had no idea what she was talking about. Not when she looked so happy. "I'm sorry, you must be mistaken." There, that wasn't too cruel and surely obeyed fae rules of politeness.

"No mistake." She cocked her head, smile still broad. "You ate from my garden: you accepted my invitation. It's only a month, and I've been *so* lonely for *so* long."

"A month? A fucking month!" Faolán's eyes blazed at me, and I swore his shoulders strained at the seams of his coat.

I opened and closed my mouth. "But I—"

"They are the rules, dear." She pointed one thin finger at the apple in my hand.

At the single bite taken out of it, such a stark white against the crimson red, I couldn't deny it.

That was when I placed the "something else" that was off about her appearance: her arm cast no shadow on the ground. No part of her did. And the diffused light in the forest tinted my pale skin with a cool blueish tone, but the light hitting hers was yellow and warm, like it came from a clear, sunny day. What the hells that meant, I had no idea.

"Come now." She held out her hand, palm up, as though she expected me to take it.

So a mouthful of apple meant I had to stay in an old woman's cottage for a month? I didn't have time for that. I had to find Ari and save her.

I stared at Faolán and silently asked, "What do I do?"

He hadn't told the woman she was wrong or denied that I was tied to this invitation I'd apparently accepted. Did that mean I had to take her hand and go with her? Did it—?

"Oh, for fuck's sake." He blasted out a breath that was many shades harder and angrier than any sigh I'd ever heard. With a swoop of his huge hand, he snatched the apple from me. Eyebrows clashing together, he took a bite.

"Wait, what...?" I stared as he chewed, his jaw working as he glared like he would rather be murdering me. "What are you doing?"

As he swallowed, the red burn on his throat rippled.

Face hard, he ducked closer. "I promised to protect you, didn't I?"

I blinked. He was getting himself trapped in… whatever this was, so he could stay with me and keep me safe. Burning his throat on iron and now this? Fae took their vows far too seriously.

"Two guests," the woman squealed. "Come now, come, my dears." She held out both hands and beamed as we took them. "You can call me 'Granny.'"

Then the world shifted.

A Welcome

W hen the world stopped spinning, I stumbled, stomach still churning, spasming. Whatever had just happened was *not* right. Not right at all. Gravel crunched as I ducked to the side and puked my guts up. All this for a bite of apple that hadn't even stayed down.

"Huh." That was Faolán, not far away. "Maybe this won't be so bad."

I wiped the back of my hand over my mouth and straightened.

And blinked.

Because this was no old lady's cottage in the woods, like where I'd got the iron knife, this was... It loomed four storeys high, narrow windows dark. The sun cast it all in silhouette, so even as I squinted and raised my hand to block out the brightness, I couldn't make out any detail of the turrets piercing the sky.

But I saw enough to know this was a *mansion...*

maybe even a fanciful castle like Ari's pa had shown us in his books.

"Welcome to my humble home." Granny, as she'd dubbed herself, swept her arms wide. Her white teeth gleamed in the light.

The golden light. Exactly the same as when she'd stood in the woods. And here, her feet were on the floor. She turned and started for the front door, beckoning for us to follow. Not floating, but walking.

Had she ever really been in the forest, or had that just been an image of her?

Frowning, I turned to ask Faolán another silent question, but he stared after her, and in the space between us, he held out the pouch of mint leaves.

With a muttered "Thank you," I took one, and we started after Granny.

"A month?" I spoke softly. "Isn't there any way of getting out of this? Or leaving sooner?"

"Nope." He didn't take his eyes off her as we crossed the gravel drive.

"I don't have time to stay here a whole month. Ari needs me."

That brought his gaze to mine. "No, little flower. Right now, you're trapped in an unknown entity's home. *You* need you."

My eyebrows shot up, eyes widening. "You said this wouldn't be so bad."

"We don't know what she is." He shook his head and gestured to shapes carved into the stone above the door. They were almost letters, but not like the ones

Ari's pa had taught us. "That's the language of spells. And I'd bet my arse there are more on the walls around the whole estate that mean we must stay until our month is up." His brows drew lower as his gaze followed the text. "It's a ceremonial script. Fucking old. A geas against speaking of..." His eyes bulged. "Oh shit."

Seeing him taken aback turned my blood cold. "What?"

"It's a geas against speaking of..." He opened his mouth, but no more words came out. He tugged on his collar and swallowed, but when his mouth opened again, still nothing came. Sweat beaded on his temple. "I can't say."

We passed under the carved spell and into a grand entrance way. "This way," Granny called from the top of a sweeping staircase. "I'll show you to your room."

Faolán made that low sound in his throat. "Nothing we can do about it now," he muttered, angling towards me as we crossed the hall. "No harm in making the most out of a comfortable bed and some decent meals."

A month. The very idea fisted in my empty stomach. Ari would be on her own. I had to find a way out of here. I couldn't leave her to that fate.

Eyes burning, I started up the staircase.

"Rose." Faolán stopped.

That made me pause and meet his gaze.

His eyes were hard again, almost in that look of certainty, but there was something else, something edged. He placed his hand on my shoulder, its weight strangely reassuring. "Whatever happens here, don't let your guard down."

GRANNY SHOWED us to a bedroom bigger than my family's entire house. I tried not to stare, but this place was huge and the decoration wasn't like anything I'd ever seen. Every surface had been painted or gilded in gold, black, or a crimson red the same colour as the apple I'd eaten. Dozens of candles cast the room with a warm, flickering light. Everything gleamed—even the fabrics glistened, all fine silks and thick velvets. Twisting vines patterned the lush carpets and wall hangings, as well as the drapery over the bed.

The one, very large bed.

The ghost of Faolán's weight and the heat of his breath on my lips washed over me.

I'd married him. It was for survival. And it complicated things.

The marriage was for a year and a day, but nothing could stop me from grabbing Ari, taking her back home, and leaving him in Elfhame. But now we were stuck together for a month—a fucking month.

We definitely couldn't do anything, even just for fun. Even if I somehow found myself fancying a bit of something as rough as him. Admittedly, my body had responded to his last night, just for a moment. But the last thing I needed was for him to catch feelings—or *think* he had.

Humans. Fae. Tragedy. End of story.

At least he hadn't shown any desire to call in our bargain or make the most of the "pretty human" now bound to him.

"I'll leave you two to settle in to your room for the next month. You'll be able to leave at dawn after your thirtieth night. In the meantime, the house will look after you. Supper will be along soon. If you need anything else, just ask." Granny smiled from the doorway and disappeared.

Faolán scratched the back of his neck, staring at the closed door for long seconds. "Hmm."

I hefted my bag onto an armchair by the fire. "What do you think she is?"

"Not sure. Just remember what I said—"

"'Don't let your guard down.' Got it."

His eyes narrowed on me, then he threw his backpack onto the sofa that matched my armchair. "She'd better be quick with that food she promised. Now, if I'm right..." He opened a door I hadn't noticed, half-hidden in a wooden panel, and groaned. "Oh, Stars a-fucking-bove. Jackpot."

"What is—?"

He disappeared before I could finish, and a moment later the sound of running water drifted through the open door.

Running water? Wow, this place really was fancy. I'd heard the Hawthornes had it, but had never *seen* such a thing. I hurried over, about to peer inside, when the door shut in my face.

"Suppose it's your turn first." I sighed. He *did* look like he'd been on the road a long time, so I busied myself exploring our room. A fire roared in the hearth, warming the space, so I pulled off my cloak and opened the wardrobe and...

It was full of clothes already. Faolán hadn't even opened his bag yet, so they couldn't be his.

I peered more closely. Brocade and satin, gauzy chiffon and organza, all in colours so rich it was as though I'd never truly seen the world before. Midnight blue velvet studded with silver stars. Slippery golden fabric, so heavy it could be made of real gold. Deepest, darkest black. And plenty of that crimson red that wove through the house's decor.

When I pulled out a piece of wine-red velvet so soft it made me gasp, I found it was a gown. It didn't tug on me in the same magic-touched way Ari's sewing did, but it was so beautiful, I couldn't help but hold it up, careful not to let it touch my dirty clothes.

I looked into the mirror that stood next to a tall chest of drawers. Grimy, strawberry blond hair coming out of its braid, I was a mess, but the gown? It would be pretty damn close to a perfect fit.

And a midnight blue suit alongside it was cut wide enough to fit Faolán. The fae lord who'd taken Ari was tall and broad, but nowhere near as big as Faolán, so not all fae men were his size. It didn't *feel* like coincidence, either.

I grabbed another garment. A gown in my size. And the next? A jacket in his.

Worrying my lip between my teeth, I shook my head. "What *is* this?"

The rattle of wood on wood had me turning on my heel with a gasp.

But there was no one there.

I peered behind the wardrobe, under the bed. No one hiding. I held my breath, listened.

Another rattle—or more of a clatter, perhaps—from the tall chest of drawers.

Something was in the drawer.

INK & SILVER

The drawer jiggled again.

Heart beating just a little too hard, I crept closer and grabbed a hefty candlestick. That seemed a safer bet than my iron knife—if we were stuck with Granny for a whole month, I didn't want to insult her on the first day. I blew out the candle and deposited it on the side, never taking my eyes off the drawer.

When I was in arm's reach, it went still.

Candlestick raised, I pulled it open.

Despite my tight muscles, there was no movement within, no creature, just...

"Oh!" The sound fell from me in a breath that fluttered the delicate items inside.

I put the candlestick down, transfixed by the frothy lace and fabrics so lightweight, my breath had disturbed them. A black nightdress that looked like it would fall apart if I looked at it wrong. A tiny pair of... "Is this meant to be *underwear*?"

Castors squeaking, the mirror slid out from beside the drawers. I almost inhaled the underthings, I gasped so hard. The mirror tilted, revealing my reflection.

My eyes were so wide, I could see the whites all the way around the sky blue irises, and my mouth formed a perfect *O*.

I held my breath and peered around the mirror. Nothing behind it—no *one* behind it.

What the hells was this? Maybe I should ask Granny.

"The house will look after you," she'd said.

I worked my tongue around my dry mouth. "Is this... are you the house?"

The mirror tilted up and down, creaking, and the drawer I'd opened shuffled.

I stared at these objects moving *on their own*. Either it was the house or someone had put together some sort of intricate pulley system—an invisible one, at that.

I *was* in Elfhame, so... "The former it is." Nodding, I gave a shaky laugh. "Nice to—uh—meet you? I'm Rose. Can you speak?"

The mirror swivelled side to side, the motion like a head shaking.

"Do you have a name?"

Stillness.

Did my question break some rule of faerie that I didn't know?

Then the mirror rolled from left to right on its squeaky castors, slower. Was that uncertainty?

"Then, can I call you House?"

The up and down tilt again. That had to be a nod.

So the house had created these clothes. And did that mean it was trying to give me this tiny wisp of underwear?

Tied at the hips with satin bows, it was beautiful, but... "I'm not sure it's the best idea for me to wear this...." I held up the sheer nightdress. "*Or* this. He's"—I glanced at the bathroom door—"well, we're married, but... not *really*."

After a brief pause, another drawer slid open. Inside, I found a nightdress made of soft linen. A flounce of lace decorated the low neckline and hem, but it wasn't see-through.

"Much better. Thank you." I patted the chest of drawers.

The mirror wheeled back into place, then a clatter of crockery came from near the fireplace. On the table by the chairs had appeared a tea service, steam drifting from the teapot's spout, and a plate full of sausage rolls and little pies.

I groaned at the savoury smell of herbs and spices and perfectly baked pastry and threw myself at the table. "Thank you, House. Did you make this yourself?" Or was there a chef hidden away in a kitchen somewhere? I had no idea of the building's layout. I'd have to explore.

The plate slid towards me. I took that as a *yes*.

I put down my makeshift weapon and it was only now I took a closer look. What I'd thought were golden branches and twigs... No, I'd never seen twigs with joints like that. And branches didn't have bulbous ends that looked like they would fit perfectly into a socket. The candlestick was made in the form of dozens of tiny bones, vines growing between them. I shivered and backed away. What an odd choice of decor.

And it was only now, as I looked a little more closely at *everything* that I noticed the crack in the mirror's frame, the tattiness of the curtains, the threadbare patch on the armchair.

Still, the house was bigger and more luxurious than anything I'd ever seen, and most importantly, I had food—food that smelled wonderful, at that.

Mouth watering, I picked up one of the sausage rolls, and the cheerful blaze in the fireplace stilled. The clock on the mantlepiece stopped.

It was as if the house held its breath.

Ma always did that when she invented some new cake or pastry and gave it to us to try, waiting on our verdict. It warmed my chest and ached in my heart all at once. How were they doing without me?

I raised the sausage roll in a salute to the fireplace, then took a bite. The pastry crunched, its buttery scent coating my mouth a split second before the rich meat inside hit my tongue, salty and rich with pepper, sage, parsley, and just the right amount of thyme. I couldn't help but groan. It rivalled even Ma's best work.

"Incredible," I muttered before devouring the rest of the sausage roll.

The fire leapt back to flickering life, and the clock resumed its steady *tick tick tick*.

The food kept me occupied until the bathroom door opened again.

Faolán came through, towelling his hair, and the breath caught in my throat, nearly making me choke on my sip of tea.

He'd tied a towel around his waist, but that was it. Even that stopped far short of his knees, giving me a generous eyeful of thick, muscled thighs as he stepped into the room.

And above the towel...

If there had been any doubt whether that bulk under his clothes was all muscle, it was gone now.

But I hadn't predicted the black and grey ink etched into his skin. An organic pattern covered the expanse of his chest—leaping and intertwined shapes. Were they creatures? I couldn't tell from here. They ran down his arms, dancing with the intriguing shadows that flexed as he rubbed the towel through his hair. The ink faded out to ghostly grey, then nothingness by the time it reached his wrists.

Amongst the tattoos, dark hair flecked his chest and the packed muscle of his belly, trailing down beneath his towel. A path my gaze couldn't help following, though it snagged on something else that also cut through the tattoos, silvery pale in the candlelight.

I swallowed the tea and sucked in a deep breath, face suddenly hot.

"Sorry to hog the bath." It was Faolán's voice, but when he pulled the towel away from his head—the man in the doorway was *not* the man I'd married yesterday afternoon.

He'd shaved, revealing a square jaw and strong chin

lined with candlelight. His hair had been brushed and also trimmed to his shoulders, leaving the damp lengths to frame his face.

"I needed that." The sigh he gave was one of such pure relief, I believed him. "Been on the road far too long." The edge of an apologetic smile teased his mouth, which I could finally see properly. Not too full, not too thin, with an angular cupid's bow.

It was a mouth that promised something hard and unyielding. Something that made me press my thighs together.

Because, damn it, he was far more attractive than he had any right to be and more *neat* than I'd ever expected. And yet...

Even trimmed and clean, a rugged edge clung to his solid lines and sheer size.

Still beastly, but a gorgeous beast.

"Oh, food, thank the gods." He came closer, and although his steps were silent, I felt each one tremble through the floor. His scent reached me first: bay and mint, woody and fresh.

The candles flared brighter, their golden light playing with the planes and shadows of his body, making the inked shapes seem to move.

It was only now I realised they were wolves. Stylised versions, sketched in rough lines, but those dark eyes, the large ears, the sharp teeth—definitely wolves. Playing and fighting, twisting together, leaping and howling.

And the silvery lines? Scars. The ink overlayed them,

following their angles, as though the tattoos had been designed to work *with* the slashes.

Who had done that to him? My jaw tightened. And why? Something about the repeated shapes, the similarity, and the way they covered him so thoroughly told me he'd taken a bad, *bad* beating.

"Rose? Are you all right?"

I blinked up at him, opened and closed my mouth. I'd been staring, wordlessly.

"Uh. Yes. I… I've never seen tattoos like that. They're beautiful."

"Mm." He nodded acknowledgement, surveying the plate of food. Another platter appeared, this one twice the size.

I gestured towards them. "When Granny said the house would take care of us, she meant it literally."

"Looks like it." Eyebrows rising, he nodded more enthusiastically before popping a sausage roll in his mouth, whole. "Stars above." His eyes widened as he chewed. "These are fucking incredible."

"That's what I said."

"Mm-hmm." He grabbed one of the little pies, which were filled with venison, juniper, rosemary, and I *thought* I'd caught a hint of sweet-sharp rhubarb.

My lips quirked at the size of it in his huge hands.

With the pie halfway to his mouth, he jerked his chin towards the panelled door. "I've drawn you a bath, too."

I blinked, eyebrows shooting up before I hurried to the bathroom. "Thank you."

I'd inadvertently married the most oddly attractive

man I'd ever met, who could use his hands to kill a were-wolf or run me a bath. That was... unexpected.

This sham marriage was supposed to ensure my safety, but it felt suddenly dangerous, and not in the way the werewolf pack had been dangerous.

He was a killer, no stranger to violence. I had to remember that.

Humans and fae. Tragedy. I had to remember that, too.

And the fact I was only in Elfhame to save Ari. Even if I was stuck here for a month, I'd get right back on the road after and find her. Maybe there was a way I could get out of here and reach her sooner.

Still, when I reached the bathroom door, I glanced back at him.

More tattoos etched the expanse of his back. An arc of moons marked the phases from new to full and back again across his shoulder blades. The night sky, full of dark clouds and constellations covered his skin, fading towards a horizon formed by the towel around his waist. More scars traced silvery lines through the inkwork, many of them incorporated into the constellations, linking stars.

As he picked up another morsel from the tray, the tattoos shifted, following the flex of his muscles, making my mouth suddenly dry.

Eyes screwed shut, I dragged myself into the bathroom.

Steaming water gushed into a large bath. Large enough for two, my traitorous mind pointed out.

"Nope," I muttered to myself. "Not happening."

The bath stood at the centre of the room, clawed brass feet resting on the tiles. Even the taps had matching claws as though a huge bird clutched the bath's edge. Foam frothed so thick, I couldn't see the water's surface.

For me, "a bath" meant a copper tub in front of the fire and waiting my turn after all my brothers and sisters so I could attempt to get clean in murky lukewarm water with a scrap of plain soap. For my birthday one year, Ari had gifted me a tiny round of lilac and honeysuckle soap, with strict instructions that it was only for me to use. I'd treasured it, using a tiny amount each time and hiding it away from the rest of the house. Eventually it had run out.

Now, the scent of lilac and honeysuckle wafted through the room, cut through with something citrus— orange? I let out a soft laugh. Somehow the house knew my favourite combination of scents, *and* how to add another to round them out.

"Amazing." I shook my head and turned off the taps.

"By the way…"

I whirled and found Faolán standing there, still clad in only a towel, filling the doorway.

"I used a bit of that and that"—he pointed at a shelf with two dainty bottles—"for you, together with a dash of orange, but if you want to add anything else, there's more in the cabinet."

"You…" I blinked at him, at the little, labelled bottles. "You picked those out?" The idea of this hulk of a man pouring those into my bath was both amusing and... sweet.

With a shrug, he cleared his throat, the sound gravelly. "I caught the scent of lilac and honeysuckle on your hair and cloak—I figured they were ones you liked. Orange works well with them." His face screwed up. "Call it a peace offering for diving in here first. Also, use that shampoo." He pointed at another larger bottle on a stand by the bath. "The mint makes your scalp tingle."

Then he was gone, the door clicking shut behind him.

My gorgeous fae beast of a husband whose body looked like the model for a statue also knew how to pick out incredible scent combinations.

And I had to share a bed with that.

I was in so much trouble.

When I emerged from my bath, Faolán had, mercifully, put on some clothes. A black shirt and trousers, simple but neat and perfectly tailored. He stood at the mirror, fastening a button.

"Not a dirty, stinking dog after all," he muttered with the bitter edge of a smile.

"I never called you—"

"Not you." He huffed and shook his head.

Someone else had called him that, and something about who'd said it or how they'd said it had made it stick with him. I gripped the tie of my dressing gown. He'd smelled of the road before his bath, yes, but he didn't *stink*.

"I am sorry, though."

He raked his fingers through his hair, pulling the lengths from his face, then canted his head at me. "For...?"

"Your appearance scared me at first."

He snorted and grabbed a comb from the chest of drawers. "I get that a lot. And in my line of work, it's useful."

I narrowed my eyes as he combed his hair even though he'd clearly already brushed it. "But not the full picture, I think. The flower was kind. And the bath was thoughtful."

"Mm." He stood back and shrugged, replacing the comb. "Didn't want you to bolt."

But when he turned to face me, there was no hardness in his eyes.

Yes, I had to crane my neck to meet his gaze, and if I tried, I was sure I wouldn't be able to get my arms around him. Although he'd only just shaved, the promise of stubble already shadowed his cheeks and jaw. But this neatness in his combed hair and the shirt with its sleeves carefully rolled up to his elbows—it suited him far better than the road worn clothes and dirt.

"Hmm." I tugged at my lower lip, and he shifted as I turned his own sound back on him. *Ha*, he didn't like it when the tables were turned. I grinned. "Now you look more like your personality." Not *entirely* a beast.

He gave me a long look, slight crease between his eyebrows.

We didn't say anything more about it. I dressed behind a screen, and a note appeared from Granny together with more food. "'I'm sure you're tired, so here's an informal supper,'" Faolán read out. "'We'll get to know each other better tomorrow.' Hmm." He frowned out the window and glanced at the mantlepiece where the clock *tick tick ticked*. "Night's drawn in quickly. Must've lost track of time."

We ate by the fire. Despite the sausage rolls and pastries, Faolán still devoured a large plate of chicken. Not a speck touched his shirt or marked his cheeks or chin.

Then there was nothing else to do but go to bed. Miraculously, it was large enough to not only fit Faolán comfortably, but for me to also stretch out and not come close to touching him.

Some part of me twinged with disappointment at the fact, but I'd barely registered it before sleep closed in, as sudden as a clap of thunder.

***

I woke in the dark. Something wasn't right. I'd never fallen asleep so quickly in my life, for one thing. Though maybe that was just exhaustion from all that had happened the past few days. But still, something in the room felt... different.

I waited for my eyes to adjust to the dim light creeping around the edge of the curtains.

Faolán was gone.

I touched his side of the bed. Cold. I sat up, pulling the blankets closer and peered around the room. No sign of him.

"Faolán?"

The bathroom door was open, so he wasn't in there.

I called for him again. No reply.

A chill crept down my neck. I thought I'd seen some softness in him earlier—the man who killed with one hand and shrugged it off. Had I been stupid and let the sight of his body and the handsome face revealed after his bath cloud my judgement?

Yes, he'd promised to protect me, but fae could twist bargains. By his own admission, they could twist the truth.

Maybe he'd brought me here to Granny deliberately. For all I knew, he could be working with her.

But working with her to do what? What might they want with me? I had so little information, it was hard to say, but one thing every story about the fae agreed on—it wasn't anything good.

I ran through all those tales. Granny could boil me up in a stew. Maybe she'd feed me to some sort of monstrous pet. Maybe she'd trade me in a deal with some worse creature to get herself eternal youth—for some reason too many women in stories wanted that. None of them ever asked to be rid of their periods or the risk of dying in childbirth. Seemed unrealistic to me.

Still, stories were the only clues I had about Granny and her intentions.

Maybe she and Faolán would play with me for years, keeping me trapped here, and when they finally freed me, I'd stumble home and find a hundred years had passed. Worst of all, some part of me would miss their exquisite torture and the taste of faerie food, and I'd pine away, driven mad for wanting something I could never have.

With Faolán gone, this might be my chance to escape. What proof did I have that the geas keeping me in the house was real? None. Only his word.

I opened the curtain a crack and dressed quickly in the dim light. I hadn't unpacked my backpack, and I threw in a few extra items.

The halls were empty when I slipped out. House didn't make a sound. Did it know what I was doing?

Beneath my boots, the twisted vine pattern on the carpets seemed to writhe in the darkness, making my steps speed up. Shadows loomed left and right. They were only wall hangings and doorways or a tall clock *tick tick ticking*. None of the clocks here seemed to *tock*.

However much I told myself what the shadows were, they still seemed to shift as I passed, making the hairs on my arms strain to attention.

But a few minutes later, I found my way outside, where I paused, gasping in deep, cool breaths.

Overhead, the sky was dark, the stars only faint against the blackness. A sliver of moon cast a dim, cool light.

Strange. It was a full moon when Ari was taken and that was only three nights ago. The moon shouldn't be a thin crescent yet.

But this was faerie. Nothing could be trusted here, not even the moon, apparently.

Certainly not Granny or Faolán. Hadn't he told me

not to lower my guard? Maybe that was a shard of truth poking through some deeper deception.

Fuck.

I didn't know. Who he was. Where I was or why. Where Ari was. How the hells I was going to find her. What lay out there.

I didn't know *anything*.

I rubbed my arms.

Was *in here* worse than *out there*?

If Faolán was working with Granny, then probably, yes.

I ran across the driveway, gravel crunching under my feet. In ten yards, I would hit the grass and that would be quieter. I could follow the road through the woods out of here. If there were gates, I'd climb them.

Eight yards. Six. Four. Two. Then I was on soft, silent grass. Thank the—

Something moved in the woods.

I froze.

Between the trees, darkness and more darkness.

Barely breathing, I inched the dagger from my belt. Whether or not I believed half of what Faolán said, my iron knife had bothered the werewolves. It sat in my boot. I would only draw it if I had to—if I was prepared to use it, as he'd said.

A flash of something—an eye reflecting dim light— then a growl, and a creature burst from the undergrowth.

Huge. Grey. Teeth bared in a long, snarling muzzle.

A wolf.

My blood ran cold.

But my muscles flared like tinder catching light. I shot right, but the beast shadowed me, its great body standing between me and the road. When I darted left, thinking to circle through the forest and hit the road later, it did the same.

Every time I turned, it blocked the way.

I tried again, but it snapped at the air inches from my hand, its hot breath brushing my fingertips. My heart lurched into my throat, blocking the yelp trying to leap out.

It was too fast. Too big. Too dangerous. I'd never get past it.

I didn't dare bend and draw my dagger—didn't dare take my eyes off it for an instant.

It came closer, and I had no choice but to back away. Much as my instincts screamed to run, I couldn't; the moment I turned, it would be on me with those huge, pale teeth.

My heel crunched into the gravel. The wolf continued slinking towards me with a low growl. Two yards onto the drive. Four yards. Its growls softened and it let the gap between us open up. Six yards onto the gravel. Eight. Now it only bared its teeth with no sound.

It was herding me back to the house.

I groaned, shoulders sagging. This had to be Granny's watchdog. I shouldn't be surprised that she'd have a wolf do that for her.

Sure enough, when I edged up the steps to the

entrance, the wolf stopped. It watched as I opened the door and backed into the house.

I hurried to the nearest window.

When I peered out, the wolf was gone.

Last Night I Saw

I slept right through to morning, when House opened the curtains, letting in a stream of sunlight. With a groan, I pulled the blankets over my face. Although I'd fallen asleep quickly after my adventure with the wolf, my eyes were gritty, like I hadn't slept at all.

Judging by the grumbles coming from Faolán as he sat up, he felt the same. No surprise after his night jaunt.

I pulled the blanket down far enough to narrow my eyes at him. "Where did you go?"

He screwed up his face and knuckled his bloodshot eyes. Dark stubble flecked his jaw and cheeks—actually, it was probably too long to count as stubble anymore. "Uh?"

"I woke up and you were gone."

His face screwed up even more, and he scrubbed his hair, shaking his head. "I slept right here all night. Not that I feel like I slept at all." His voice rasped. "Are you sure you weren't dreaming?"

Nothing about it had felt like a dream. Though... the floor had shifted, and the shadows had moved, so maybe?

If he was working with Granny, I didn't want to alert him to my suspicions, so perhaps it was better not to mention my escape attempt.

"I looked out the window and saw a—"

But nothing more came out, like I was reaching for something that wasn't there.

"I saw—"

The words twisted just out of reach. It was like the time I got into a fight with Sienna Smith after she'd tried to steal Ari's ball. I broke her nose, but she winded me, and I'd stood there, lungs twitching, trying to breathe, but nothing came.

I couldn't even...

What had I been trying to tell Faolán about?

I shook my head. "It wasn't a dream. I... there was something I saw and I can't say."

Faolán made his customary low hum. "The geas. Above the door. I read it, but... I can't tell you what it said." He scrubbed his face, jaw flexing. "Can't even remember it properly—there's a blur over the words in my memory."

That was how my brain felt. Even now, as I tried to reach for last night, for the thing I'd seen at the forest's edge, a fog rolled in, sweeping away the details, until all I could remember was the way my heart had pounded in fear.

With that still on my mind, I washed and dressed, then brushed my hair. If anything, the memories drifted further away. Maybe it *was* a dream—they always faded as the day wore on, didn't they?

Faolán dressed in a crisp grey shirt and close-fitting trousers. Scowling into the mirror, he rubbed at his freshly shaved cheeks.

"You said there was a spell stopping us from leaving." I wasn't entirely sure I believed him, particularly not if he was working with Granny.

"Mm." He combed his hair, each stroke methodical.

"What would happen if I tried to?"

He shrugged and pulled his hair back into a knot. "I haven't seen the spell on the walls, but at best?" He tied the knot in place with a leather thong. "It would shoot you back inside, probably with some burns and broken bones."

"Probably" and "at best"—he was hedging. That could be a way of getting around the no lying rule.

I cocked my head at him as I braided my hair over my shoulder. "And at worst?"

Mouth flat, he lowered his chin and gave me a level look. A few strands of hair had already pulled free, falling in his face. "It would kill you."

No direct lies, and I couldn't see how that could be an indirect one, so that left only one possibility that had me shivering. It was the truth, and I'd narrowly avoided possible death.

Once we were ready, House showed us through the corridors, moving the carpets, rippling the wall hangings, shuffling the paintings and ornaments to lead us to a dining room.

"Ah, there you are!" Granny beamed at us from the head of a long table and spread her arms wide in welcome. "Come sit, come sit. You're just in time for breakfast."

A dozen platters of food appeared, steaming. Toast, muffins, and fruit piled high. Ham, bacon, and sausages. Sautéed mushrooms, steamed spinach, and roasted tomatoes. And eggs, so many different varieties: boiled, scrambled, poached, fried, pickled, omelettes, baked in little earthenware pots, devilled with flecks of vermillion paprika, even little pastry cases that had been filled with beaten eggs before baking.

Amongst the plates sat a large, round pot of tea and a taller pot of something that smelled richer and darker, a little fruity, a little bitter. Its spout steamed, so it was hot, but it wasn't something I recognised.

Granny watched as we joined her, smile not dimming for a second. "My dear guests. How lovely. Did you sleep well?"

No, but *manners*. "Yes, thank you."

Faolán grunted. Not a lie, I supposed. Not *really* an answer, either.

She leant across the table towards me. "I'm sorry if it seemed I tricked you with my invitation, Rose dear. I'm trapped in this house by a very old curse, you see, and I grow lonely stuck here by my self."

So she hadn't come to us on the road—it must've been only an image of her sent magically. That explained the odd light and the way she'd floated.

We ate, and I couldn't help but marvel at the amount Faolán put away. Such a large body required a lot of fuel, but still, it was impressive. He piled his plate high three times and had toast and buttered muffins on a side plate.

I even caught Granny eyeing him as he went in for more toast from a rack that never seemed to empty.

When I asked, she explained the tall pot was coffee. I'd seen the Hawthornes' cook buying bags of it at market, and there was a coffee shop near Madame Froufrou's atelier, but it was too expensive for us.

I poured her coffee and one for myself, then tea for Faolán. With a little sugar and a dash of cream, it was... I shook my head after the first sip. Rich. Indulgent. And so many layers of flavour, I couldn't pick them all out.

Oh, gods, I'd been missing out. Had Ari tried it yet? Was the fae lord treating her well?

A low growl of irritation came from my right, tearing me from my delicious new friend. "Damn tiny bastards." Faolán glowered at his teacup, pinching the handle between finger and thumb.

When I raised my eyebrows at him, his face screwed up.

"Can't fit my finger through this stupid hole, *and* I'd need ten of these to get a decent drink."

In front of him, a large mug popped into existence— so large, it was more like a vase with a handle than any drinking vessel I'd ever seen.

His eyes widened, and I swore a smile flashed across his face. "That's more like it." He scooped up the mug, which fit his hand perfectly, then emptied the teapot into it.

When he returned the teapot to the table, there was a gurgling sound, and steam poured from the spout. Just like the never-empty toast rack, House didn't let the tea run out, either.

Much as I wasn't keen on being trapped here for a month with two people I knew so little about, I appreciated House's attentiveness. Did it need help or did it just make things happen as effortlessly as they appeared? Did it think like a person? Did it *feel*?

I nudged Faolán. "Say thank you, then."

Mug an inch from his lips, he gave me a sidelong look and raised one eyebrow. "I'm not thanking a house."

"Why not? It did that for you. It's been very kind, in fact." I tugged on his sleeve and he immediately smoothed the crease. "All these clothes in your size."

With a huff, he lowered the mug. "I. Am. Not. Thanking. A. House."

"I thought fae were particular about manners."

"The house is a *thing,* not a person, fae or otherwise."

"Is it?" Eyebrows raised, I turned to Granny.

She watched us over her coffee cup, amusement in the glint of her eyes and curve of her mouth. The curve tugged higher before she blew on her drink and took a sip. With a tilt of her head, she shrugged, as non-committal as one of Faolán's grunts. "Probably best not to offend it."

Lips pursing, he flicked a glare at me and the triumphant look I undoubtedly wore. "Fine. *Thank you,*" he muttered, practically into the mug, before taking a gulp.

I patted his shoulder. "There, that wasn't so hard, was it?"

HOUSE

After breakfast, Granny gave us a tour around the endless hallways. We walked through a library with bookcases that soared three storeys high and chains that secured the books in place.

The thought of climbing to fetch a book from the top shelf made my head spin. And why on earth would books need chaining to the shelves?

We poked our heads into parlours so choked with dust and cobwebs, they clearly hadn't been used in years. A card room was similarly disused, the green baize of its card table almost completely hidden under a layer of blackish powder, a handful of cards scattered across the floor.

In another room, we found a glass sitting on the edge of a billiard table, some kind of mahogany-coloured liquid inside. Balls dotted the table's surface, a cue discarded amongst them, as if someone had abandoned the room mid-game. In an ashtray sat a half-smoked cigar.

The halls were clean, but now I looked more closely in the daylight, I spotted tatty edges to the heavy drapes and threadbare patches on the carpets. In some corners, black mould crept in from an old leak.

How long had Granny been here to wear the carpets so thin on her own? Then again, the billiard table, the card room—had there once been others here? Or were these the evidence of previous "guests"? She'd said it had been a long time.

Granny asked us about ourselves, where we were from. I told her a little about Briarbridge, how we were a family of bakers and I had a dozen brothers and sisters. I didn't mention any names. I knew what the stories said about True Names having power, and I didn't want to risk sending any fae creature after my family, even if Granny really did seem to be a lonely old fae, stuck in this house.

When she turned her question on Faolán he grunted, "Tenebris."

"A visitor from the capital?" Granny's eyes widened, an eager light entering them. "My, aren't I lucky to have someone from the very heart of the realm in my home? Tell me, does the Night Queen still insist on wearing black *all* the time?"

A twitch of the skin around Faolán's eyes. "I thought you were trapped here."

"I haven't *always* been trapped here."

"Mm."

He didn't answer her question about the Night Queen.

But Granny wasn't so easily evaded, apparently, as she opened the next door before smiling up at Faolán. "And what brings you so far from court?"

"Work."

It went on like that, her questions, his one-word answers, half-grunted. I tried to be friendly and respond more fully, albeit heeding his advice to not let down my guard. But Granny didn't ask anything too invasive, certainly nothing that seemed dangerous. They were all exactly the sort of questions I'd ask strangers if I'd been alone for a long time.

She also spoke about how this wall hanging was made by some old fae with a name I couldn't pronounce and that sculpture of a naked woman bearing herself to the moon was carved by somebody else. The reverence with which she spoke the names told me I should've been impressed, but Faolán and I exchanged glances that said he was as clueless as I was.

Abandoned rooms and storage cupboards, she opened every door we came across and showed us inside.

Except for a set of double doors so wide, three Faoláns could've stood shoulder-to-shoulder and still not touched the sides.

I caught him eyeing them, but he said nothing.

I glanced back as we passed without Granny saying a word about who'd carved their pure white surface. The shapes had grown indistinct with age—lumpy forms that merged together. That was perhaps an eye. This, a misshapen hand.

"What's in there?"

Without slowing her pace, Granny smiled at me. Or at least, her mouth curved and her eyes crinkled, but everything about it was stiff. "We don't go in there."

"How come?"

"Because we don't."

It was the kind of non-answer I gave my brothers and sisters when they hit that particular age when they could ask "Why?" a hundred times in an hour. I'd do my best to answer and explain, but eventually they'd *why* even my patience to death and I'd snap "Because."

Finally, she led us to a huge conservatory that clung to one side of the house. It was so tall, entire trees grew inside, twisted forms with broad leaves unlike anything I'd seen near Briarbridge or since arriving in Elfhame. Their dark branches carved up the sky and merged with the black metal frame of the structure. Thick swathes of pale—was that moss?—hung from their boughs, almost reaching the floor in places.

A small table with two chairs sat on a patio beneath their shade, like someone had set it up to take in the view.

I wasn't sure it was a view I wanted to take in.

Just like the lighting on Granny had been "off" when she'd appeared in our path, so many things about this house were... not quite right. The abandoned rooms, yes, but also smaller things that I couldn't always place.

The last step coming down the stairs was a little

higher than the others, meaning I lurched into the hallway.

A quarter of the doorhandles didn't open when I turned them, so I had that momentary jolt of my heart as it seemed I was trapped. But when I turned it for the twelfth time or so, it opened smoothly as though nothing had been wrong.

And that wasn't even mentioning the things that were *almost* normal. The room where the floor wasn't *quite* flat. The clocks that didn't *tick-tock*, only *tick*ed. The creaky floorboards and hinges.

Only, I'd never heard a floorboard sound quite so much like a distant shriek.

We saw no sign of another soul in the entire place. I didn't even see any of the spiders that had created all these webs, and there was no birdsong outside. No servants, either, only House.

By the time we'd trudged around the entire place, up steps and down narrow passageways that threaded beneath narrow staircases, my legs ached as much as they had from walking across Elfhame for a full day, and it was time for lunch.

AWAKE & NOT

That night, I awoke again, except...

Evening light peered through the open curtains, and candles lit the whole room. No spiderwebs lurked in the corners, and a sense of something *different* dragged at me—the sense that I had something to do.

"We need to get ready for the ball." Faolán's voice, soft, thoughtful. I found him standing by the fireplace, a frown etched between his eyebrows.

I blinked at him, taking a moment to register—the furniture was all new, with no threadbare arms to the chairs, no chip in the table. By the time we'd gone to bed, his facial hair had grown into a trimmed beard but now it was freshly shaven.

"What ball? How do you know?"

He shook his head, the frown deepening to dark, scored lines. "I just do. Come." He opened the wardrobe and rifled through.

I squinted at the windows, at the indistinct shapes outside and the violet dusk.

The change in time, the old furniture made new, the odd sense that I had something to do.

This was a dream.

No harm in playing along, and I'd never been to a ball, so this could be fun.

I slid out of bed and reached the wardrobe just in time for Faolán to turn, holding up two gowns. One was deep wine red velvet with an off-the-shoulder neckline. The other draped to the floor in blackened emerald green satin.

"Hmm." I canted my head. "Not sure either of those will fit you."

His eyes narrowed. "I meant for you."

I'd known that, of course, but I raised my eyebrows at him. Picking out dresses?

"Or there are plenty more, if you want something different."

"No, I just..." I shook my head. "I didn't have you down as having an interest in such things."

A flicker at the corner of his mouth. "Am I only allowed to like knives and road rags?"

"That..." I opened and closed my mouth. "That wasn't what I meant. I just... you're..." I gestured to him. "You're very masculine. Where I'm from, most men look down on women for being interested in clothing—they say it's frivolous."

His lips pressed together. "And yet, I bet they don't complain when women look good in what they wear."

I laughed. "You'd win that bet any day of the week."

After a nudge from him, I took the red velvet, and he nodded as if I'd chosen well before handing me a pair of dainty suede shoes in the same colour.

When I emerged from behind the dressing screen, he stood before the mirror, tying back his hair. Black trousers clung to his muscled thighs and, I couldn't help but notice, his backside—his wonderfully round backside.

I clenched my hands and dragged my gaze upward. A tailored jacket that Ari would've been proud of accentuated the angles of his shoulders and the narrowing line to his waist. It wasn't velvet but some other rich fabric that had been dyed the same wine red as my gown.

The idea of matching outfits made my belly do a little flip. Which was silly. Because of course Dream-Faolán would do something thoughtful like that—he was my invention.

Still, my imagination had conjured up a really quite impressive bottom for him. Well done, me.

It was only when he shifted to one side that I pulled my attention from it again, mouth dry, and met his gaze in the mirror.

Another flip in my belly.

The lines of his face were still hard, but something about seeing him dressed so smartly with his hair so carefully knotted at the back of his head softened it all —or maybe it was the hazel of his eyes. Again, I could picture his teeth and claws and the forceful savagery of his physique being used as a shield, just as he'd used his size and strength to protect me from the werewolf pack.

In this light, I noticed a faded scar on his chin. Except, I must already have noticed it, since this was a dream and I couldn't know things here that I didn't already know in the real world. Perhaps I'd invented it.

His eyebrows rose slowly, the rise echoed in his chest as he took a deep breath. "Well." He held my gaze a long moment before turning and looking me over. "I've never seen a rose look quite so beautiful."

I gave him a coy smile as though his praise didn't make my heart stutter. Dream-Faolán was still a man of few words, but he knew how to make them count.

But when I caught sight of myself in the mirror, any pretence fell away as my mouth dropped open.

I hadn't touched my hair, but it was pinned high on the back of my head, leaving the curled lengths to trail down from there, with tendrils loose around my face. And I didn't own any cosmetics, but a rosy flush covered my freckled cheeks and tinted my lips even darker. It emphasised the creamy pallor of my skin and the sky blue of my eyes. The gown clung to my breasts, my waist, my hips, and down my thighs, before flaring out and draping around my lower legs so I could actually walk.

I'd never...

I shook my head. My body was always something to *use*, a tool for work or flirtation. I'd never seen it look like this. Hells, I'd never seen so much of it—we only had a small mirror at home and looking down at yourself wasn't the same as seeing your body in a reflection.

While staring at all the details my dream had magicked into my hair and makeup, I'd stalked closer to the mirror, and now Faolán stepped behind me, so close I could feel his warmth. He lifted his hand and I held my breath, waiting for it to land on my waist.

But he let it drop without that contact, and I exhaled my disappointment. Dream-Faolán wasn't subject to my every whim. *More's the pity.*

His breath brushed my bare neck and shoulders, as he asked in the mirror, "Are you ready?"

THROUGH WHITE DOORS

Again, House showed us the way by moving furniture and objects in the hall until we stood before the white double doors Granny had refused to open during the tour. My heart thudded a little heavier, a little faster, and I drew a long breath of anticipation.

When we walked in, the ball was everything I'd imagined from the stories. Music, incredible gowns and suits, free-flowing drinks, and dozens of beautiful couples sweeping across the dance floor. There was no sign of the dust and disrepair we'd seen during our tour of the house with Granny. No sign of Granny, either.

Taking it all in, I leant closer to Faolán so he'd hear me over the music and chattering voices. "Have you ever been to anything like this?"

"At court, a few times, yes." His flat tone spelled out his distaste.

I cocked my head and smirked at him. "When you can't avoid it?"

"Mm." He nodded, eyebrows drawn low as a pair of fae sauntered past, both their gazes lingering on me. I more felt than heard the rumble in his torso. When they'd disappeared into the crowd, his frown shifted to something more thoughtful than irritated. "Have you?"

I lifted one shoulder and looked away, face warming to admit my inexperience. "Never."

"Ah." He nodded and scanned the room. "Then we'd better make sure you get the full experience. First, drinks." With a jerk of his head, he led me to the nearest footman with a teetering tray bedecked with a dozen different types of glass.

I chose something raspberry-flavoured and so sweet I couldn't taste the alcohol, he took a tumbler of honeyed whisky, and we wandered around the huge ballroom as we drank. The vine pattern I'd seen elsewhere in the house continued here through the inlaid floor, weaving and twisting, thorns piercing.

It was only when we reached the edge of the crowd that I realised the walls were covered in huge, floor to ceiling mirrors. No wonder it seemed there were so many people—they were reflected on and on, and I couldn't even hazard a guess at the true number.

We paused to watch a game of cards where the stakes had grown high—stacks of gold and gems, as well as little black boxes with gold locks. When I opened my mouth to ask what was inside, a cheer erupted as a small, blond fae showed their hand, revealing a royal flush.

"Cheat!" Their opponent slammed his hands into the table, rising. "You damn cheat."

"Time to move on." Faolán steered us away, placing himself between me and the disintegrating card game.

Couples glided across the dance floor, bodies close together, mouths moving in soft, private conversations. A woman laughed, head thrown back, revealing the pale column of her neck. Teeth revealed in a wolfish grin, her partner bent closer and kissed her throat.

That wasn't like the stories or my imaginings. Balls were meant to be stuffy—at least the ones the Hawthornes and their like threw were. Maybe, in faerie, things were different.

And, as real as the velvet of my dress felt, this was a dream. It was hard to remember that when Faolán's arm seemed so solid under my hand and the raspberry of my drink still left its flavour on the tongue, sweet and tart.

"Do you want to dance?"

We'd reached the edge of the dance floor and I realised it was my feet that had steered us here as I'd watched. I raised my eyebrows at him. "Do *you* want to?" Real life Faolán surely wouldn't—he didn't seem the type, especially if he avoided balls.

"I asked if *you* wanted to. This is your first ball, not mine."

I shifted my shoulders, suddenly uncomfortable, though I couldn't say why. He seemed to want to show me everything a ball was, and that involved dancing. "I don't know the steps, and I wouldn't want to force you—"

He huffed. "You couldn't force me to do anything, little flower. Come." He tugged me onto the dance floor.

My heart leapt as I hurried to keep up. What were the moves? I turned left and right trying to watch what the others were doing.

"Don't worry." He pulled one of my hands to his shoulder, held the other in his, and cupped my waist. "The steps aren't hard."

And, strangely, they weren't—it was as though my feet already knew them. So this wasn't one of those dreams where I arrived in the kitchens, ready to help Ma and Pa with the day's baking, to find not only had I completely forgotten how to mix bread dough but also I was on a stage failing so spectacularly in front of all of Briarbridge and, suddenly, naked, too.

The ballroom blurred, leaving only us and the dancers, the freedom of gliding movement, and the tickle on the back of my neck and shoulders where my hair swung behind me.

Faolán wasn't even scowling as though he hated every minute.

This was a strange dream, but not a bad one. I smiled and let the colours and sounds of the place swirl together, enjoying the feel of my limbs knowing what to do like this was as familiar as kneading dough.

The vines on the floor seemed to pulse with the music, like they were arteries and music their blood. At the centre of the dance floor, the thickest vines wrapped around a grey heart, weaving through it, piercing it. The blood seeping from the wounds reminded me of the healed injuries I'd seen amongst Faolán's tattoos.

"Faolán?"

"Hmm?"

"I want to ask you about something, but... I don't want to upset you."

Tucking in his chin to look at me, he raised an eyebrow. "I don't upset easily."

"I'll bet, but... but if you don't want to answer, please just tell me. I don't mean to pry, it's just... It's been playing on my mind."

His eyes narrowed a fraction. "Then ask, Rose." His grip on my waist flexed, pulling me that bit closer. "I won't bite."

My breasts skimmed his torso as we followed the dance's steps. Much as the touch of him felt solid enough, brushing my nipples, sending little streaks of sensation through my nerves that felt *so real*, this was a dream. It was meaningless for me to ask dream-Faolán when I'd only get the truth from the real, waking man. Still, I could treat this as a practice.

"Your scars"—I tensed, fingers tightening on his hand, his shoulder, but he only dipped his head in acknowledgement—"what happened? Who did that to you?"

"Hmm." He nodded thoughtfully.

That was all the answer I'd get. His usual low hum that was no answer at all. I had no right to expect—

"I was young, barely an adult." He frowned, gazing

out past me. "It was a village where they didn't like…" He opened his mouth, closed it, then shook his head. "They didn't like *my kind*. Didn't want one dirtying up their streets." His nose wrinkled, baring his teeth for a second.

Was he talking about humans attacking him for being fae? Or was it that he worked for the Night Queen and had found himself amongst the Day King's followers? Or was it down to his beastly side? Either way, the idea burned the back of my throat. I squeezed his tight shoulder, thumb running along his collarbone.

"Pitchforks and torches—I'm sure humans have the same thing." His mouth curved without humour.

I'd seen the seed of that as a child. The group of kids gathered around Ari because she was different, their hands raised, fingers gripped around stones.

And when the creeping death came stalking through Briarbridge, I'd seen full-blown mobs gathered, searching for the sick, determined not to become one of them, terrified of the plague. So terrified that it stripped away their humanity and made them do the unthinkable.

It had started off as marking where the sick lived and making them stay in their homes. Just a warning, a sensible precaution.

But then as more had died, as the full horror of those black tendrils working their way through victims' veins had truly hit, terror gripped their hearts and crushed them.

They'd gathered, an overwhelming wave and swept through town. Where they found death, they lit fires.

They burned down houses, even a whole block on the edge of town. Sometimes, it wasn't just the dead they burned, but the sick still inside as they waited for death or the slim chance of recovery.

They were still alive enough to scream.

I slipped out of the house. I wasn't stupid. I knew I couldn't stand against a whole mob. But I might be able to stop them hurting Ari. Her parents had already died by this point, and she was sick. I'd delivered food to her, but that night, I ran from shadow to shadow and beat the mob to her cottage. Praying they'd forget about her, I scraped the mark off her door, blunting my new dagger.

It was worth it.

So, yes, I knew about pitchforks and torches.

Stomach a tight fist, I nodded to Faolán, who surveyed me in silence. "We do."

"Then you understand how they chased me out of town." His jaw clenched, and the shoulder under my hand turned so hard, I thought he would stop there, but he went on. "They wanted rid of the 'dirty, stinking dog.'"

My heart clenched in a painful beat. The comment he'd made in the mirror. He carried their words, just like he carried the scars they'd left on his body. "They are wrong, you know."

His gaze slid to mine, the flecked green and brown unfathomable. "Oh, *I* know that." His mouth twisted. "Doesn't mean there won't be more like them." He shrugged. "I know what people see when they look at me. I know what you saw when we met."

I opened my mouth to apologise again, but he gave a soft growl.

"You admitted it. I don't blame you for it. Understandable, I suppose." He cocked his head to one side. "But I know to expect it now, and I keep up my guard. No one will catch me unawares and beat me half to death again." His brows lowered, and his jaw ratcheted tighter still. "And although they might think it, that doesn't mean I have to *be* it."

He fell silent, and we flowed with the music, gliding and turning. I let my feet and his sure grip on my waist and hand lead the way as I went over all he'd said—or all my imagined version of Faolán had said.

This was a dream and yet, it *felt* true.

I sought his gaze again. Even the pale verdigris and gold flecks in his eyes were there. Had I really paid so much attention to how he looked that I could conjure him this clearly? "That's why you jumped in the bath right away, isn't it?"

One side of his mouth rose, this time softer than his earlier bitterness. "I won't be what they call me. My work takes me on the road sometimes, but travel dirt makes me... grouchy."

He'd still been pretty grumpy about the tea cups this morning and that was after his bath. I arched an eyebrow.

He huffed out a short breath. "Fine, *more* grouchy than usual."

I chuckled and pulled closer into him, our bodies flush in a way they hadn't been since he'd held my iron blade to his throat. His brows rose, but he didn't pull away, and I didn't feel a need to explain.

This confession, even if it was just a dream—it made sense. It made *him* make sense. No wonder he'd trimmed his hair so neatly and took his time choosing his clothes. Everything he picked out matched perfectly, even our outfits tonight.

At my waist, he stroked the velvet of my gown, making me suddenly aware of the bare expanse of my shoulders and how his fingers might feel there—skin-to-skin. The hair on the back of my neck rose.

He dipped close, the shadow of a frown between his brows as his gaze swept across me. "What's wrong? You're covered in goosebumps."

"Not wrong..." I shook my head, chills rippling through me at the hard set of his body against mine and the way his masculine scent wafted around me.

Could I? *Should* I? Because my body wanted to know how his mouth would fit upon mine, since his chest pressed into me so perfectly.

I bit my lip, drawing his gaze, and that gave me the same hard certainty I'd seen in his eyes when he'd promised he wouldn't harm me.

This wouldn't be over-complicated, because married or not, this wasn't real. I could enjoy my dream.

"Not wrong," I said, "but maybe right."

Breaths coming quicker, I danced onto my tiptoes and tilted my head back.

His chest reverberated, though there was no sound

save for the music keeping our feet obeying its constant rhythm.

I gripped his shoulder, using it to steady myself so I could reach higher.

Like he understood, a smile flickered on his mouth before he dipped lower, eyes fixed on my lips as though he were a hunter and that his quarry.

I wouldn't mind being his prey.

IN A BALLROOM

He closed in. His breath was hot upon my face, brushing my lips before his warm, firm touch. It wasn't soft, but I knew he could kiss harder—much, much harder—and that thought, together with the press of kiss after kiss, burned through me.

I forgot about holding his hand in the proper dance pose and slid my palm to his cheek. His stubble—already growing despite his being clean-shaven when we'd left our room—prickled my skin, and I couldn't help but hum my pleasure into our next kiss.

My husband could be a gentle beast, but I wasn't sure I wanted gentle.

Something in my body language must've given my wish away, because his other hand closed around my back, and he pressed me against his body just as his mouth opened against my lips, which parted at his command.

His tongue swept in, assured as it swiped mine, and his lips crushed rather than explored as they had before.

Then my feet were no longer on the floor, and there was nothing soft left.

I looped my arms around his neck, seeking more, encouraging the hard command of his mouth on mine. I opened to take his tongue deeper, to invite his invasion, the cut and thrust like this was a sword fight that I wanted to lose. There were whimpers—they were mine —and a low rumble of approval or maybe pleasure in his chest.

I gave as good as I got. I met his swipes. I nibbled his lip. I ran my tongue along the hard length of his canines as I clung to him for dear life.

Thank the gods I'd chosen this dress, because my skin burned even with my shoulders and arms uncovered. Every breath seared as I drew them against his lips, not wanting to break from the devastating force of his kisses even for something as vital as air.

Because, good gods, somehow these determined kisses, the prick of his claws on my back, the unyielding planes of his body flush against mine... they were vital, too.

Eventually we broke apart. It might have been minutes later or years. Was this how mortals lost track of time in faerie, caught up in fae kisses that tasted of mint and honeyed whisky?

We'd come to a stop, but the dancers flowed around us, like water past a stone. His chest heaved against mine as his gaze flicked between my eyes. One hand slid up my back and when his fingertips reached the top of my dress and then bare skin, I shivered and pressed all the tighter against him.

Even with the surreal elements—the shift in time to evening, the house being different, the presence of all these people, and the inexplicable knowledge we had a ball to attend—his touch, his body, the softness of his hair as I toyed with loose strands at the back of his neck… It made it easy to forget this was a dream.

He huffed, and the corner of his mouth curled. "This is much better than my usual dreams."

I blinked. "What?" People in dreams didn't say things like—

Gong!

It reverberated around the room, through our bodies, and when Faolán set me on the floor, I felt it there too.

At the front of the ballroom, a petite woman stood on a dais. Her white skin was even paler than mine—the colour of the sheets on our bed. Blue-black hair curled around her face in a long, loose mass.

And what a face. For a moment, I couldn't breathe, it was so exquisite. A wide mouth with full lips parted in a smile, revealing perfect, white teeth, complete with fae canines. Her small nose matched her pointed chin, and large, sapphire eyes surveyed the room, waiting for us to fall silent.

Just as I drew a breath, my attention trailed down her slender body, and my lungs stilled again. She wore a black gown, but it was as though it had been cut from scraps of night, flowing down her body in a veil so sheer I could see the pink tips of her nipples and a dark strip of hair at the apex of her thighs.

None of the fae around us reacted like I knew the Hawthornes would, in gasped shock or pearl-clutching scandal.

I gripped Faolán's sleeve. The sight of her, the feel of her magnetism rolling across the room, sweet upon the air, it had me clenching my thighs together, wanting, wanting, wanting, building on the fire Faolán's kisses had stoked in me. He was an anchor stopping me from running to her.

"Dear guests," she said with a flash of those perfect teeth. Her long, elegant hands spread in a gesture of welcome that beckoned me.

Faolán held my arm, and I realised I had taken a step forward.

My chest heaved as I shook my head. What *was* this? What had such a hold on me? I tucked into his side, planting my feet on the floor.

"Stay close to me," he murmured in my ear, the heat of it making me shiver, then he took my hand, grip as tight as a vice.

"My friends, it is time to begin." When she gestured to the side, two servants opened a pair of doors hidden in the mirrored walls.

The crowd flowed in and would've dragged me with them, if not for Faolán's immovable weight shielding me.

He narrowed his eyes at the darkness through the doors. "Let's have a look."

Rather than leading me, he placed a hand on my shoulder, the unexpected skin contact making my breath hitch, and placed me before him, steering us through the throng.

Every sensation was too much. The warmth of him at my back. The rough skin of his hands. His breaths disturbing the hair on top of my head. The voices and footsteps of the crowd, and their eyes upon me.

I found myself straining for a glimpse of the woman who'd spoken, to no avail.

Fae charm. Of course. That was the thing pulling me towards her. Faolán had said he had no talent for that, but clearly our host did.

I leant back into him as we shuffled through the doorway, and he looped an arm around my waist. I fought against the desire to arch back into him and was grateful that our shuffling gait prevented it.

But my body cried that this was how it would feel if he took me from behind and that I should let him—beg him to—and bury my face between that woman's legs at the same time.

Fuck. Fuck. Fuck.

Fae charm was a dangerous thing. A glorious thing. A thing that had its claws in my muscles and nerves, toying with me like I was a puppet.

Eyes closed, I took long breaths and trusted Faolán to steer me through the crowd. It was only then I realised the floor sloped away—we were walking down. Granny hadn't shown us a cellar or mentioned one, but a house as large as this surely had one.

Also. I had to remember—this was a dream.

I sighed in pure relief as the air grew cool and dank, quenching the fire that had swept across my skin.

Although I still couldn't catch many words in the conversations around us, there was a general tone of excitement running through the guests' voices.

After maybe five minutes, Faolán drew us to a stop, his grip on my shoulder and around my waist tightening until I was hard against him. His "Hmm" rattled into my spine, jangling along my overwrought nerves.

When I opened my eyes, we were in a large, round chamber that dropped away towards the centre. The other guests occupied plush velvet chairs in inky black that worked their way down to that central space in tiers with nine aisles radiating out. We slid into seats at the back, Faolán's on the aisle. I kept hold of his arm, still not entirely trusting myself not to climb across the audience to reach that woman the next time I spotted her.

The low conversation continued, though everyone's gazes kept turning to that empty central area, making the air buzz with anticipation.

I craned my neck so the ceiling filled my vision—raw rock that glittered faintly in the light of the torches lining the aisles and surrounding the central stage.

Faolán squeezed my shoulder. "Are you all right?"

I massaged my temples as I turned to him. "I think so."

Damn it. He was too close and so fucking gorgeous,

and when I licked my lips, I could still taste the honey from his kisses. Despite the cool air, heat raced across my flesh again.

I'd had lovers, some almost as handsome as him, but I'd never felt as overwhelmed as I'd been since that woman appeared in the ballroom.

Even as I swallowed, my hand crept to his knee. "I can't..." I closed my fingers into a fist, but it still rested on the solid muscle of his leg. "I'm sorry, I don't know what's happening to me. *Is* this fae charm?" When I looked at him, his eyes were fixed on my hand.

The knot of his throat bobbed before he replied. "Yes. Hers. Not mine." His voice came out gravelly.

Fuck. Even his voice hummed in me, low in my belly. What would it be like to have his head between my legs as he spoke in that tone?

I squirmed, hooking my ankles around the legs of the chair like I could tether myself in place. My fingers had opened and slid up his leg. Maybe he could distract me. Higher, higher. My fingers curled so the tips traced his inner thigh.

His muscles solidified, then his hand closed over mine, clamping it in place. "Little flower," he growled.

A pathetic whimper escaped my parted lips at the sound. It was as though he made the very air shake, vibrating across my skin like a lover's caress.

Nostrils flaring, he stared ahead as his chest rose and fell in a deep breath. "Much as I might enjoy this, I'm not going to take advantage of you being under the influence of charm. And much as there are things I'd love to do to you, I'm only going to do them if and when you *want* them, not because your body's telling you you need them."

Need. Need. Need. I did. I needed release, relief, to be splayed across a bed—or any other surface—and filled. I needed him.

My fingers flexed, but he held them in that same spot, not letting me trail higher.

Some part of me knew he was right to do that. Her tiny ounce of control kept my other hand gripped to the arm of the chair. But she was a small voice trapped in a cage and the rest of me raged at being denied.

This was a battle I both wanted to lose and feared failing.

A distraction might help. I stared at his hand fastened over mine. "If it's not to take advantage of me, then why?"

"Why what?"

"Why are you doing this?" It was a nonsense question, since this was a dream, but I prayed talking, however nonsensical, would help keep my mind from the bulge in his trousers and what he might do with it if I asked, begged, *anything*.

I blinked, jolting upright. No, I was staring at it now, mouth watering. That wasn't... "Why help me now? Why help me then? Why marry me?"

He opened his mouth, but I leapt on, stopping the predictable answer before he could voice it.

"To keep me safe, I know. But what do *you* get from

being married to me? Why bother to save me from the werewolves? *Why?*"

"Hmm." His jaw flexed as he threw me the briefest glance. "Fine. No harm in saying here, I suppose." He shrugged and squeezed my hand. "Because I could see how determined you were—how bloody pigheadedly, foolishly, plain *stupidly* determined you were to save your friend. So I knew marching you back to Albion would do no good."

"You could've left me. Let the werewolves have their fun." I shuddered at the thought and leant closer to him.

"No," he sighed, shoulders sinking, "I couldn't. Because I know what they would've done. And I couldn't live with that on my conscience." He shook his head, gaze drifting into the distance. "Not just death, but the pain, the cruelty, the screams. Even if I didn't inflict a single injury, I would've still been responsible for your death."

I blinked up at him. His stupid comment at the time about not wanting to ruin his day by listening to my death screams—there'd been a speck of truth in it. "Damn it, Faolán. Why didn't you tell me that in the first place?"

"I told you Bastian was the Night Queen's right hand, yes?"

I nodded, though I didn't see what that had to do with anything.

"He does the Night Queen's dirty work, and I do *his* dirty work. My reputation, my... size, they help me keep the work a little less dirty when I can. Can't have half of

Elfhame knowing I'm a soft touch." He lifted one shoulder with a rueful smile.

Reputation. I could've laughed. Almost did. Instead I prodded my elbow into him. "You mean, it was all for—"

Gongggg!

BENEATH A BALLROOM

It shivered through the air, dragging out longer than the previous gong had. It pierced my eardrums, making me jolt, too much to take in my heightened state. It buzzed on my skin, obliterating the distracting effect of our conversation, forcing my eyes shut.

The sound was fading, just a soft reverberation in the air when I could open them again.

As the gong shivered away to nothing, shapes appeared on the sunken stage, bit by bit, materialising into existence.

An altar at waist height. A small, round table. And *her*.

Her charm flooded the room, flooded me, making my pulse spike. I bit my lip. My nails dug into the velvet upholstery of the chair's arm. Faolán's hand crushed mine into his thigh.

Her smile... Wild Hunt take me, but it called to me,

beckoning, promising. She wouldn't deny me as Faolán did. She wouldn't keep me still. She would welcome me, free me, give me all the satisfaction I craved... and then more.

I found myself on the edge of my seat as she opened her arms and the audience fell silent. I wanted to be in those arms. I would throw myself into them, kiss them, let them entrap me, let them crush me, let them break me. I didn't fucking care, so long as I was in them.

Her sapphire eyes turned to me and her smile broadened. Her lips glistened in the torchlight as though she'd just licked them. Her tongue. Her mouth. What pleasure would they give me? What could I give in return? My body, my heart, my soul—anything she asked.

Anything.

My legs straightened, and I was off my chair, starting for the aisle.

Then I wasn't.

Arms banded around my waist, and I was sitting again, on something warm.

A sigh blew against my ear, sending every hair on end. "Sorry, little flower, but this is for your own good."

I squirmed but he gave nothing, keeping my arms clamped at my sides. Inside her cage, that aware part of me sagged against the bars in relief. With a huff, I sank into him.

Surrender.

That caged part of myself managed to seize control long enough to whisper, "Thank you."

Smile fading, the woman in black turned, arms still

outstretched. She took in her entire audience, who sat rapt, straining forward in their seats with lips parted.

"I promised you an evening of sheer perfection." Her voice was low and rich like the velvet of my dress, but somehow it still reached us at the back, as though she were murmuring in my ear.

I shivered, and Faolán's arms tightened around me. I let my head sink back onto his shoulder. I couldn't trust my own body, my own mind, even, but I could trust in his solidity. Maybe, after all he'd just told me, I could even trust him.

"I promised you ultimate pleasure." A hint of that smile played upon her full mouth.

My body throbbed in response, and I found myself arching back into Faolán. The urge to grind into him gripped me, and I had to bite my lip against it.

"I promised you the greatest Calan Gaeaf celebration you've ever witnessed." Her smile snapped into place, full of pride, at the exact instant her arms snapped out to the side.

Something appeared on the altar. Something appeared at the bottom of each set of steps. They faded in slowly, so I had to stare and wait, battling my drying eyes that wanted to blink. But if I blinked, I might miss the moment the forms solidified—or I might miss something that wonderful woman did.

And that would be a tragedy.

Then, they weren't *things* appearing, but *people*. Nine men and women, perfectly naked, one at the end of each aisle, and a tenth on the altar.

She lay there, dark hair spread across the stone surface, breasts spread by gravity, dark nipples pointing at the ceiling. Even at this distance, I just knew even that small detail, like I'd just known I was meant to be somewhere when I'd awoken in this dream.

The humans each faced outwards, expressions serene. But their chests heaved like they felt the same desire that I did. Except because of where they stood and the fact they were naked, I tasted the bitter envy that said their desires were going to be acted upon.

When the sapphire-eyed woman nodded, nine fae rose from the front row. Three men, three women, and three that I couldn't determine. Each wore white robes that flowed behind them as they approached the naked people.

Our host raised her chin and stood over the altar. "The nights grow long." With a smile gentler than her previous ones, she caressed the prone woman. At the touch, the woman's back arched, and a pang of jealousy lanced through me. "The nights grow dark." The host smoothed hair from her partner's face.

I let out a grunt, pulling against Faolán's hold, even though part of me knew I didn't want to be down on that stage. Why, I couldn't say, but just as the air hummed with tension, with anticipation, it trembled with something else...

The same thing I'd felt in the forest with the werewolves. The same thing I'd felt the night the mob had swarmed the streets of Briarbridge. The same thing I felt hurrying home before dark on the night of the new moon, knowing the Wild Hunt would ride abroad as soon as the sun set.

Danger.

Our host bent over the altar, and I could tell by the way her partner lifted her chin that she could feel the caress of her breath.

Sapphire eyes flicked up to the audience. "The nights are ours." With that, she bent over her prone partner and claimed her lips in a deep kiss that had my hips thrusting back into Faolán's.

He growled, and I absorbed the sound, biting my lip harder to keep from whimpering in return as his body stirred against me.

Down on the stage, our host's hand trailed down over the woman, between her breasts, over her solar plexus, down to her belly button...

I held my breath, waiting for her fingers to trail lower —her clawed fingers, I noticed—but they stopped at her belly and gripped and...

I blinked. I choked on a gasp or a shout or something that was trying to claw its way in or out of me, because her fingers *sank in*.

Faolán went rigid beneath me. I think he stopped breathing.

Blood welled from the spot, across pale skin—the host's and the prone woman's—and onto the altar.

It had to be some trick. Some stagecraft. Mummers had visited Briarbridge who did strange performances that seemed to defy reality and logic when taken at face value. After, Ari and I would pore over the details as we drank in the tavern, and sometimes we'd work out how it was done with smoke and mirrors, pulleys and misdirection, or a hidden vial of red ink.

This had to be the same, because the woman lying on the altar—the victim as that caged part of me wanted to call her—didn't cry out in pain. Her body arched into the host's touch, and she kissed her back with writhing fervour.

But the host's hand had disappeared, and by the angle of her elbow, I could tell she was reaching up into the woman's rib cage.

At my back, Faolán's chest expanded, and his long inhalation tickled my ear.

Our host cupped her victim's head, lifting it from the altar, holding her closer, taking her mouth in an ever-deepening kiss.

"Shit." Faolán's voice was less than a whisper.

A moment later, she straightened and her sapphire eyes flashed as she withdrew her hand from her victim's body.

With a triumphant yet hungry smile, she raised it.

Crimson and dripping, still throbbing, she held aloft the woman's heart.

Faolán murmured something else, but I couldn't fathom anything because my brain was stuttering on what I was watching.

No. It couldn't be. This was a show, a performance, a...

The sapphire-eyed woman lifted her victim's head, smile gentling.

This was the moment she'd kiss her again and invite her to sit up and they'd wipe off the blood to reveal the woman had no wound. It was a pig's heart and pig's blood and this had all been a ritual for show and symbol.

Not real.

Not real.

The heart in her hand was still beating when she held it in front of her victim's face, showing her what she'd done. The woman's eyes widened, her mouth dropped open and blood trickled out.

"The night is ours." Our host nodded towards the nearest aisle, and it was only then I saw that the fae in white were now spattered in blood where they'd done the same to their nine naked victims.

Despite the warmth of Faolán curled around me, rigid, my blood ran cold. Not just cold—frozen.

This was no show.

And maybe this wasn't a dream.

"I've got you," Faolán breathed into my ear. "I won't let them hurt you."

Our host—our beautiful, terrible host—lifted the heart, which still beat sluggishly.

Her sapphire eyes fixed on mine as she opened her mouth, revealing all those perfect, white teeth.

No. No. No.

She took a bite. Blood flowed over her hand and down her chin.

I screamed, and the dark theatre shattered.

AWAKE

I woke up screaming.

Bolt upright, I searched left and right, breaths heaving, throat raw. No blood. No bizarre theatre. No sapphire-eyed woman who both terrified and turned me on so much I didn't know what to do with myself. Just the dim light of our bedroom.

It wasn't real.

"Rose?"

Faolán was here.

Thank the fucking gods.

I flung myself into him, even as part of me said that he wasn't the same Faolán who had kissed me at the ball or comforted me in that terrible theatre.

But his huge arms closed around me all the same and he let me curl into his lap as tears of pure terror streamed down my face.

"It wasn't real," I whispered against his chest. "It wasn't real."

"I've got you." He stroked my back, my hair. When my breaths had slowed, he grazed my cheek with his knuckles. "What's wrong? What wasn't real?"

"A dream. It was just a dream." I half laughed, even though my heart still pounded against the inside of my ribcage. "You were in it. We went to a ball and—and it was nice until..." I rubbed my chest like it was *my* heart that had been ripped out. "She ate—"

"Her heart."

I flinched and stared up at him. "How did you...?"

His expression usually veered somewhere between long-suffering low-level irritation and a full scowl, but I'd never seen him look this grim. Mouth flat, eyes shadowed, jaw tight. Under me and around me, his every muscle was tense. "You saw it too. The Calan Gaeaf ritual."

I swallowed, nodded.

"I thought it was a dream." His gaze flicked to my mouth as though he was remembering our kiss. "But if you saw the same thing..." His frown ratcheted deeper.

"We woke up, though. It had to be a dream."

"Hmm." His shoulders lowered. "Maybe." His eyes narrowed, glinting in the dimness. "House?"

A soft rattle from the fireplace.

"Did you put us in the same dream?"

Another rattle, then the fire flared into life.

He huffed, rolling his eyes. "Magic house. It's always the bloody magic house."

I half-laughed, half-sighed my relief and let my

fingers trace one of the lines inked on his shoulder. "I'm glad you were there."

His gaze slid from the fireplace to me as his brows rose.

"I was scared, but you made me feel safe. And"—I looked away with a lopsided smile—"I had fun before that. It might've only been a dream, but I'm still claiming it as my first ball."

"Huh." It wasn't quite his usual flat hum, and it didn't go as far as a full-blown chuckle, but something in between. He pulled me closer, the movement so subtle he might not have been conscious of it.

Suddenly, I was very aware that I only wore a light-weight nightgown and he a pair of shorts. He cradled me so well, his broad shoulders curving around me like a shield. Except shields weren't so warm and didn't have this layer of soft flesh that rose in goosebumps under my hands.

I followed the silvery line of a scar with my finger-tips. The ball might've been a dream, but he had been real. That meant his reason for helping me and the story about that mob were also real. My heart clenched—my jaw, too.

"Rose," he rumbled, and I felt it in every part of me.

Dragging in a breath, I met his gaze.

"I'm glad I was there to protect you. Not sure I'd have told you about my scars if I'd known it wasn't a dream version of you I was telling, but..." He pressed his lips together as though unsure how to continue—or whether he should. "You made me feel safe enough to tell you."

My heart went from shrivelling at what had seemed like his regret, to filling. The taciturn, grumpy Faolán had opened up a crack to me and wasn't now, in the cold light of day that crept in around the edges of the curtains, trying to deny it or close back up.

Fuck. It made me want to kiss him all over again—for real, this time.

But I'd kissed him because I'd thought it a dream. That wasn't complicated—there were no consequences of dreams. But now? This?

This could get very complicated.

Still, my traitorous fingers planed along his shoulder, up the side of his neck. They didn't understand complicated.

I cleared my throat and opened up a little distance between us—distance where I wasn't sitting in his warm breath, half pressed against his broad chest. "I'm glad you told me, and I'm glad you felt safe with me." I smiled even as I forced my muscles to obey orders to slip from his hold and the bed. Each movement was stiff, but I marched myself into the bathroom and closed the door.

I bathed, scrubbing for longer than was necessary and splashing myself with cold water, before returning to our room and choosing an outfit for the day. Faolán gave no input on my clothing. He didn't speak to me at all.

If it really was him in my dream, that meant the care and attention, the determination to not be what they said—that was all him, too. And my admiration of him was all real.

And he really had helped me for my sake—the only selfish angle being to spare his own conscience.

No sooner had I emerged from behind the dressing screen, than the air before the fireplace shimmered.

I froze, eyes wide. "Faolán?"

Dark lines appeared, two vertical, two horizontal. Smoke—no, *shadow* poured through.

"Hmph. About bloody time," he muttered, coming to my side. "Don't worry, little flower. Just a visitor."

The lines connected, forming a large rectangle—a door, I realised just before it swung open. Inside was darkness, pure shadow, then through stepped a man.

I stared. I couldn't help it.

With his straight nose and full lips, he was handsome. Almost beautiful, though the faint scar running through one side of his mouth and down to his chin stopped him quite crossing that line.

But where Faolán was all rough-hewn lines, like a stone wall or one of Ari's sketched designs, this man—another fae—was solid, sharp edges like a finely carved statue or something wrought by the blacksmith.

Where Faolán was a shield, this man was a blade.

Where Faolán felt safe, this stranger felt decidedly dangerous. I edged closer to Faolán, and I reached for my hip where a dagger would normally sit.

The fae's black hair ruffled in a breeze coming through the doorway. It reflected no light, as dark as coal or the night sky, whereas his eyes—

I blinked.

They *glowed*. Only softly, a silvery light tinged with

some pale colour—yellow or green, perhaps—but that was definitely a glow.

"Hmm." He arched an eyebrow, taking in the room with those odd eyes before turning them to Faolán as the door closed behind him. "You have some explaining to do."

A Visit

I could hear Faolán's teeth grinding. "You took your time—I tapped for you *days* ago."

"I've been busy. And... what is this place? I thought you were—" His silver eyes snapped to me. "And who is this?"

"A long story."

"And does this long story have a name?"

I cleared my throat. "And a voice." I cocked my head and gave a smile that was more than a little sarcastic. "Rose."

He inclined his head. "Bastian."

I turned to Faolán. "Is this the 'boss' you mentioned?"

He wasn't the only one who could talk about someone like they weren't there.

"'Boss'?" Bastian chuckled, taking in the room. "Is that what you call me when I'm not around? Careful, Faolán, that almost sounds like respect."

"Hmm." Faolán scowled. "I have to use terms others will understand. Saying you're the prick I sometimes listen to takes too much breath."

I tensed, expecting a reaction from Bastian at being called a prick.

But his teeth only flashed, sharp canines included, as amusement glinted in his metallic eyes. "I've missed you, too." He cocked his head, the skin around those eyes crinkling. "Oh. *Oh.* You're *stuck* here, aren't you?" He laughed, and the more he did, the more Faolán scowled.

"Well, don't just giggle about it—get us out of here." He gestured at where the door had appeared.

Chuckles fading, Bastian shook his head. "There's nothing I can do about it." His gaze trailed over the ceiling and he smacked his lips softly as if tasting something. "This is old, *old* magic. No, whatever spells are on this place, you're stuck here for the duration." He raised an eyebrow. "How long?"

Faolán's jaw flexed so much, it was a wonder he managed to speak. "A month."

Bastian's cheek twitched, and he opened his mouth.

"Don't." Faolán bit out the word.

The cough that came from Bastian sounded suspiciously like an attempt to hide another laugh. "Wouldn't dream of it, old friend. And escape?"

Faolán shook his head. "I checked the walls. Trying to leave early would mean death."

A chill ran through me. I had a vague memory of trying to escape that first night, but something had stopped me. Thank the gods. If I'd succeeded, I'd have died.

But Bastian had come by choice. I frowned at him. "But now you're here, aren't you trapped, too?"

"Just being here isn't enough. Hmm." He eyed the room and licked his lips as though flavour lingered on them. "You accepted an invitation and that's what got you stuck. My guess would be it was some sort of food." His gaze slid to Faolán.

"Mm." My husband's arms folded, a solid wall over his chest.

"How you got yourself trapped by such an obvious charm, I can't fathom." Bastian shook his head. "Really, Faolán, I thought you knew better."

His words prickled me, and I folded my arms, mirroring my husband. "He was helping me."

Faolán's face tightened in a wince.

Bastian's eyebrows rose as his attention returned to me. "Oh, *really*?" His gaze flowed over me, evaluating. "And why would he be doing that, I wonder. Faolán?"

"You can mock me all you like when I get back. In the meantime, there's something strange about this place."

"Oh?" Bastian's amusement disappeared as he looked between us, eyes sharp.

We told him about the ball we'd seen in our shared dream, though we left out the part where we'd kissed. Mercifully, Faolán also didn't mention the way I'd reacted to the sapphire-eyed woman's fae charm.

Bastian's brow crinkled as he pursed his lips. "I'm not so sure that was a dream." He eyed the ceiling and walls. "You said the house *does things*, has some sort of awareness?"

I nodded, half-expecting something in the room to move in answer.

"It may be that you're seeing its memories."

"Memories?" A chill crept through me. "Then that really happened?"

He shrugged and tossed his head. "Perhaps." He stalked to the window. "It would help if I knew where you were."

Faolán growled, eyebrows low and fierce. "I'd love to know that, too. But she transported us here. I just know the wall to her gardens"—he flicked the briefest glance to me, disapproval unmistakeable in the flat set of his mouth before he continued—"is about a day's travel from the skyshrine on the edge of clan territory."

"Hmm, that's something, I suppose. I'll see what I can find out." Bastian peered outside before turning to us with a smirk. "In the meantime, you're both stuck here."

I gave Faolán an apologetic smile as his arms tightened over his chest. "Looks like you're stuck here with me. Sorry." I raised my hands and explained to Bastian, "He hates me, you see. I make him *terribly* grumpy."

He huffed out a breath through his nose. "Oh, no, he's always this cheerful at work."

Faolán grunted. "I am when the job goes so bloody wrong."

Bastian chuckled and fingered the candlestick I'd picked up as a makeshift weapon on my first day. "Well, there's nothing you can do about it now, and this place is better than your tent. You might as well make the most of it." His eyes narrowed at the wall. "Is that a bathroom through there?"

"Mm-hmm."

With a flash of canines, Bastian grinned. "Then what are you complaining about?" He clapped Faolán on the shoulder. "Between that and…" He raised one eyebrow meaningfully. "*All* this place has to offer, I'm sure you'll find a way to pass the time. I, however, still have my freedom." He tugged his cuff. "I'll see you in a month."

"Wait." One hand reaching out, I lurched forward. "I came here to find my friend. If you work for the Night Queen, you might've heard about Briarbridge's Tithe being collected."

"The Tithe?" He exhaled, expression shuttering.

Faolán lifted his chin. "I said I'd help her."

"Of course you did." Bastian sighed and shook his head. "Who'd guess you were such a soft touch under all those muscles? I suppose that means *I* should help her or else you'll just be distracted by this little quest for another month when you get out of this place." He canted his head at me. "Well?"

I explained about Ari and the fae lord who'd taken her and did my best to recite exactly what he'd said when he'd first appeared.

"A threadwitch with white hair?" He waved his hand. "She's perfectly safe. She has a workshop in Tenebris, in fact. Excellent work. Lysander chose well."

"She… what?" My heart beat harder as though I

needed more blood in my brain to piece together what he'd just said. "She's... safe and well?"

"I have an appointment with her next week. I had to pull strings to get it—her work is in high demand."

Already set up with a workshop and clients? After less than a week? That didn't seem right. Maybe he was deliberately talking about another threadwitch with white hair—twisting the truth so he wasn't quite lying, but was telling me what I wanted to hear. Maybe he thought that would make me go home and leave Faolán in peace to do his work.

Jaw clenching, I shook my head. "I won't believe it until I see it."

Bastian scoffed. "I suppose you didn't believe..." He opened and closed his mouth, eyebrows pulling together. "Hmm. So, I can't talk about... Huh. *That's* interesting." His gaze fell distant as he rubbed his lower lip.

"What?"

Hands tipping so the palms faced me, he shrugged. "I can't say. But I'll see if I can get your friend to accompany me here. Can't imagine Lysander will be too pleased about that—barely lets her out of his sight."

She was his prisoner. And I was trapped here, unable to help her.

That fucking apple. Why had I been so stupid as to take it?

"Well, I'm getting the hells out of here, since I have the luxury of leaving this place. I'm sure you'll find some way to pass the time." Even as he smirked, he wrinkled his nose. "Really, Faolán. Try not to get killed by any of these dream-memories." He shook his head with a *tsk* before gripping thin air like it was a door handle and giving it a twist.

The rectangle shimmered like heat haze; shadows curled from its edges, wafting like smoke, then he pulled the door open.

He paused there and turned to Faolán. Holding his gaze, he dipped his chin. "Stay safe."

"Mm." Faolán shrugged.

The corner of Bastian's mouth rose, and he nodded to me. "Until next time, Rose."

Then he stepped through the dark doorway and was gone.

A Kind of Normal

Over the following days, we sank into a routine. I ran through the house and gardens each morning, keeping myself fit so I could rescue Ari as soon as I could leave this place. Then I bathed and joined Faolán and Granny for breakfast. She didn't often join us for dinner, instead sending a note saying she was too tired but that we should enjoy our meal. House looked after us in all things. And each night, we found ourselves in strange dreams that might've been events from the house's past.

Sometimes they were just odd, like the party where strange music played but we couldn't find the source.

Other times, they were nightmares like the ritual.

But at least I didn't face them alone—Faolán was always at my side.

When I asked Granny one morning, she nodded and said she had strange dreams, too. "It's part of the curse that keeps me trapped here. A punishment."

"For what?" I asked, leaning forward over my coffee.

"I upset the wrong person." She gestured towards the front door. "There are some things we can't speak of in this place." With an apologetic smile, she returned to her black pudding and grilled tomatoes. Over coffee, she asked what we'd dreamt of, and as I explained, her scowl grew deeper.

I glanced from Faolán to her. "What's wrong?"

She huffed and glowered at the chandelier over the table. "You're my guests: I don't want this house and its dreams frightening you."

After breakfast, Faolán took me to the gardens where he'd gathered a variety of logs from the woodpile and some pieces of rope.

"What's this?" I eyed a series of loops formed by one length of rope. Nearby, a thick coil was pinned to the ground.

He trod on the hook holding the coil, pushing it further into the ground. "Training."

"Blood from a stone, you are." I scoffed. "For *what*?"

He shrugged. "Whatever it is you go running for every morning. Figured you need more than just speed."

Joining Briarbridge's guard. It seemed silly now. Hells, Briarbridge and its concerns seemed silly, distant. The idea they'd let me, a woman, join the guard's ranks —that was downright idiocy.

"Hmm." I shrugged, expecting him to prod for more of a reply, but he only nodded and set to work explaining my first exercise.

He started gently, letting my breakfast go down as I jumped from one log to the next. When I'd mastered doing that slowly, he made me run across them at speed, and when I'd mastered that, he changed their pattern, moving them further apart.

The loops of rope, I ran through, only allowed to put my foot in each once. I had to uncoil the thickest rope with its middle fixed to the ground and flick it up and down, so ripples ran along its length. Finally, he had me lifting logs of various sizes and squatting as I held them.

My arms burned. Sweat bathed me head to toe. My legs ached.

And I fucking loved it.

Yes, I was exhausted, but it was glorious. The kind of exhaustion that seared my veins and sparked in my brain. Even in movement, it let my mind be still.

There was nothing else. No friend stolen by the fae who may or may not be safe and well. No family who was missing my help. No nightmares waiting for me in bed.

Just movement and muscle and trust in my grip.

The next morning, when I rose for my run, Faolán joined me. He looked tired but he was fast and fleet, his steps silent, and at some point it became a chase. I had no hope of evading him, even with the head start he gave me, but that didn't matter. It was training; it was practice. It was a test of my skill.

My heart was already pounding when he slipped out from the shade of an oak tree, but when he bowled me over, turning so he hit the ground first, it leapt in a loud and frantic beat. Of surprise or excitement, I couldn't be sure.

I laughed as we rolled across the grass, somehow free even though his arms held me trapped.

We came to a stop side-by-side and paused there on our backs, catching our breath. Above, the sky was clear and bright, the dawn's pink just fading, promising a warm spring day. Nearby, he had set up equipment for another morning of exercises.

"This is a strange kind of new normal we've settled into." I panted, pushing hair from my face.

His head tilted a fraction towards me as he gave me a sidelong look. "What's your... *normal* normal?"

I huffed. "Boring. Up in the dark to help Ma in the kitchen shaping loaves and making pastry while Pa gets the ovens to temperature. I slip out at dawn for a run while the dough has its second proof." The island of silence in my day. "By the time I get back, my brothers and sisters are waking up, so I help with nappies, break-fast, and getting everything in the ovens." I stretched, imagining the morning sun that peeked through the trees and kissed my skin was the warmth from the ovens I'd grown up with.

"Baking, baking, baking, feeding kids"—I waved a hand, feeling his eyes upon me and the weight of how dull my life was—"I told you it was boring. I mean, the older ones are big enough to help with the littles now. And thank the gods, most are out of nappies now."

I'd been an only child for almost five years before my

first sibling came. Had to admit, I'd got used to it—having Ma and Pa to myself was a luxury I hadn't appreciated until their attention grew more and more divided.

"The rest of the day I help in the shop and teach my brothers and sisters to read." My face heated and I angled away from him. "Ma and Pa can't, you see. Ari's father taught me and some of the others, but..." I shook my head. "He isn't around anymore to teach the smallest."

"And after all that?"

"Well, dinner is chaos. Not even organised chaos, just pure, unadulterated chaos." I snorted. "Food everywhere. 'She's taken my sausage!' 'He stole my roll!' 'Rose, tell him, he flicked gravy at me!'" Exhaling, I closed my eyes as my ears rang at the memory of all those arguments. "Between the three of us—Ma, Pa, and me—and with help from the older ones, we generally manage to get them under control, but sometimes the bigger ones are just as bad. Teenagers—*so* emotional."

He made a low sound that I'd worked out was his version of a chuckle. "And after dinner?"

"Honestly? I'm knackered. But there's cleaning to help with and dough to be prepped for the next day. One or two nights a week, I do get away though." The ringing and the chaos faded and my body eased into the ground and the soft grass. "I go to the tavern with Ari."

I had to close my eyes because they suddenly stung.

Yes, I had rescued Ari from the bullies and dozens of fights, but truthfully, she saved me every day.

No wonder I couldn't let her be taken. If she disappeared from my life, what would become of me?

I swallowed, throat thick and salty, unable to go on. She needed me to survive Briarbridge, but I needed her just as much. She was mine. Our evenings out together or when I went to her place for a little quiet—they and my morning runs were the only things I had, the bright stars in the night that allowed me to draw constellations and impose some sense of order in what would otherwise be chaos.

Without her, there would only be the dark.

"Hmm." Faolán's rumble hummed through the silence at last. "I hear a lot of 'help' in your normal. I don't hear much *you*."

I flinched.

Once, before I had quite so many siblings to take care of, I'd found a wasps' nest. In my attempt to point it out to Ari, I'd knocked into the great, papery mass, and they'd come for me. We ran, of course, Ari leading us to a pond, but before we leapt into the cool water, half a dozen of the little bastards had stung me. When we got home, Ma patched me up with vinegar, which stung almost as much.

Each of Faolán's words was a barb that hurt as much as the sting and the vinegar put together. Not least of all because they were true.

Wincing, I pulled my arms around myself as if they might shield me from him seeing that truth so easily. It couldn't be helped, though—what else was I meant to do? "They need me."

Being needed wasn't quite the same as being loved and cared for as I'd been before my brothers and sisters came, but it was pretty damn close.

I rolled to my feet and muttered, "Are we training or what?"

WANT

If Faolán's plan was for our training to send us to bed too exhausted to dream, it failed. Our new normal continued, dreams and all, and he didn't raise the subject of my old normal again.

It still gnawed on my mind though, even as I sank into a bath one evening almost two weeks into our month here. They had to be managing without me, didn't they? Or was the house in uproar? At least they knew I'd be back thanks to the note I'd left.

I nibbled my lip, staring at the tiled ceiling and its pattern of vines.

What if home was... just the same? What if they weren't just managing without me but *thriving*? That was a possibility I hadn't even considered each time guilt twinged in my belly.

Thriving or sinking under the chaos, which was worse?

Did it make me terrible to even *think* their thriving without me might be a bad thing?

I closed my eyes and rubbed my face, letting the steamy water run across my skin and drip down my neck.

Drip, drip, drip.

It echoed. Faded.

Drip, drip...

Sucking in a breath, I opened my eyes. The candles had burned low. I must've fallen asleep.

And although my muscles were loose, a deep tension coiled inside me. I'd dreamed... of something...

Breaths. Sighs. Cries and moans. A touch. Slick skin.

Snatches of moments, tantalising, teasing.

I huffed, rippling the water. I remembered enough to know it had been a good dream—a *very* good dream— but now my skin was afire and that tension low in my belly throbbed, dissatisfied.

Even though the water had cooled, my skin burned as I climbed from the bath and dried myself. I bit back a whimper as I towelled between my legs. Every part of me was too tight, too achey, too sensitive to the towel, to the tiles beneath my feet, even to the air wafting as I moved.

The silk dressing robe made me gasp, pebbling my nipples to hardened tips that pushed against the fabric.

I paused at the door and swallowed. Just like in the dream with the sapphire-eyed woman, I needed to get a grip on myself. I couldn't walk into the bedroom and jump onto Faolán at first sight.

"We're married. That makes it complicated, and I

don't have time for complications." I pressed my palms and forehead to the cool tiles of the wall. "Besides, fae and humans end in tragedy."

They were the reasons why I hadn't kissed him again since that first dream. They still stood, even if my resolve was wobbly right now.

With a nod, I opened the door.

As I entered the bedroom, my gaze sought him out at once. Traitor.

He sat by the fire, mug of tea halfway to his mouth. He stopped dead. The candlelight painted his hair bronze and his skin gold as, slowly, slowly, he turned to me.

Again, I was struck anew by the crooked nobility of his face, the beastly beauty. The fire flashed in his eyes, more than gold, more than dawn, more than flame. Although there were faint shadows beneath them, he'd never looked more alert.

He lifted his chin, and his chest rose as he took a long breath. It rose further still, as though he tried to take in as much air as possible.

Then he was on his feet, his mug set aside, forgotten. "Rose." His raw voice hung in the air as he closed the distance between us, his eyes intent on me like I was prey.

Did it count as prey, as hunting, if I let him catch me?

I'd fallen still—I didn't know when, only that I watched him come closer, closer, closer, hardly daring to breathe.

And I didn't pull away when he buried his fingers

into my damp hair, claws scraping my scalp. I only gasped.

He lifted his chin and inhaled again, deeper, nostrils flaring. A slight vibration travelled from his hand to the back of my head, as though he made a sound so soft I couldn't hear it. "I scent the desire on you." He blinked, and when his gaze lowered to mine, it was dark, his eyes hooded and flecked with still more golden fire.

He knew. He knew that I craved touch, heat, gratification—*him*.

My breathing came in little gasped pants as though my lungs didn't fully know how to work.

"I know this isn't a real marriage; it's only to keep you safe." His gaze skipped from eye to eye, down my face to my parted lips, then beyond them to my throat and heaving chest. "But I want to satisfy my wife."

I couldn't move. Could barely think. The throbbing in my body thundered now—it was a wonder it didn't rattle the floorboards.

Maybe... But... No... Yes...

He bent closer, and my lips tingled in delicious anticipation of his kiss. I swayed towards him. But he only brushed his nose to mine, taking another deep breath. When he exhaled, it shook, laced with a groan.

Somehow, my fingers found their way to his chest, tangling in the front of his open-necked shirt. They were already trying to answer for me. Tilting my head back, I took in air that tasted of mint and bay leaves, the familiar earthiness of tea, the rich warmth of evergreens, and something sweet I couldn't quite place.

"You spend so much time worrying about other people's needs, you don't pay attention to what *you* need. You don't listen to your body or your desires. I can smell what you want, what you need. Let me provide it." He shook his head. "Fuck, Rose, I'm yammering like a damn idiot, but I can't help it. We may only be wed for a year and a day"—his nose brushed my cheek, my jaw, and his grip shifted on my hair, making me shudder—"but can't I please you in the meantime?" He held still, hot gaze on mine, but I could feel the tension thrumming in his hand and chest and knew he was containing himself, waiting for my answer.

Perhaps I'd been thinking about this all wrong. Being married to him didn't complicate things. It simplified them. We both knew we liked each other but that this is only a matter of convenience until I found Ari and took her home.

There would be no awkward proclamations of love.

I wouldn't be here long enough for the tragedy.

This wasn't a romance: we were telling a story of a different kind.

So I nodded. "Yes." Gods knew how I formed the word, but it raked the air, raw in my throat with pure want.

"Hmm." The flicker of a smile caressed his mouth, then it was on mine.

Hot and hard, he kissed me, just as he had in our shared dream. He kissed me with his lips, his tongue, his teeth, with every part of him—his grip coming around my waist, his body pressing against mine, his hand in my hair positioning me to his will.

Every part.

And when he took that new angle and deepened the kiss, tongue demanding, I gave.

I gave him my mouth. I gave him the whimper I'd bit back earlier. And I gave him the arch of my body as I sought every point of contact I could find. His belly, his chest, his hardening cock, the fronts of his thighs, and the glorious rasp of his stubble scraping my chin, making me his just as much as his tongue did.

By the time he pulled away, the world was a haze, my breaths ragged, my pussy wet and aching. I staggered forward, trying to stop him escaping, but he chuckled, the sound soft and dark.

"Don't worry, my little flower, I'm not stopping any time soon." He backed off a step. "This way."

Hands on my shoulders, he propelled me towards the fireplace and pushed me into one of the armchairs.

I stared up at him, cheeks aflame—not with a blush or shame, but with sheer desire for the man standing before me, silhouetted by the fire. He could fuck my mouth right now, drive into me, gripping my hair, and I'd take every inch I could. He could give me that pleasure he'd promised, then take his own however he wanted.

As long as he made me come, I didn't care.

He sank to his knees and kissed me again.

When he pulled away, I licked my lips. Honey. That was the sweet note I'd tasted on the air earlier. He must've been eating some of House's honey cakes with his tea.

He hooked a claw under the edge of my dressing gown and pulled one side open, baring my breast to the air. The muscles of his jaw feathered as his gaze trailed over my naked skin, leaving goosebumps in its wake.

I gripped the chair's arms and bent forward, seeking his lips again. "Faolán." It was a prayer, a plea, a wish that he would do everything to me that he knew how.

Part of me knew this was all a reaction to the heightened circumstances of this house—being trapped together, the frightening shared dreams, whatever I had seen in the bath—but I enjoyed him. His presence, his taciturn conversation, his companionable quiet. The way he pushed me when we trained. The fact he'd protected me from the werewolf pack and from the sapphire-eyed woman at the theatre below the ballroom. The way he looked; the way his body moved. It all pleased me.

And that was nothing to do with this place. It was all him.

Maybe that did complicate things.

But maybe I didn't care right now.

Before I reached him, he placed a clawed finger on my lips, the tip tickling my cupid's bow, and pressed me back into my seat with a slight shake of his head. Then that claw trailed down over my chin, my throat, my chest, dragging on my flesh just enough that it sent shards of sensation through every inch but didn't break the skin.

By the time he reached my nipple, I was trembling.

He circled once, twice, then ran the pad of his finger over that aching tip.

I had no shame, no pride, nothing, as I arched with a shuddering moan.

It was the tiniest thimble of water on the fire raging through me—the tease of relief.

He gave a hum that sounded like approval before bending and closing his mouth over that same spot. I squeezed my eyes shut but the fire's sparks still danced behind my eyelids as he enveloped my nipple in hot, wet heat. The flick of his tongue. The scrape of his teeth. The moment of suction before he went right back to the start.

It killed me. I was a melted mess writhing against the chair's back, tangling my fingers into his hair, holding him to me, because if he stopped, I might break something.

Not stopping his torment, he chuckled onto my nipple, the vibrations of that making me lurch, before he tugged open the other side of my silk robe.

Eventually, he pulled away and looked up at me. Seeing him peer up through his lashes, the gesture coy and so alien considering he was usually above me, made my head spin.

When he coupled it with a grin that flashed his teeth —an unbridled grin, not his usual half-smile—I knew I was done for.

"Rose." He shook his head, gaze ravaging me in places I wish his touch would. "I think you already know you're beautiful... stunning, when we go to those balls and parties." The grin faded and his throat bobbed. "But

I like you best like this." He yanked the tie of my robe undone and slid the sides apart below my waist. "No, actually, like *this*."

His teeth flashed in something more feral than a grin as his gaze dipped to the auburn hair between my legs. Thumbs grazing down the inside of my thighs, he splayed me open.

He had to see my wetness glinting in the flickering candlelight—the same light that caught in the gold motes of his eyes. He had to see how much I *wanted,* the sheer state he'd built me to with that wonderful mouth of his. He had to see it all.

And I? I wanted him to. I arched into his gaze and spread my legs as far as I could, pressing against the velvet arms of the chair.

"Mm." As though approving and goading me on, he dug his claws into my flesh, not quite breaking the skin, but lighting my nerves with glorious sensation. "Yes." The breath of the word brushed my skin, doing nothing to cool my unbearable heat. "Exactly like this."

Then he bent to my aching centre and licked.

I cried out. Loud.

Because his tongue was molten and firm and surprisingly rough. It dipped into every groove and fold and finished on my throbbing clit, which he ran his full length along, lifting me towards a trembling peak.

With just one swipe of his tongue.

Oh, dear gods, I was well and truly done for.

He did it again, and I screamed.

"Don't stop," I whispered, barely able to get words

out between my panted breaths. I gripped his hair in case he hadn't got the message, but he didn't fight my grip in the slightest—if anything, he buried his head deeper between my thighs.

When my eyelids fluttered open, I gasped. Not because of him, but because the room around us bristled with candlesticks, the poker from the fire, the pointed end of a tail comb, all of them floating mid-air, all of them pointed at him.

Oblivious or uncaring, he continued his assault on my pussy.

"House," I said as I realised. My scream; maybe it thought he was hurting me. But—I jolted as his tongue dipped inside me—but this was anything but pain. "Not... not bad..."

Faolán's eyes popped open, and he pulled away just far enough to speak. "What do you mean, 'not bad'?" Then his eyes widened as he saw the makeshift weapons trained on him. He went very still.

"He isn't hurting me, House."

The weapons sank an inch but didn't return to their homes.

Seemed that was enough for Faolán, because he gripped my thighs afresh and thrust his tongue into my pussy.

"Oh!" My leg shot out as I made a sound that was almost a note from a song.

House's weapons rose again, trained on him.

"Not hurting," I huffed out as every part of me tensed, pulling that low-in-my-belly tightness from in the bath towards the peak I sought. "These aren't bad cries."

His tongue delved deeper inside—deeper than I thought possible. Had it just got longer? But then he curled it forward, and I no longer cared because he hit a spot that made sparks rain across my vision.

The weapons hovered.

"Not bad cries..." I panted, teetering, tightening, desperately trying to cling to my line of thought and ability to speak. "But good." The last word came out on a groan as my fingers knotted into his hair.

The weapons lowered an inch.

"So... fucking... good."

A hum of pride from Faolán reverberated into me, and I exploded on his tongue.

Behind my eyelids, flame roared, like a scoop of flour thrown over fire—bright, consuming, terrible, glorious. My body was everything, nothing, scattering apart like that same flour, drifting on the wind, then burnt to ash.

But Faolán didn't let the tension fade there. When I dragged my eyes open, the weapons had vanished, and he was still driving his tongue into me, through me. Merciless. So beautifully cruel.

Only this time, his molten hazel eyes were on me, watching as the tension built and I arched, and he stoked my flames higher, higher, higher. With a low sound of satisfaction, he palmed my breasts and ran a blunt claw over my nipple with pressure that was just the right side of pain.

I fell apart again, unable to do much more than

whimper on an outward breath that tore through me just as he did, pulling me apart with pleasure until there was only that and his eyes on me, the flesh around them crinkling as he smiled against my pussy.

Head lolling, I sagged against the chair.

"Faolán." This time it wasn't a plea, but gratitude.

Except, he didn't stop. Instead, he hooked my thighs over his shoulders—I was too spent, too boneless to resist—and feasted all the harder, his lips closing around my clit as he sucked and flicked with his rough tongue.

He didn't stop until I came another two times and whimpered that I could take no more.

I'd never done such a thing and would've sworn an hour ago that I never would. But here I was, begging him to stop.

He smiled and licked his lips clean. All that must've addled my mind, because I was sure he did it with a tongue that was too long.

I blinked, and it was gone before he kissed me so gently, so sweetly that I had to wonder if this was the same man who'd invaded my mouth and core with such merciless command. The honey of his lips mingled with my musk, a heady, private taste whose sharing felt even more intimate than everything else he'd done to me.

"Is my wife satisfied?"

He asked it to check whether he could take his own pleasure now. Hells, he'd more than earned it, and I still stood by my earlier thought that he could do whatever the fuck he wanted to me. My limbs felt like jelly—pretty sure they no longer contained bones—so I wouldn't make much of a partner, but I could try to please him as he had me.

So I nodded.

He smiled, the expression as gentle as that last kiss. "Good." He pressed his lips to my brow and gathered me into his arms.

With a sigh, I snuggled into his warmth and strength, revelling in the feel of him all around me.

While I drifted in and out of a blissful haze, he tucked me into bed and pulled off his shirt. If my muscles had cooperated, I would've explored the planes of his chest that I'd so admired, but I could only watch his body through my heavy lashes. He tucked into bed beside me, wearing those lightweight shorts, and put his arm around me, making the crook between his arm and chest my pillow.

He stroked my hair. "I'm calling in our bargain."

If I'd had more energy, I would've laughed. He didn't need to use his favour if he wanted me to fuck him. Not after that performance. Truth be told, not *before* that performance, either. Though that was after the bath and whatever dream had teased me; maybe I'd feel different in the morning. Still, right now?

Right now, he could have me any way he wished, bargain or no bargain.

More fool him for wasting his favour on something he could already have.

I arched and gave him a sleepy smile, letting my hand trail to his stomach in lazy circles. The muscles went taut under my touch. That power felt good—not as good as his tongue had felt inside and upon me, but still good. "Oh?"

He played with a lock of my hair, which had dried into waves before the fire. He tickled it from freckle to freckle along my arm. "Tell me what you want, Rose. Not from my body, but from life. From everything."

I blinked, my caress of his stomach falling still. What I wanted. I blinked again, swallowed, but I couldn't find any words.

I didn't *have* any words.

To delay answering or to distract him, perhaps, I grazed my touch lower down his belly and past the waistband of his shorts until my fingers traced his hard outline. It was just as thick and long as I'd have expected from his overall size. I had to swallow again.

He captured my wrist and pulled my hand up to his chest, where he trapped it with his own. "What do you want, Rose?" His voice was soft, but it contained a note of warning that rumbled into my palm.

I scoffed softly, disturbing the hairs on his chest as I looked up. He met my gaze, not quite scowling, but intent, serious. "Don't *you* want me?" I arched into him and draped my leg over his thigh.

His neck corded. "Like you wouldn't believe."

"Then why don't you have me?"

"Mm." His nostrils flared as he shifted but didn't push me off. "I'm *trying* to be noble." He let out a soft growl as though not all of him agreed with the decision. "I'm not taking advantage of whatever got you hot and bothered in that bath."

"Hmm." My eyelids grew heavy, and I fought their closing, but found myself losing the battle and let them shut. "My noble beast." I huffed at my own joke, snuggling against him.

His arm tightened around me and he resumed playing with my hair. "What do you want, Rose?"

So he hadn't forgotten his question. Sleep pressing on me, I let out a breath that matched the rise and fall of his chest. The dark came, creeping across me, but I managed to answer before it closed over my head.

"I don't know."

WAKING

ouse sent us pleasant dreams that night and I woke warm and well-rested. With a weight around my waist.

Ah.

Yes.

Complications.

But—I eased away and looked back at him—sound asleep. Maybe not a complication. Maybe just an instinctive response to having me close. We'd shared a bed for a couple of weeks now, and a few times I'd woken snuggled against his great mass. It didn't have to mean anything. Just like last night didn't have to mean anything. He'd said himself that he just wanted to give me relief.

"Mm." His arm tightened, pulling me against his chest.

Admittedly, it wasn't the worst place to be. But...

I tugged on his hand—it was like trying to wrestle a whole ham.

"Rose?" His voice was muffled and soft with a note of sleepy confusion that wrenched on my chest. The great and grumpy Faolán, all soft and vulnerable like a child. "You're still here." He sighed, ruffling my hair, and pulled me close again, nuzzling into the crook between my shoulder and neck.

His warmth, his touch, the way that last comment and sigh sounded like relief... It slid through my veins, easing my muscles, like the creeping effect of good, strong spirits.

He still wore those shorts, and although I couldn't smell his desire as he had mine, they did nothing to hide his interest. I indulged, letting myself nestle against him, tilting my head to give him better access to my neck.

Last night, he'd held back because of the outside influence that had turned me on so much, but right now the tension pulling my thighs together was all thanks to him. All he'd done last night. The strength and vulnerability I'd seen in Faolán the protector and Faolán the man who'd been attacked by a mob. The care he'd shown me in those little ways between his gruff exterior, and the way he helped me train even if he didn't know what it was for.

If I asked him now, would he deny me?

Except...

All those things that made me want to ask again? They were him. Not just the crooked charm of his handsome face or the solid muscle of his impressive physique, but *him*.

His personality; his spirit. His *self*.

And that was a far more dangerous thing than a quick fuck with an attractive man.

Shit.

I was the one being complicated.

Shit!

I tugged on his hand, even though part of me wanted nothing more than to put it between my legs and arch back into him. But it was that part of me that was the problem.

He released me, and I wriggled away, making the excuse that I wanted to go for a run before breakfast.

Problem was, I could run all morning, all afternoon, and all night, but I couldn't outrun my feelings.

THROUGH A DOOR DARKLY

Faolán stood waiting at the end of my route, ready for training. And much as I'd feared it would be awkward or that he'd try to turn things sexual, it was the same as every morning—professional even. Albeit, I caught myself staring at his mouth a couple of times as he explained an exercise, and once or twice, I was sure his usually appraising gaze softened as he saw *me* rather than just the imperfections in my technique.

But we said nothing about last night. Clearly, he was happy to leave it as a husband satisfying his wife.

I just needed to remember that was all I wanted.

However incredible it had been, I couldn't afford to want something with him. I had to keep my head so I could go after Ari once we were free of here.

Breakfast with Granny and lunch—the day went as normal. Granny excused herself from dinner, as she often did, and we ate in our room; the little table for two by the fire was far cosier than the cavernous dining room. Maybe because it was the two of us or maybe because it understood what we'd done last night, House sent us a rather delicious bottle of wine with our supper.

I snorted to myself as I poured a second glass. Maybe it was an apology for threatening Faolán.

He rubbed his bloodshot eyes. House's dreams had to be taking a toll on him. "What's that for?"

I cleared my throat and took a sip of wine to delay replying. For all that the day hadn't been awkward, we hadn't spoken about last night and the line we'd crossed. I bathed my tongue in the wine's flavour, rich and fruity like brandy-soaked cherries, but that only brought to mind *his* tongue upon me, inside me, reaching places it shouldn't have been able to reach.

I shifted in my seat and squeezed my thighs together. *Not thinking about that. Not thinking about that. Not thinking about that.*

Faolán's gaze stayed on me, the remnants of his supper, which had been a whole chicken with roasted veg and thick gravy, forgotten. He lifted his chin, chest rising.

Oh, shit. Could he smell what that one thought had done to me? That was how it had all started last night. I cleared my throat and fixed my gaze on the wine glass.

"I was laughing at House." I glanced at the fireplace, as though there were a third person in our conversation —that would make it safer, right? Make it feel much less like it was just me and him in our shared room, a few feet away from the chair where he'd fucked me with his tongue, and a few yards from the bed he'd taken me to after. "House, why do you keep sending us such horrible memories, but then you threaten Faolán with a poker and decide *that* warrants sending the best wine I've ever tasted by way of apology?"

"Hmm." He swirled his wine. "It *is* good wine."

And this was where he'd joke about it not being the best thing he'd tasted in this house. That was what my tavern conquests would say—one of them had made almost that exact joke. I'd laughed like it was funny and didn't make my entire body cringe.

But when Faolán said it, my cringing would be tempered by the memory of his mouth on my nipples and his head between my legs as he tasted me. I squirmed in my seat.

He canted his head and shrugged. "Maybe House has no choice about the memories."

I blinked at him. No joke. Of course not. Not for Faolán the gentleman who'd refused to fuck me when I'd offered myself entirely. "What—uh—huh?"

"Do you choose what you dream of? What old memories your sleep self dredges up? Maybe House is the same and we're just carried along by accident."

I frowned at him, at my plate, then speared a floret of broccoli. As I chewed, I examined the fireplace, the vine decoration weaving around it with thorns digging into the pillars that held up the mantlepiece. "Granny said she's stuck here as punishment. It could be House is punishing her and we're just caught up in it."

Faolán watched me, a crease between his brows as he

wiped his mouth with a napkin. His beard had grown back over the course of the day, but it was neat as though freshly trimmed. I liked it best at this length—it emphasised his jaw and softened the hardness of his face. It suited him, both his appearance and personality.

Neither of which I was supposed to be focusing on. Gods damn it. I tore my gaze from him and pushed my plate away. Maybe I should sleep on the settee tonight. Even in that huge bed, I didn't trust myself not to seek him out in the dark.

"Hmm." At last he nodded and discarded his napkin on the table before leaning closer. It was only a small table—barely big enough to hold our two dinner plates, cutlery and glasses—and he had to sit with his legs stretched out to the side, since they wouldn't fit under it. I refused to look at those long legs, thick with muscle, on the periphery of my vision.

But Wild Hunt take me, it was tempting.

As were his lips, close enough that I could lean forward, take his cheeks in my hands and kiss him.

I gripped my napkin.

Faolán canted his head, mouth skewed to one side in thought. "Punish her for what, though?"

The atmosphere shifted, pressed on my ears. He straightened, attention darting to one side.

The air rippled. A shadowy door appeared.

"Is it Bastian?" I stood, waiting for him to step through. Maybe he had news of Ariadne. We hadn't heard anything since his visit almost two weeks ago. Was she really safe? Was she—?

"Rose!"

Someone came through the shadow door, but it wasn't Bastian.

White hair, tawny skin, large, dark eyes, then a pair of arms were fastened around my waist, and all I could do was blink.

My knees, my outward breath, my chin—they all shook, because it was her. At least it *looked* like her, smelled like her, felt like her. "Ari?" I reminded my arms to work, closing around her petite form. She was solid. Real. "It *is* you."

I bent over her, eyes stinging as I buried my face in her hair.

For all my determination to battle through all of Elfhame, for all my fight and optimism, for all that I'd risked to get here, some part of me had feared I'd never get to do this. And that was the part that broke as I squeezed her.

"Of course it's me." A chuckle laced her words, but the way she sniffed gave away that she was crying too. "Good gods, woman, where the hells have you been? I *told* you not to come after me." She swatted my back. "You could've got yourself killed."

"Where have I...? *What*?" I pulled back far enough to give her a frown. "You're the one who's been in Elfhame, doing gods know..."

Then I looked up and saw *him*.

All beautiful and tall, though dwarfed by Faolán—I suspected most fae were dwarfed by Faolán—with that dark, magpie-sheened hair and black eyes that stayed on Ari.

The fae bastard who'd taken her. He stood to one side as though waiting for his property to be returned.

Teeth gritted, I kept one arm around Ariadne, holding her close, and reached for...

Except I had no blade on me. The iron knife was hidden at the bottom of my bag, and I didn't wear my dagger around the house.

I had to settle for shooting daggers at him with a glare instead. But the moment I could get to that iron knife...

Jaw aching, I forced my attention to Ari and a small, tight smile to my face.

She smacked her lips as if tasting something, a frown threading between her eyebrows.

I stroked hair from her face; it was usually soft, but this was even softer and smoother, like a sheet of silk. "Are you all right? Has he hurt you?"

She licked her lips, the frown deepening, then exchanged a glance with the fae lord. Checking what she could say in front of her captor?

My veins sizzled. What the hells had he done to her in the space of a couple of weeks? I would end him.

A frown mirroring hers creased his handsome face as he met her gaze. "Something's off," he muttered, so softly I wasn't sure I was supposed to hear.

She dipped her chin in a single nod, then blinked up at me as if only just aware that I'd spoken. "Am I—?" She scoffed. "Of course he hasn't hurt me. And... you're asking if *I'm* all right? Wild Hunt take you for even asking that, Rose Miller: you're the one who's been missing for six months!"

I laughed.

She didn't.

Neither did the fae lord nor Faolán. My husband swore and his dark eyebrows smashed together. When he glanced at me, his expression asked whether my friend usually spoke as if she had a screw loose.

But other than the anxiety that dogged her, Ari wasn't one for flights of fancy or anything worse than white lies.

Which left one possibility.

"Six months? I don't..." I shook my head. "I left to find you the day after *he*"—I speared the fae lord with a glance—"took you. And I've only been in Elfhame a couple of weeks."

Ari shared another look with him, and his lips drew flat before he spoke. "Time must move differently in here. The place reeks of magic."

"I went back to Briarbridge to see you." Ari looked up at me, dark eyes large. "I wanted you to know I was safe. But when I got there, you were gone."

He nodded. "And that was months after the Tithe."

My chest tightened because Ari's watery gaze confirmed it. And if I'd been gone months... "Ma and Pa? The littles? Are they...?" But my throat closed around the words.

Ari's smile trembled. "They're doing well, but they're scared for you. They thought..." Her throat bobbed as she swallowed and shook her head. "The older ones are helping with the littles. They're all mucking in with the chores." She raised her eyebrows as if she knew.

Which of course she did. She knew me better than anyone. She knew it was guilt constricting my chest. She knew I should be back there helping, not living in this strange luxury in the middle of Elfhame.

Her jaw went hard—an utterly alien look on her. "As soon as Bastian said he'd found you, I made him open the door to bring us here."

My eyebrows shot up. "You made…?"

The fae lord who'd taken her crossed his arms, eyebrows drawing low and darkening his whole expression. He muttered something I didn't catch.

"Don't mind Ly." Ari huffed something that was half sigh, half chuckle. "He's furious that he now owes the Serpent a favour."

A low rumble emanated from Faolán, and when I glanced back at him, his brows were tight together in an even darker glower than the one Ly wore.

It made my fingers itch to smooth his face, to ease the tension working his jaw side to side. But I didn't want to release Ari, so instead I cocked my head at her. "The Serpent?"

"He means Bastian." Faolán's voice grated through the air.

"My beloved wife tipped our hand." Ly narrowed his eyes. "And when that man sees a hand, he can't help but bite it." One eyebrow arched, he looked at Faolán.

Blinking, Ari turned from Ly to Faolán's fisted hands.

"I wouldn't believe everything you hear, Lysander," he growled.

Lysander gave a dismissive snort and shrugged one shoulder. "So now I owe the Queen's Right Hand, which…" Shaking his head, he exhaled, and the tightness of his expression faded. "But I'm pleased to finally meet you, Rose." With a smile that warmed his eyes, he inclined his head. "My wife has told me so much about you—around her frantic fears, that is." He gave her an indulgent look and the smile she returned was…

It was a punch to my gut, because it was utterly radiant. She was good at pleasing her captor. Did he get angry if she didn't play the part?

"Wait," I breathed. "Did he say 'wife'? He made you marry him? We can get you a divorce—it just needs both sides to agree. Faolán told me. We'll make him—"

"Happily married." Her expression had gone from confusion to amusement. "Through choice. No bargain or coercion."

I stared at her, opened and closed my mouth, tried to speak. Nothing came.

"Mama was wrong." She sat me on a chair by the fire and took the settee before explaining how she'd started off hating Lysander but that her view had changed over the course of months. The fact it was months still made my head spin. She told me how he'd given her space and quiet and had recognised her worth, and that she'd even rescued him from an enemy using her magic because *she loved him*.

I could do little more than blink as she went on. It

was only after all that they'd married and performed a ritual that meant she'd live as long as he did. Her bronze cheeks flushed at the mention of the ritual, but I couldn't pull my thoughts together enough to quiz her on it.

Ari loved the fae lord who'd stolen her. He'd... *rescued* her. And she him. And now they would be together for the rest of their lives.

No tragedy.

And me? I believed it.

How could I not? She practically glowed with happiness, and the looks she shared with Lysander lit their eyes up and made me look away, because they were too private, too personal. Too loving.

I wanted to be looked at like that.

I wanted to be loved like that.

I *wanted*.

The rest of their visit was a blur of hugs from Ari and brief explanations of meeting Faolán, our fake marriage, and what had happened here in the house. And all the while, the world sat in a hundred puzzle pieces that my mind stuttered to try and fit back together. Love and happiness, not death and tragedy.

We grabbed an old almanack with blank pages in the back and counted out the days we'd been here—tonight would be our fourteenth—and the six months that had passed in the outside world. By the time our month was over, it would be a year since I'd left Briarbridge. The thought stung my eyes, but with death spelled into the garden walls, what could I do about it?

Ari clasped my hands and told me she'd let my family

know I was… well, if not safe, at least *not dead*.

"Now, Faolán," she said as she stood from the settee, "promise you'll bring Rose to me as soon as you're free of this place." Although she was a fraction of his height, she lifted her chin and met his gaze boldly.

Who was this person? What had happened to my timid friend?

But tension rippled through her jaw, and her breathing came a little too deep. She was counting her breaths, willing herself to be strong and bold as she faced my giant of a husband.

It only made me love her more.

And when he stepped forward, took her hand, and bowed over it, it made me *something* him more too.

Not love.

Not love.

But…

It was a softness in my chest, a warmth in my belly, a tightness in the back of my throat.

Lysander stiffened as Faolán touched her, but he held himself taut and still. The tension between the two of them was palpable, but that shouldn't be any surprise considering Lysander clearly had a dim view of Bastian and Faolán worked for the man.

But Faolán covered Ari's hand with his own. "I cannot deny you, my lady. I promise."

Ari shot her husband a triumphant look, thanked Faolán, and barrelled into me again. "I'll see you as soon as you're free of this place." She jumped up and kissed my cheek. "A couple more weeks, yes?" Her expression darkened as her shoulders sank. "Well, *your* time. Another six months for us."

"As soon as I can get to you, you won't be able to get rid of me." I grinned and ruffled her silky hair.

Lysander opened the shadow door and waited for her. He smiled and bade me farewell, then his expression cooled as he gave Faolán the barest nod.

Arms folded, Faolán returned the gesture.

Ari paused at the threshold and looked back at me. For all she'd been full of joyous smiles for most of her visit, there was none of that now. Lines darkened between her eyebrows as her lips pressed together. This was the worried Ari I knew all too well. "Stay safe, Rose. You hear me? I'm going to be really pissed off if I have to command you back from the dead."

I cracked a grin. She did not, expression remaining flat and serious.

Did she *mean* it? I cocked my head. "Wait, can your magic *do* that now?"

She shrugged. "I don't want to find out." Then she stepped through the door.

Faolán's eyebrows rose as he shot Lysander a sharp glance.

Lysander canted his head. "I wouldn't be surprised," he murmured before disappearing into the darkness.

After his wife, who he loved and who loved him.

Ari had been taken in the Tithe and yet seemed *happy*. Not just happy—joyful, glowing, more confident.

I watched the shadow door close, but it felt as if a much larger door had opened.

UNDER GLASS

Despite my mind buzzing with thoughts of Ari and Lysander and their happiness, I still fell into a deep, dark sleep the instant my cheek touched the pillow.

Either House had no control over its dreams and they spilled over into my mind or it really was a cruel tormentor, because when I opened my eyes in a corridor, I was alone. No Faolán. No partygoers. No *anyone*.

The house was dark and quiet, the only light a wall sconce by the glazed door leading out into the conservatory. On the wall behind me, where there should've been another door, there was nothing, just vine-decorated wallpaper.

"Faolán?" I ran my hands over the wall, but there was no sign of an exit. I called his name again, louder.

Was that...? Just quietly, distantly, perhaps behind many more walls, I thought I caught his voice calling me. Or was that wishful thinking?

I paused, listened but heard nothing more.

Fine. If there was only one way out of this room, I'd take it and loop around to find him.

Out in the conservatory, it was a little lighter, with a full moon shining through the glass roof, casting grey shadows beneath the bent trees. The moonlight flecked the hanging moss with silver and lined the branches; it barely reached the floor.

Ahead, a faint sound, a song drifted between the tree trunks. Haunting and soft, it made tears prick my eyes. Sorrowful. Mourning. Even though I couldn't pick out the words, I knew it was a lament.

I hadn't realised my feet had carried me closer until the song grew louder, and I caught the cracking of the singer's voice, the soft sobs between the verses, and the splash of water that was her only accompaniment.

There had to be some way I could help or comfort her, at least.

I picked my way along the path that wound between the trees, sometimes stumbling over their twisted roots. In places the path squelched, and in others it rose onto a timber boardwalk, crossing boggy ground. I kept one eye out for a door that would take me out into the night, but I couldn't even see the conservatory's glazed walls, never mind an exit.

Eventually, the way ahead brightened as it opened into a clearing. Silvery light glinted off water where a stream cut through the indoor garden, snaking between large stones worn smooth over ages.

And there, on one, sat a woman. Like everything, her

hair seemed grey in the moonlight, but I swore it held a hint of warmth, like it was really a chestnut brown or red. It sheeted around her, hiding her downturned face, spilling into the water like it was just another tributary leading into the stream.

Bent over, she worked as she sang, dipping into the water, scrubbing against a rock, dipping and scrubbing, dipping and scrubbing. At her side sat a basket piled high with clothing. A washerwoman.

I wasn't quiet in my approach, but she didn't look up; she only focused on her work and her song. Scrubbing and singing, scrubbing and singing.

At last she reached the end of her tune and instead busied herself muttering over her work. In this light, her hands and bare arms looked grey where they poked out from the veil of her hair, with just a hint of pink at her rough elbows.

The bones of her arms jutted from her flesh, so skinny it was a wonder she could still work. I could count the bumps of her spine through her thin white shift where she bent over. The poor woman shouldn't be doing all this work; she was much too frail.

"She's dead. She's dead." She shook her head, rocking back and forth as she worked.

The crack in her voice broke my heart. I picked my way through the rocks littering the riverbank, moving slowly, keeping my arms wide so she'd see I wasn't a threat. I only wanted to help. "Hello?"

She didn't look up, didn't pause in her washing, just

kept at her rocking and muttering. "She's dead. She's dead."

"Are you all right?"

Still no response.

Now I was closer, something in the square set of her shoulders felt oddly familiar. Her voice, too—it picked at the back of my mind, a scorched version of a voice I knew. It tightened my chest and stung my eyes, tugging, tugging, tugging on recognition. "Do I know you?"

Nothing.

"Can I help?" Even though she'd been working the whole time I'd been here, the washing still overflowed from her basket. Maybe if I did some for her, it would allow her to rest and mourn as she was so clearly trying to do.

"She's dead."

I reached her basket and eyed it. Would it be rude to just take an item and start cleaning? It might help her understand that I wanted to help.

Next to the rock she sat upon, the stream swirled into a wide pool. The moonlight barely gleamed on its surface, leaving only a dark reflection that gave no hint of how deep it might be.

"She's dead." Her hair rippled as she shook her head and wept.

"I'm so sorry." I took another step closer, fingers itching to touch her shoulder in comfort. "Who do you mourn?"

She went still, head still bowed, then muttered something that wasn't "she's dead" over and over.

I edged closer and leant in. "What's—?"

When she looked up, I knew why she seemed so familiar.

That face, so much like my own. Large eyes, a proud jaw, nose a little too broad to be considered pretty.

My mother.

But… beneath those large eyes pooled purple shadows. Her skin sagged on hollow cheeks and crinkled around her too-skinny throat. My mother wasn't this old, had never looked so haggard.

She stared at me, eyes milky, and pulled her hands from the water. Face crumpling, she grabbed handfuls of her hair and tugged. The skin on her knuckles cracked, dark blood seeping out, dripping in the stream, staining her pale hair. Her fingers had been wet so long, they'd gone beyond wrinkled.

Gods, how long had she been here? "Ma?" I hurried forward, vision blurring as I reached for her poor hands. I knew it wasn't her, but I couldn't help calling her that. Not when she looked so similar.

"My girl."

"That's right, Ma, your girl is here. I'll look after you." I gasped at how cold her flesh was when I tried to disentangle her fingers from her hair.

She shook her head, grip tightening, resisting my efforts. "My girl is dead and gone," she wailed.

I sucked in another breath. Oh no, not Peony. Please don't say something had happened to—

"Rose is dead and gone."

I froze.

"Rose is dead." She said it over and over, louder each time.

It was as though the cold in her had seeped into me, stilling the blood in my veins, the breath in my chest. I opened my mouth to tell her that I wasn't dead, that I was right here, but my tongue wouldn't work.

"My girl is dead and gone. My Rose. She's dead."

Then the pool erupted.

FROM THE DEPTHS

Icy water crashed into me, stealing my breath, sending me stumbling backwards. My calf hit something hard, and for a wild moment, my arms windmilled as I tried—and failed—to keep my balance.

With an "Oof," I landed on a rock, my backside stinging.

The water ebbed, sheeting off me as I blinked it out of my eyes.

And blinked and blinked.

And kept blinking, because... *Please gods say I'm not seeing this.*

In the pool stood a creature.

At the top, regarding me, was a long head, pale, bone white. Hollows and holes gave way to nothingness, and I could see all the way to its interlocking jaw.

It was a *skull,* not a head. From the long shape, it could've belonged to one of the horses that farmers near Briarbridge used to pull their ploughs.

Except I'd never seen a horse with sharp teeth made for tearing flesh.

And horses' eyes weren't glowing pits the colour of a frozen lake.

They bored into me, and I couldn't look away, but I took in the rest of it in the periphery of my vision.

Instead of a mane, strips of flesh and straggly pond weed hung from its neck, some bloody, some rotten, most long enough to reach the pool and float across its surface. Its powerful shoulders rose above the water, bare bone pale against dark flesh, mottled with moss and green scum. As it strode from the depths, I caught a glimpse of hooves with wicked sharp edges.

Ma's wails rose, losing their words, but gaining in volume, pounding in my head.

Over it, one thought circled: *Not a creature. A monster.*

For long moments there was only my heaving breaths, the drip of water from my hair and clothes, and the slow unfolding of the monster as it rose, taller and taller.

I could've sworn it stood on four feet, but when it stepped into the shallows, it rolled its shoulders back and where had just been hooves were now clawed fingers with thin membrane webbed in between. And those shoulders were no longer the powerful quarters of a horse, but the square shoulders of something that was almost, but not quite, a man.

Rose. You need to move.

I blinked. Some corner of my mind wasn't frozen in shock, and it was right.

My muscles creaked as I scrambled against the rock, pushing myself to my feet as one hand went to my waist. Where there was no dagger. Damn it.

Fists would have to do. I had to protect Ma.

But my actions must've alerted the thing to the fact it had lost the element of surprise, because where its movements so far had been unhurried, now its hand darted towards me.

I'd barely formed a fist when those clawed fingers closed on my forearm.

Four pinpricks of pain opened up in my skin, one for each of those terrible claws.

Letting out a ragged cry that was all my pain and fear, I punched its wrist. My knuckles groaned as I hit again and again, but its grip didn't loosen, even as my knuckles grew raw and bloody.

I kicked and stamped. I tore at its rotting flesh. I roared at it to leave us alone.

Ma still sat there, rocking back and forth as she started her song again. A lament for *me*.

I'd gladly die if it bought her a chance to survive. "Run, Ma. Run."

But she didn't even get up.

"Please. Run!"

She only sang.

That fell glow in its eyes fixed on the warm blood forming four thin rivulets to my elbow, my armpit, soaking into the wispy silk of my dress, transfixed, like it enjoyed the sight.

It was playing with me. It could rip me apart in an instant, if it really wanted to.

It was down to me. I had to save Ma... maybe myself, too. But Ma first.

The beast towered above me and it hadn't even finished unfurling its shifting frame yet. It wasn't just bigger than me, but bigger than Faolán even.

I couldn't pull myself free, it was too strong.

My strikes to its hand and forearm had had no effect. And I couldn't even reach its head to punch it in the nose or claw out one of those glowing eyes.

But another vulnerable spot was coming closer as it took another step from the pool, its hoofed foot finally clacking on the rocks of dry land.

Who knew if this fae beast was male or female or whether such things even had concepts like sex, but it was my best option... my only option.

Just out of reach from where I stood, but if I swung...

Rather than punching it again, I fastened my fingers around its wrist. Its mouth opened, the few bits of sinew and muscle on its face twitching as though it smiled. Maybe it was laughing at me for thinking I could pull its grip away.

But that wasn't my plan.

All my weight on that left hand, trying to protect my right arm from ripping any further on its claws, I swung both legs back.

It cocked its head, and its face twitched again. A long, black tongue snaked from its mouth, writhing in the air as it hissed a horrifying laugh.

But I'd committed, and I was past being afraid of its laughter—it had its damn claws in me, what was a laugh compared to that?

My feet reached the apex of their backswing, and I pulled tight the muscles of my belly and the fronts of my thighs, bringing my legs forward.

I flashed the beast a fierce grin before turning my focus to my target: the weed-shrouded area between its legs.

The soles of my feet connected with something as solid as rock, jarring my bones, jolting my joints.

But the beast screeched.

It pierced my ears, shrieked over my skull like nails over stone.

For a moment, all I knew was that sound. No sight, no feeling, no taste or smell. Just that splitting sound.

Then the grip on my arm loosened, and the world was here again, with my feet back on the floor and the monster bent over around the spot where I'd kicked it. I gasped at the withdrawal of those slender claws.

I was free.

I didn't need to know anything else. I turned and ran. One arm cradled, I scrambled over rocks. The rolled and clattered under my feet, but I would not fall.

I would not.

"Come on, Ma," I called, but she didn't even look up from her work. "Get up!" I reached out, a few feet away. We just needed to get out of the conservatory—surely the monster couldn't follow us through that little door.

Then darkness and bone blocked my way.

My heart and stomach lurched. My body went cold.

How had it moved so quickly?

I'd barely told my feet to turn, to get me away, when its glowing eyes flared.

I didn't have time to gasp.

Its claws closed back around my arm and sank in.

Tighter. Deeper. Lancing through skin and muscle, piercing veins, spilling my blood in a thick, bright tide.

I choked and shouted something incoherent to Ma as it pulled upwards until my arm was taut.

An inch more and all my weight would be on those four claws. Amid the pain, I could *feel* the fibres of my muscles tearing and splitting.

My face, my neck, my shoulders and back—every part of me was slick with blood or sweat, and some places both. Hot and cold at once. Grey blotches spread across my vision like dough rising out of control, threatening to blot out everything.

I hung in its grip, the final ounce of energy I had left going into keeping my tiptoes on the floor, holding a fraction of my weight.

I had nothing.

I couldn't save myself or Ma.

My head dipped, grey darkness filling the edges of the world, leaving just a circle visible—the monster's hooves sinking into the silty banks of the stream and my toes straining.

The drip of water, the drip of blood. The slow thud of my pulse. It all formed a macabre accompaniment to

Ma's lament and the scrape, scrape, scrape of her washing. Why didn't she run? Why didn't…?

No. That wasn't Ma. She wasn't that old. This was some old lady, some old fae who looked like Ma.

Somewhere far away, the song shattered. Then came a tinkle that sounded like bells.

And I teetered, grey creeping in, threatening to swallow me whole.

MONSTER & BEAST

The monster roared and snarled, except... the sound didn't come from in front of me. It had a friend.

I blinked, face tingling, toes barely touching the ground as I fought to cling onto thoughts as they scattered in the face of this ringing agony.

Not bells. And not the song shattering.

Glass.

First breaking, then hitting the ground.

I lifted my heavy, heavy head and caught a flash of something metallic and beautiful, before the grip on my arm twitched.

The pain rose a pitch with that slight movement and there was a sound, a weak cry. My mouth was open, so I guessed it was mine.

Then there was a moment of freedom, no grip pulling me taut, but only for the briefest instant before gravity claimed me. I slammed into the floor, but even that bruising impact paled against what the monster had done to me.

With a wet thud, something else fell beside me.

I had to blink at it several times before I made sense of the white bone, the jagged flesh, the inches and inches of slender claws.

The monster's hand. Severed. Bleeding a sludgy green-black blood.

As if that realisation were a door opening, the grey tunnel of my vision expanded.

Blood-spattered rock. The liquid dripping down to mingle with the mud. Hoof prints, but no sign of the monster. A sword lay in the dirt, its blade covered in the monster's blood.

I had no time to lie and catch my breath, though, because nearby there was a snarl, a shriek, and the crunch of bone.

I scrambled to my feet, cradling my injured arm, and found the clearing around strewn with torn flesh, that pond-scum coloured blood, and *pieces* of the monster.

At the centre of it all, the huge form of Faolán.

I let out a breath that was more than half whimper. That roar wasn't another monster, but him. Thank all the gods.

His bare back was to me as he bent over something on the floor. He looked even bigger than usual, dominating the open space, painted silver by the moonlight.

"You hurt her." His body heaved with great breaths that steamed the damp air of the conservatory forest. "You fucking hurt her."

What the hells was he doing? I circled around, squeezing the slices in my arm to staunch the blood, but not daring to look at them. Even the thought made my knees weak.

And when I reached Faolán's side, I fell to them.

He had the monster—or part of it. No limbs remained, but its eyes still glowed with that fell light, even as they stared up at him, wide and *afraid.*

Part of me—the part that had been sure I was going to die tonight—relished its fear.

"You hurt her. Now you die." Teeth bared, nose wrinkled in a brutal snarl, Faolán took hold of its jaw in one hand and the top of its skull in the other.

I must've lost too much blood, because I could've sworn his claws were longer than usual.

His thumb dipped into its eye socket, and the monster let out a shriek, its tongue twisting through the air like it had earlier.

Only it wasn't laughing anymore.

Faolán's shoulders and arms bulged, straining as he pulled.

And he tore.

And he ripped the beast in two.

Its tongue fell still.

The glowing eyes guttered out.

Faolán lifted his head and bellowed.

The moon edged every snarling wrinkle of his face with silver. It painted his fangs and the gore smeared across his chest and covering his arms to the elbows. It lit in his hazel eyes and bathed his muscles in its pale glow.

He *was* a beast.

Brutal and terrible and more beautiful than anything I'd ever seen.

Because he'd done this for me. It was wonderful and awful in equal measure, but all I wanted were his arms around me, because there I knew I was safe.

He'd done this, after all.

I could only stare as he turned to me. Chest heaving, face still contorted, he stared. That wildness was still in his eyes, like he wasn't entirely Faolán—at least not the one I knew.

Then he blinked and that man was back. He looked down at me, eyes wide as they settled on my wounds. "I'm sorry." He shook his head, eyes bright in the moonlight, arm coming around me.

Despite the gore, I was grateful for his strength, as I wobbled and every part of me felt far, far too heavy.

"I'm so sorry." He shook his head again, as though locked in that one reaction, over and over. "I couldn't get to you in time. I was trapped in the house. I—"

"It's all right." I managed a smile, though my voice sounded weak.

A ripple ran through his jaw before he released me and tore a strip from his shredded shirt, then wrapped it around my injured arm. The pain pulled tears from my eyes, but my cheeks were already wet—I must've cried as the monster tore my flesh.

Faolán's expression wound almost as tight as the bandage he tied. "You won't bleed to death. But we need to get you some proper treatment." His jaw worked side to side for a moment, then he straightened from where he'd been bent over me and strode to the river. No doubt to clean the blood from his hands.

Except, when he reached the rocks, he ducked, picked up his blade, and started towards the washerwoman.

I blinked, brain not fully understanding, not wanting to believe, but my legs heaved me upright. I took faltering steps, cradling my arm. "Faolán? What are you...?"

He brought the blade back, no hesitation, only swift, unerring savagery.

"No." The word scoured my throat, burning and raw, and I half fell, half ran at him.

But of course I was slower than a blade.

One strike took off her head.

I grabbed him as her body fell into the pool and stared at the black ripples radiating from the point where she'd disappeared.

It was only once they'd stilled that I could stare up at him, mouth open, unable to speak.

"Rose." He said it so softly, it cracked my heart. It would've had me sinking against him if not for the woman's blood on his knife.

"What have you done?" I shook my head, eyes burning. "Why did you...? She was an old lady!"

"An old lady?" He snorted a mirthless laugh. "Look more closely at the rocks beneath your feet."

"What the hells have the rocks got to do...?" The silt gave way to uneven ground, with stones piled around the rock the washerwoman had sat upon.

Except, this pale stone was long and thin, with a curved notch at one end.

Not stone, but bone.

And that next to it, another—the curved shape of a rib with several more piled beneath it. The tiny pebbles I'd squashed into the silt as I'd fought to keep some weight on my toes—they were finger bones.

Thin lines scraped the surface of each and every one, and I frowned, not understanding until Faolán spoke again, his voice soft. "They've been gnawed. The beast, that was a kelpie. It crunches right through bone, eats it all until there's nothing but shards left. But the bean-nighe gnaw on the ends and suck out the marrow."

My stomach turned, making my whole body flinch away from the sight and the knowledge.

Nose wrinkling, he snatched the top garment from her washing basket—a grey skirt with a narrow waist and rust-red smears down the front. "She washes the blood from her clothes so her victims aren't scared off."

He turned to me, brows pulling tight together, and a light of desperation entered his eyes, as though he needed me to believe he wasn't some monster who murdered old women. "She can't kill on her own, so she lures folk in, close enough for the kelpie to strike. And in return, he shares his kills with her." His teeth bared in a snarling smile. "Quite the team."

She was just as much to blame as the kelpie. Just as murderous. Just as monstrous. And I'd almost died in their trap.

I nodded at last. "Thank you."

His eyebrows rose in surprise.

"For saving me." I sank against him, giving in to the trembling and the weakness that spread through me with the pain, clinging to him with my uninjured arm. "Thank you," I whispered against his chest.

"You never need to thank me for that." His body tensed. "Especially not when I was almost too late. I'm so sorry." He pulled back, holding me upright and meeting my gaze, again with that air of desperation. "Please forgive me."

I snorted and leant into his hold. "I'll forgive you for being so ridiculous. Too late would mean I wasn't breathing. Your timing was impeccable." I gave him a reassuring grin, even though I had to suppress a yawn to do so.

His shoulders sank on an exhale that might've been relief, but the lines of his neck were still too tight for that. "Hmm. This isn't over yet. Let's get you inside. I need to find something to clean and treat those cuts."

Tenderly, careful not to jostle my wounds, he lifted me and held me against the broad expanse of his chest. The hairs tickled my cheek and neck.

It helped to focus on that rather than the way pain throbbed through my arm with every heartbeat.

He strode through the conservatory, each step measured and smooth. "Keep talking to me, little flower." His voice was achingly soft, stirring the hair on top of my head, making me shiver and snuggle closer to him. "I want to know you're still with me."

"I'm here. Tired, though."

Around me, he tensed. His neck corded. "I'm not sure how much blood you lost. And I don't want to find out what happens if you… if the worst happens in one of these dreams." He lifted his head. "House, it would be really helpful if you would wake us up now."

At least then I wouldn't be injured.

But we were still trapped in House's dream when we passed through the door into the main part of the house.

"Rose?" He nudged my forehead with his nose, the tight line of his mouth dipping into view.

When I didn't respond, he nuzzled more forcefully, the bridge of his nose passing over my brow.

It was such a delicious feeling, I was sorely tempted to go on not responding.

"Love? Little flower?"

Damn it, his voice with that little edge of brokenness to it cut through any temptation to stay still.

"I'm here." I patted his chest and lifted my head to smile up at him. But the expression withered on my lips when I caught sight of the fear on his face, the bright gleam of his eyes.

He was afraid. For me. And sorry that he hadn't been able to prevent me from getting hurt.

He'd ripped that monster apart with his bare hands because it had hurt me. The washerwoman was lucky to get away with plain decapitation.

He wasn't a monster.

But he was a protector. A shield. A beast.

My beast.

And I loved that.

Maybe that made me sick. Maybe I didn't care.

I cupped his cheek. "I'm here, Faolán, my beast. I'm safe with you." I tilted my head up and touched my lips to his.

Only lightly.

Only briefly.

But it filled me with warmth and let me take a fuller breath and pushed away the gnawing pain of my arm.

And after, the fear on his face was replaced with a smile. No bitterness to it. Nothing guarded. No sardonic edge or cocky humour to it.

Just a pure, happy smile.

I'd kiss my grumpy beast many more times if it would have that effect.

Heart full, grin tired, I twitched a loose lock of his hair and clicked my tongue like I heard riders do to their sabrecats. "Come on, giddy up."

One eyebrow arched. "Are you treating me like I'm your steed?"

"A *noble* steed."

"Hmm." He scowled, but started up his smooth pace again. "If I could lie, I would say I preferred it when I thought you were unconscious."

I chuckled and leant my head against his chest, limbs feeling heavier with each moment.

The blank walls had doors once again, and he kicked one open, strode out into the hall and up the stairs towards our chambers.

"You're not talking," he reminded me, a growl in his voice.

"Fine." I busied my left hand by playing with his chest hair. It was a welcome distraction from my arm. "So that was a kelpie, huh?"

He dipped his head.

"If you want me to talk, *you* should probably try being more talkative."

"Still too angry. That thing could've… Besides"—he tilted his head away and gave me a sidelong look— "you're talkative enough for both of us."

I scoffed but couldn't call him a liar. "Is that a complaint?"

"Did I say it was?"

"No, but—"

"I'm not complaining about anything you are or do, flower. Just keep talking to me. I love the sound."

I blinked. Swallowed. Felt foolishly giddy. That had to be the blood loss.

I cleared my throat. "So that kelpie didn't look like a horse, it…" But the words wouldn't come out. I couldn't say how it had changed shape, how its form had shifted from horse-like to humanoid. Its front hooves had shifted to sharp-clawed hands. I tried again, but the words danced away, and my tongue fell still in my mouth, useless and silent.

Even in dreams, the geas on this house had power over me. I just didn't know exactly what that power was.

The only way I could keep talking was by changing the subject, so I spoke about dinner and training and other things, while Faolán carried me to our room.

"I don't know if this will work to wake us up," he

said, standing over the bed. "But worth a try." He eased me onto the mattress and the moment my head hit the pillow, came nothingness.

I woke in our bed, Faolán sitting up beside me a moment later. Stubble, dark circles under his eyes—he looked haggard.

I winced as I moved, because—

"Shit."

We were in the here and now with the tatty decor, but the kelpie's slices still marked my skin in deep crimson.

They should've disappeared when I woke in the real world.

It was a dream. They were only dream injuries, and yet...

I looked up at Faolán, searching for an answer. But the way he stared at my wounds, eyes wide—he was just as shocked.

He met my gaze and I nodded, because I knew what he was thinking.

Maybe House wasn't friendly and kind but dangerous. And if injuries from its dreams carried over into real life...

Death in one of its dreams meant *death*.

OF SEELIE & UNSEELIE

Faolán tended to my wounds, applying his odd-smelling salve and bandages with all the care of a mother cat cleaning her kittens. He held me close and explained in a low, lulling voice that the salve would stop infection and speed healing. His gentle touch soothed my fear too and helped me fall into a natural sleep, curled in his embrace.

The next morning, I was still there. No more dreams had come for us, as though his arms were enough to shield me from them.

Or maybe they'd been scared off by his display of animal ferocity.

My limbs ached and with a sigh I agreed to his suggestion that we take a break from training. "For today, anyway."

The dark look he gave my bandaged arm suggested he wasn't satisfied with that response, but I pointed out that training was even more important now. "If those dreams can do this"—I held up my arm—"it's a matter of survival."

The way he scowled, I thought he was going to battle me on this, but instead he gave a firm nod. "Tonight is our fifteenth night here. Halfway." Jaw tight, he pulled me close. "We will get through this."

I placed my hand over his heart and nodded. "We will. I promise it." With Ari safe and happy, she didn't need me to save her. But like Faolán had said when we arrived, I needed myself. If I wanted to survive, I needed him too.

At breakfast, Granny eyed my bandages and gasped, clutching her chest. "My dear, what happened?"

I explained about the dream, my tongue tripping over some detail of the kelpie that I just couldn't pin down. Hadn't that happened last night, too?

Something I couldn't say. Something that my thoughts scattered from as soon as I tried.

What was this house doing to us?

Still, I smiled and thanked it when breakfast appeared on the table. It was dangerous, but we were stuck here. I could play along if that kept me on its good side. If its good side meant dangers like the kelpie, what would its bad side mean?

"I'm so sorry, my dear." Granny shook her head and dabbed her thin lips with a napkin. "I think sometimes this house dreams of things that have come before. And this place has a dark history."

Behind his huge plate, Faolán straightened and paused with his fork halfway to his mouth. "And that is what, exactly?" His eyes flitted to one side, narrowing at the house in accusation.

"You've seen it." Granny tilted her head, eyebrows pulling together. "The balls. The rituals. The strange people who used to come here with their violent desires. There's a touch of the unseelie about them, I think."

Faolán's look darkened. "Hmm. Unseelie." He said it like someone might say a curse and let his fork clatter back onto his plate with a look of disgust.

I blinked from him to her, waiting for an explanation. Stories, both fictional and historical, told us there were seelie and unseelie fae. The first were powerful, tricksy, and capricious, acting in ways that left mortals confused and groping for meaning.

The second were worse.

"I thought the unseelie had been banished from this world," I said at last when no explanation came.

"Aye." Faolán shrugged, and for long seconds I thought that would be his only reply, but then he sighed and loaded his fork with food. "But they lived in these lands before that, side-by-side with us. We're cousins, after all."

"And sometimes, they pass between realms." Granny canted her head and offered me coffee.

Faolán snorted around his mouthful of sausage. "You don't believe that, do you?"

Her eyes widened as she paused with the pot above my cup, not yet pouring. "When the veil is thin, many things may come to be."

"Hmm." He shook his head but otherwise busied himself with his plate.

I pursed my lips, watching them over my coffee. Speaking to fae was like only getting half the conversation. Even Granny's replies to direct questions felt like they hid twists that I couldn't see. And Faolán's answers rarely extended more than a sentence—often nothing more than a single word or just that *sound*.

I asked Granny about what other dangers she'd seen in House's dreams. If we had information, we could prepare. But she only shrugged and explained that she'd never faced the kelpie or any other dangers in her dreams here. I supposed the sapphire-eyed woman wasn't a threat to her, since she was fae. All the sacrifices I'd seen were of humans.

Faolán gave me an apologetic smile and murmured that it was a good idea to ask.

It didn't help us, though.

Once I finished my coffee, I excused myself. I couldn't go for a run today or train, but that didn't mean I couldn't take a gentle walk around the house and gardens.

Stuffing another slice of toast in his mouth, Faolán followed.

WE DID a circuit of the gardens, stopping short of the forest that surrounded them. Something tugged on my mind... a memory. Something I'd seen out here at night.

But I couldn't quite see it, like trying to look at a single raindrop as it fell.

Faolán kept rubbing his eyes and even though we'd slept for a long while after the kelpie dream, he looked just as haggard as he had in the middle of the night.

"Are you all right?"

"I'm fine." He said it with a tone of utter finality.

He must've realised how harsh he sounded, though, because he came a little closer as we approached the house, knuckles brushing mine before he caught my fingers. I didn't pull away.

As we walked hand-in-hand through the same corridor we used every day on our way to and from training, he stopped short.

Head cocked, he peered at a painting on the wall. "Hmm." His eyes narrowed as he bent closer and tapped a claw to the wide gilt frame.

"What is it?" I craned around him. A grand room with an even grander chandelier and mirrored walls that reflected its lit candles on and on and on into infinity. Its tiled floor depicted the swirling shapes of thorny vines. "Wait, that's the ballroom—*this* ballroom."

"Mm-hmm. And"—frowning, he glanced up and down the corridor as if confirming our location—"this wasn't here before."

I scoffed and shouldered him. "Haha, very funny. It's cute you're jumping on the haunted house bandwagon, but House definitely wins on that front." I rolled my eyes at him.

But he didn't so much as crack the tiniest smile.

"This is no joke. Either she's put it here or…" His lips pursed.

"Or House did."

He scowled at me, then returned his attention to the painting. "Wait, there's—"

"It's moving!" I grabbed his arm and stared as the ballroom's doors opened, and in walked a man. His tiny form made up of artful daubs of paint somehow suggested he was young and strong. He paused and looked around, as though expecting to find someone there.

While his back was turned, a shape emerged from a dark corner of the painting, and I gasped. A wolf. It skulked into the light, watching him.

"Behind you!" I couldn't help it. Stupid to speak to a painting, I knew, but… "They look so *real*." I ran a nail over the raised brushstrokes, unable to tear my gaze away as the man turned and spotted the beast.

"They do." Faolán's voice sounded dreamy and distant. Out the corner of my eye, I spotted him also reaching for the canvas's surface.

It was impossible to resist.

The man darted to one side, but the wolf leapt and bowled him to the floor. "You poor thing." I stroked the man.

My vision went white, then gold.

A glimpse of mirrors.

My breath seized.

Darkness swallowed me.

Then candlelight.

PAINTED

I didn't wake, I just *was*.

Fur and fangs. A thundering pulse in my ears. Breaths at once gasping and crushed by the weight on my chest of two great paws. My fingers dug into the beast's chest and shoulders, desperately trying to keep the wolf's great maw from my throat. It snarled, brown eyes fixed on me with murderous intent.

I tried to shift my grip but my hands didn't obey my instructions.

Only, they weren't my hands.

Large—far larger than mine. More like my Pa's— wide, with blunt fingers and blond hair on the back that disappeared beneath the sleeve of my shirt. A man's shirt. That covered a man's muscled forearms.

And the grunts that came from me as I struggled, not in control of my body—they were all in a man's voice. This wasn't my body, but a man's.

I tried to call for Faolán, but I couldn't even do that.

It seemed I was just along for the ride.

As the wolf snapped and growled, blasting hot breath on my face, I took in the flickering candlelight overhead and the way it reflected in the walls over and over again.

I was *in the painting*.

The man must've had the same idea as me, because he… I… *we* grabbed a handful of the wolf's fur and scrabbled at our belt until we found the smooth leather of a hilt.

Quickly. Quickly. Inwardly I winced as those teeth got closer and closer.

Our grip on the wolf's fur. It was slipping. The beast would have our throat soon. We needed to land a blow.

Blade easing out, fingers aching with how tightly they gripped that slipping fur, we let out a bellow. Our hand arced and plunged our knife into the wolf's chest.

Hot, hot blood washed over our hand and arm, and the wolf let out a shuddering sound that raised the hairs on the back of our neck.

It twisted, turned, cracked, its weight collapsing on top of us, so we could barely draw breath. It wheezed, eyes rolling. When they turned back to me, they weren't a wolf's eyes, but soft, chocolate brown, almost human. We gasped, body tensing.

Why? What did he see in those eyes?

We didn't see anything else for a long while, lost in the depths of those eyes and the accusation in them.

At last they blinked and so could we.

And that was when I saw more that just those eyes

and took in the body on top of me. Not a wolf's but a woman's.

Shallow, panting breaths. Pointed ears. And those soft brown eyes screwed shut.

"Elaina?" Our voice trembled as we shook our head. "No. No, it can't be."

But she looked up at us and... and...

"It is you." But it wasn't only her.

Just as I was myself and this man, this was Elaina *and* Faolán.

And I'd just stabbed them.

"My love." I touched their hair, flecked black and brown and sat up, pulling them close. "I... I didn't realise."

I wanted to press my hand over the wound on their side that still seeped out hot, red blood, but the man whose eyes I was seeing through didn't do that.

Elaina-Faolán shook their head with a tremulous smile. "I'm sorry." Crimson smeared their teeth and lips.

It wracked through me, that look of pain, that spilled blood—the fact Faolán had to be experiencing this pain.

"Couldn't control... myself." They winced, eyes screwing shut as an agonised grunt came from deep inside. "It burns."

We blinked at the knife lying on the floor, blood pooling around it.

Darker than steel. Colder.

It was iron.

That was why we didn't bother to stem the bleeding.

It was too late, too much. They were fae and the iron so deep in their body was enough.

And the blood.

So, so much blood.

"I'm sorry," we whispered, cupping their cheeks. "I'm sorry." Our vision blurred, and my own heart cracked.

"I know." They smiled and covered our hand. "Not your fault." With a cry, they shook, neck cording.

"Elaina!"

They didn't respond, locked in pain, in dying.

They were dying.

Oh gods.

It felt different, but if this was a dream, then Elaina might have died centuries ago, killed by her lover, killed by me. But Faolán was in there too.

And death in the dream meant...

Trapped inside the man's head, in his body, in his actions, I cried out. I flung myself at the walls around me.

It might be that this was something else. After all, we were in bodies that weren't our own, and we'd fallen into the painting rather than falling asleep.

That might mean we were safe.

But it might not.

We needed to wake up or get out of the painting or whatever this was.

Now.

"I won't leave you to go alone." Our voice cracked on a sob and our hand closed on the iron knife's hilt.

Wake up. Wake up. Wake up.

It was a shriek in the void.

But I couldn't let this happen to Faolán. It wasn't just that I didn't want him to die because death was generally sad and something to avoid.

It was that I didn't want *him* to die.

I didn't want to be without *him*.

Whatever I'd told myself, however convenient this marriage was, I cared for him.

And it felt frighteningly like... like...

But there was no time to force myself to think the word I tried so hard to avoid: I needed to save him.

House? Please?

Something stirred.

We stared into Elaina-Faolán's brown eyes as they blinked, but on the edge of my vision, in the mirrors of the ballroom, in the endless reflections of us and them and the blood and the twisting vine floor with a crimson heart at the ballroom's centre, there was another figure.

Tall. Dark. Slender. Otherwise indistinct.

But I knew it was House.

House. Please wake us up.

Elaina-Faolán blinked again, eyes staying shut longer this time. Their breaths came slower, shallower.

We turned the knife, bringing the point against our chest.

Wake up.

The threads of my shirt split. Pain pinpricked as blood welled from that point.

Elaina-Faolán exhaled, slowly, slowly, slowly. Everything about it weak.

Not much longer and they'd be gone.

Wake up!

WHITE.

Then black.

A blur of paint and gold.

A warm hand caught my shoulder.

I blinked up at Faolán. Hazel eyes. Steel grey hair falling in his face, catching on the edge of his beard. Just Faolán. No Elaina.

Sucking in a deep gasp, I touched my chest and found the round swell of breasts, not a broad, flat chest. No blood.

But...

I clutched at Faolán's shirt, ran my hands over his torso, even though it made my bandaged arm ache, and turned him around, the breath catching in my throat.

The fabric was dry. No torn hole. No blood.

I let out all the air in my lungs, though it came out sounding like a sob as I pressed my forehead against his chest.

"Rose." His hands planed up my back, claws catching in the fabric of my dress.

I didn't care. I'd live with pulled threads and little rips. I'd let him shred every item of clothing I owned, as long as it meant he was all right.

"You're alive." The words were shaky, and I tugged on his shirt to prove that he was solid and real.

Because I cared about him. Oh, good gods, I cared far too much about him.

I didn't just need to survive this place: I needed *him* to survive it.

There was a momentary pressure on the top of my head—a kiss? And then his arms encircled me and pulled me close. I flung mine around him and squeezed, pressing my cheek against his chest.

"I am." His voice was firm, reassuring, like he'd never feared otherwise, but the wild thunder of his heartbeat?

It was afraid.

THESE OLD BONES

We couldn't make sense of what had happened in the painting, no matter how much we talked about it. And it didn't help that there was an element I couldn't speak of. I saw Faolán's mouth open and close, too, like there was something he struggled to say. Something about the woman. Hadn't there been a wolf, too? But I couldn't…

It wasn't there. When I tried to speak, the memory slipped between my fingers and my tongue felt thick and heavy.

I pitied Granny, stuck here in a house that sent terrors in the night and stopped your tongue and stole away shards of memory, leaving fractured moments that made no sense. We were only trapped for a month, but she said she'd been here a long time. Even if she'd never faced danger in her dreams, the things House showed were terrifying in their own right.

I wondered how long ago the different events we'd

witnessed had happened. The sapphire-eyed woman appeared in many of the dream-memories, but she and her guests never seemed to age, so it was impossible to calculate a timeline. Faolán had commented that their clothing looked old, but was that two centuries old or a thousand years?

One lunchtime a few days after the painting incident, I asked Granny about the sapphire-eyed woman and whether she'd been at the house when Granny had arrived for her punishment.

"I never saw the woman you mention performing rituals or holding parties in these walls." She went to take a sip of peppermint tea, but paused with the rim an inch from her lips. "Though they sound fun."

I must've made a sound, because her eyes widened and she chuckled, shaking her head. "The dancing. It's been a long time since I danced." Her expression pinched as she exhaled, then took a sip from the steaming cup.

Biting my lip, I scratched my bandaged arm. Faolán said the itching meant it was healing, thanks to his salve, but at this moment my frustration at not being able to train paled against the sorrow on Granny's face. I'd taken my body and its fitness and youth for granted. I was lucky this was only a temporary stop to my exercise.

"Still"—Granny lifted her shoulders—"mustn't complain. These old bones should be dust by now." Her eyes sparkled as she chuckled.

I couldn't help but smile back. Her cheer brightened her eyes, making them seem less rheumy, almost blue.

Faolán grunted and hid a yawn behind his hand.

I went to swat him for being rude, but the way the afternoon light set darkness under his eyes and carved a hollowness into his cheeks made me stop.

Admittedly, *my* eyes were gritty most days since we'd arrived, especially when our dreams were especially strenuous, but great blue-purple shadows haunted his like he hadn't slept in weeks. And his cheekbones hadn't been that sharp when we arrived. He insisted he was fine, but the stress of this place was clearly weighing upon him.

I couldn't save him in a fight the way he'd saved me from the kelpie, but I could give some small help with this.

Instead of swatting his arm, I soothed my hand over it and gave his fingers a little squeeze.

Although we'd stolen plenty of kisses since the night with the kelpie, they were always when we were alone, never in front of Granny. An unspoken lie stood between us: if we didn't have to explain it to anyone else, that meant it wasn't real.

And, I told myself, that also meant it wasn't anything I had to worry about. Even if my heart thudded whenever he touched me and now clenched for how exhausted he looked.

Even if I avoided letting things between us go any further than kisses because of the truth behind our unspoken lie.

It was real.

It was messy. It was complicated. And if I gave in to all I wanted from him, it would only get worse. What would I do once our month was over? I couldn't stay with him in Elfhame, even if that seemed like a nice idea. Not that he'd asked me to.

Even if he did, I couldn't stay with him to see the year and a day we'd stated in our marriage vows. I didn't have time. I had to get back to my family. I had to help them.

Sure, they'd managed without me, so Ari said, but...

They needed me.

And being needed wasn't the love I'd seen between Ari and Ly, but it was as close as I could get.

Movement out the corner of my eye tore my mind back from the tangled mess of my feelings and tore my gaze from Faolán's gauntness.

Granny watched us with a small smile, slender hands cradling her cup. The arthritic swelling of her knuckles had gone down, no longer bending the joints out of shape.

Maybe having guests made House spare her from its dreams. We hadn't seen her there, after all. Most of the time I asked her about them, she only said there were certain things the house didn't let her speak of. With how pleased she'd been to have guests, it made sense that we gave her a break from the nightmares. I didn't begrudge her that.

I reminded myself that over the following week as we had still more dreams. Knowing the risks, we were much more careful now, not giving in to curiosity to follow sounds, sticking together at all times. Our plan to simply survive seemed to be working. No matter what we tried, we couldn't avoid the memory-dreams, though—they came for us eventually.

Twice, we woke in the part of the house we'd been dreaming about, looking around in confusion, but usually we found ourselves in bed with the sun rising.

I still had a few normal dreams—of home, of Ari, of spending time with Faolán. A couple of times I dreamt that I woke and he was gone from our bed. Maybe that was fear of what might've happened if I hadn't saved him in the painting.

Maybe, part of me whispered, it was that I feared losing his companionship, his solid presence, the way he made me feel with his kisses. The way he looked at me like he wanted me—not my help, not what I could do for him, but *me*.

Because much as I'd cursed spending thirty nights here, as the days ticked by, I found myself less relieved at my impending escape from this house and more heavy at the thought of losing *him*.

Because being without him in my life would be worse than waking without him in my bed.

I didn't dare ask what he dreamed of outside of House's memories.

Instead, I ran him sweet smelling baths and massaged his temples and scalp. I made him calming chamomile tea and made him lie on the settee while I read from storybooks I found in the library. Anything I could think of to ease his exhaustion and stress, I tried. But he still looked so tired.

By the time I'd marked twenty-eight days in the old

almanack—two days before freedom—the slices on my arm had closed into red scars, and he declared I could start some gentle training.

I threw myself into it, grateful for the distraction and at the same time grateful for the excuse to spend every moment I could with him.

A Different Kind of Party

That night, House didn't spare us from its memories. But perhaps it had picked up on my wants, longings, fears, because when we woke in the dream, we were naked in bed, with two outfits laid out on top of the sheets. A loose sleeveless gown for me, the pale green fabric a whisper away from being see-through, and for Faolán just a pair of trousers, which it quickly became clear were very, *very* tight.

I tried to bite back laughter as he glared in the mirror at the trousers clinging to his legs. Still glowering, he hunted through all the drawers and wardrobe.

They were empty, and I failed, my laugh coming out in a strangled guffaw. "I think House just really wants you to wear those." I raised my hands, helpless. "Unless you want this?" I gestured at my gown, which it turned out dipped so low at the back, it almost exposed my backside.

The flicker of a smile edged his mouth as he surveyed

me, the brown and gold flecks of his eyes catching light. "I much prefer that on *you*."

That fire in his eyes spread to me, making my skin too hot, despite the lightness of my outfit, and I bit my lip. "You do?" I gave him a playful grin and turned to give him a full view, brushing my hands over the loose mass of fabric, holding it taut over my body. "What bit do you like?"

When I returned to facing him, he was suddenly very close, having moved across the floor on those silent feet of his. His eyes were molten now, gaze sliding across my shoulders that were bare save for the thin straps. It wasn't a touch, but it jolted through me all the same, making my tongue forget the other teasing comments I'd planned.

His hands flexed at his side as he took a long breath. "I like all the places it isn't."

I hadn't even worked out a reply to that when a gong sounded in the distance and the door to our room swung open. Sharing a look of concern, we tried not to go, but our feet were treacherous, carrying us to the door the moment we were distracted, then down the hall, until eventually we sighed and obeyed the gong's summons.

Faolán took my hand, threading his fingers between mine, and squeezed. It made my back straighten.

Whatever House decided to throw at us tonight, we would face it together.

AGAIN, House took us to the great white doors that led to the ballroom. Music whispered through the door, mingling with laughter and another sound... A moan? I shrank away, stomach knotting at the prospect of more sacrifice, more torture, more and more of the sapphire-eyed woman's cruelty.

I went to exchange a look with Faolán, but he stood stock-still, eyes fixed on the doors, nostrils flaring. His grip on my hand grew hard, as did the naked expanse of his chest, making the wolves tattooed there flex and writhe.

My throat clenched at what might have such an effect on him. "What's—?"

The doors swung open.

Rather than a mirrored room with the vine-tiled floor, the ballroom was a heaving expanse of flesh.

I had to blink a few times to truly understand what I was seeing.

Naked bodies, dozens—maybe a hundred of them, maybe even more, upon each other, under each other, tangled together. Their groans and gasps rose and fell, interspersed with cries and laughter, murmured conversation and bellowed commands. They were fucking. All of them. And in so many different ways.

The only people who weren't were the dozen musicians on a low stage at the far end of the room, though they wore no clothes, just masks.

I hadn't even realised we'd moved, but Faolán raised my hand to help me step over a fae's legs, and the ballroom doors closed behind us.

We picked our way across the room, between the couples and groups, and even some who took their enjoyment solo, our bare feet padding in a silence that didn't disturb the music's low thrum or the people fucking.

The rhythm trembled in the air, vibrating into my body, tugging low in my belly like *I* was one of their instruments.

I fought to keep my breathing even as I stared left and right.

A masked woman lay on a *chaise longue*, blond head lolling off the end, eyes closed as she groaned. And she groaned because, because another woman, this one with red hair, was bent over the arm of the *chaise longue*, face between the blond woman's thighs. Meanwhile a man thrust into *her* from behind.

My mouth dropped open. My eyes might've popped out of my head.

So much flesh. So many fae bodies, thick and thin, curved and angular, some naked, some part-clothed, others with gowns hiked up around their waists to allow access for hands, cocks, tongues, and I even spotted one man thrusting his toes between a fae woman's legs.

Splayed and bent, standing and kneeling, everyone here was consumed with frenzied desire and each wore a mask. I wasn't sure if I was relieved or disappointed to not recognise the sapphire-eyed woman amongst them. Mask or not, I would've known her in the crowd.

The very air heaved, a kind of electricity filling the

room like the moments before a thunder storm finally broke on a scorching day.

My heart joined the music's heady rhythm, the creak of furniture being tested to its limits, the cries building into one glorious tune that hummed in my very bones. I blinked from one fae to the next as we passed from the ballroom into the smoking room.

Which, it turned out, was full of yet more fae fucking each other's brains out.

I swallowed and tried not to think about the fact that Faolán was a blazing presence at my side, his skin radiating heat like an oven. Or maybe I was simply hyper aware of him, just as I was hyper aware of my feet whispering over the silk rug and the waft of the lightweight gown over my skin.

In tight silence, eyes straight ahead, breaths so deep they made the wolves on his chest expand and contract in a way that held me mesmerised, he led the way through the room. I didn't know where he was aiming for, and I couldn't pull my tongue off the roof of my mouth to ask.

We only stopped when a cool grip closed on my arm. A handsome faun-like fae with knobbly horns lounged against the fireplace and gave me a slow smile. He raised his eyebrows in question, then jerked his chin towards his crotch so I couldn't help but notice the enormous erection that emerged from the fur below his waist.

Couldn't help it.

And also couldn't formulate an answer. Because

what the hells did you say to that? "No, thank you, not today" didn't seem to cover it.

With a low rumble, Faolán closed in and stood over the faun, the stubble on his cheek rippling as he clenched his jaw. Slowly, his head tilted.

He didn't have to say anything, the faun just swallowed, eyes wide, then released my arm. Shrugging, he gestured for us to pass before turning to a nearby woman and bending her over a table. He threw her loose gown over her head before thrusting one horn in her pussy and the other in her arse, fucking both orifices all in one go.

It took me a second of staring to realise Faolán was on the move again and I had to hurry after him.

Suddenly the loose voluminous lengths of my dress made sense. Ease of access.

My heart sped, and I don't know if I imagined it, but I swore the music's pace increased, joining me in the dizzying spin. Faster. Faster. Faster. My breaths, too.

Faolán said nothing, just stiffly crossed the room, aiming for a door that led to a courtyard.

When he opened it, a cool breeze came in, pressing my gown against my thighs and teasing my nipples, making my breath seize. Still, I was glad for the slight chill—with any luck, it would quench my burning skin.

But outside, we found no respite. The benches, the flower beds, even the large urns that functioned as flower pots were all being used as props for more fae to fuck on, over, or against.

Jasmine and honeysuckle scented the night air, mingling with smoke from the torches and the musky scent of flesh and sex. It filled me, drawing that familiar tension low in my gut that still thrummed with the music.

But I didn't want any of these people who were bared to me, even as they beckoned when we passed, even though they were beautiful, even though, technically, none of this was real.

My body yearned for the beast at my side. I fought to keep my gaze from him, but it kept flicking that way, resting on his thighs displayed so beautifully in those tight trousers or his naked chest, before I managed to pull it away.

"What is this?" I finally managed to ask, once we'd completed a circuit of the courtyard and found every room that led off it similarly full of amorous fae.

Even with the moans and whimpers around us, I heard the deep breath he took in and out before answering. "Another kind of party."

"I don't think this is one even the Hawthornes have been to." Grinning, I dared a glance at him. But that was my fatal mistake.

YOURS

It was beyond deadly, because my beast was beautiful and looking at me with darkened eyes that could've burned a hole right through my dress, right through my soul.

And good gods, I wanted him. Not just sex, but *him*. His protective instinct. His vulnerability. Even his grumpy gruffness and that "Hmm" that was the most infuriating answer to any question but had somehow become one of my favourite sounds in the world.

Wild Hunt take me, because I was well and truly lost.

A tragic story waiting to happen.

Except Ari and Ly had no tragedy. Maybe human and fae didn't automatically mean that.

I pulled him to a stop and placed a hand over his chest, covering a pair of circling wolves. His heart thundered under my palm, as fast as mine, a pounding accompaniment to the music's solid rhythm. "Faolán." It was all I knew how to say, but it didn't convey what I needed to. My tongue was clumsy, my head too foolish for words, my heart too loud to allow my voice box to work. All I could do was stare up at his hazel eyes, breaths heaving, silently asking.

Maybe he felt the same, because he said my name in return and cupped my cheek. His touch was such a relief, I sagged against it with a voiceless sigh.

I burned to hear him say it again. I would've scorched myself to ashes to hear him cry it out as he came. It wasn't even down to the party going on around us—it was something I'd wanted for a long while now.

His fingertips stroked the sensitive skin behind my ear, making me shiver as his gaze trailed over my face like he was trying to decipher something.

"My love, my little flower," he said at last, dropping my hand and cupping my other cheek. The pad of his thumb skimmed my lower lip, a tease that I felt in every inch of my body.

I stepped in and tilted my head back, tugging on his waistband with my newly freed hand.

The corner of his mouth twitched as he understood my silent demand and bent low enough to kiss me. But he didn't. He stopped a finger's breadth away.

"Rose." His voice was low, but somehow blotted out all the cries in the courtyard. Or maybe it was just the power of him saying my name. Even if it wasn't my True Name, it had a hold over me—at least, when he used it, it did. "I asked you before. I called in our bargain. You said you didn't know. Now I'm asking again. What do you want?"

I hadn't known before. But now? There were too many answers.

"I want to train." I left out the *with you* part. That felt too raw, too vulnerable for a starting point. "I want to be strong enough and fast enough to fight and be useful and be taken seriously and protect others." That was what my wish to join Briarbridge's guard had been about. "I want to be more than a baker. More than someone else's helper. I want to be someone who's respected." I'd never thought it before that moment, but as the words came out of my mouth, I knew them to be true.

I trembled at that. At the things I didn't know about myself—hadn't until coming here, until having space and time, until being *asked*.

He remained silent, watching me. He didn't look disappointed by my answers and the fact they hadn't included him.

But I wasn't done yet.

My tongue worked around my mouth as I dragged in breaths, voice not knowing where to go next.

"I wanted Ari to be safe and happy... and she *is*. And... and I want that. I want to be loved like that. I want a home. It doesn't have to be somewhere like this"—I shrugged to indicate the mansion we'd been living in for the best part of a month—"just somewhere that is... mine." I almost said *ours*. "Somewhere that is a *home*. Whether that's a cottage or a tent, I don't care."

The corner of his mouth flickered at that, and I pressed my hands more firmly against his chest. I could've sworn his heart thudded a little harder at my last comment.

"I want a hobby. And time to do it." I huffed out a breath, almost laughing. Again, I never knew I wanted that before, but here we were. "I don't know *what* hobby, but isn't looking for one half the fun?"

He nodded in silence, fingers easing back into my hair, tracing delicious lines across my scalp.

"And..." I dragged in a breath, not sure how to say it.

But really, wasn't it simple?

I wanted him.

But that was too raw an admission. Too dangerous.

Maybe it wasn't his heart hammering, threatening to drown out all other sound, but mine. Still, I had to swallow and go on, because apparently now I'd started wanting, I had a long, long list.

"I want to hear you cry out my name as you come apart." My cheeks heated to admit what I'd thought when he'd said my name moments ago. "I *really* want to know what that sounds like. I want to feel you inside me, again. I want to be held by you. And I don't want these things because of someone else's fae charm or because of a dream or because we're surrounded by people fucking, but because of *you*. I've wanted you for days, weeks now, however much I've tried to stamp down that feeling.

"And I want things *for* you, too." My eyes stung as I said it, as my fingertips found one of the smooth, silvery scars that criss-crossed his body. "I want you to be happy. I want you to never be told you're a dirty dog or looked down upon or made to feel you're less than."

He shifted, weight slanting to his heels, but I grabbed his bearded cheeks and held him in place. Maybe he didn't want me, maybe he just wanted sex, that wasn't important right now, but this was.

"Because"—I gave him the slightest shake—"you are not."

Under my hands, his jaw turned solid.

"You are *more*. When I first met you, I thought you were a beast." I gave him a half smile. "And you are, but what I hadn't realised is that being a beast is no bad thing. It took a beast to scare away the werewolf pack. It took a beast to rip apart the kelpie and end the washerwoman's trap. It took a beast to make me *want* for my own sake. If that's what being a beast is, then I'll take beast over beauty any day."

I swallowed, throat thick at my litany of admissions, at the treatment he'd faced. I just had one more want to get out—for now, at least. Who knew what dam I'd broken open—one want seemed to lead to another, to another, to another.

"Faolán." I ran my fingers through his beard, fighting the desire to pull him to my lips. If he felt the same, then soon. But not yet. "I want every inch of the beast you are."

Silence for one breath. Two. Three.

Then there was no room for breaths—not between

us, anyway, because his lips were on mine and he backed me against the courtyard wall, fingers tangling in my hair. "Rose," he whispered against my mouth, "I *am* yours. Your husband. Your shield. Your beast." He kissed me again, again, again, like he was trying to prove what he said was true.

And as he couldn't lie… Well, the sentences formed by his tongue had to be truth, but the thrust of that same tongue into my mouth obliterated all thought, except for the repetition of his words in my mind.

I am yours. Your husband. Your shield. Your beast.

And his kisses were every bit those of the beast I wanted. Hard. Deep. Devouring. Catching my breath and holding it hostage as he pinned me against the wall.

Somehow I'd managed to wrap my legs around his waist, and I could feel how much he wanted me, too. It was dizzying, glorious, the hard press of him against the soft sensitivity of me. But…

"There's one more thing I want," I panted, lips grazing his.

He pulled back, pupils so wide, I could've fallen into their depths. "Hmm?" He raised an eyebrow, then pressed his lips, his tongue against my throat, sending a wave of goosebumps across my skin, making my body hotter and hotter. "What's that?"

I threaded my fingers through his thick hair, pulling strands loose from the knot. "I want to wake up so we can do this in reality."

"You want this?" He grabbed my backside and ground into me.

My dress did nothing to dampen the sensation, and I shivered at the slick wetness he made pool at my core. I nodded and arched into him. "Wake up," I huffed. "I want to wake up."

And I did.

WONDER

Surrounded by drifting fae lights, alone at last, we stood in the courtyard. Him in his tight, tight trousers, me in the loose folds of my semi-sheer gown. I didn't question it. Didn't want to. Not when I could feel him for real, hold him for real, kiss him and make him mine *for real.*

And I didn't delay that, leaping into his arms, wrapping my legs around him, anchoring my lips to his, opening to let his tongue sweep into my mouth.

Much as the memory-dreams felt solid, there was something they lacked compared to this. Here, I knew his hands really were squeezing my arse, holding me hard against him. Here, I knew he really was kissing me like our lives depended on it. Here, I knew he really was mine and that it wasn't just some shade of our awareness trapped in a haunted house's nightmares.

It seared through me, hot and bright and beautiful. I squeezed him tighter, rocking against the hardness that strained at his trousers, tugging on his hair, meeting his tongue swipe for swipe as it plunged into my mouth.

Somewhere beyond the depth of our kiss, there was a sense of movement, and moments later, my backside landed on something solid. I gasped at the cold, realising it was also wet, and Faolán pulled back far enough to grin at me, before trailing his lips to my neck. He'd sat me on the edge of the fountain, its water gushing against my bottom and over the edge of the shallow stone basin, flowing into the grate below.

Truth be told, the cool was welcome after all the heat he'd stoked in me. And that heat rose even higher as he sucked and nipped at the sensitive skin between my neck and shoulder, making me shiver.

Somehow, I managed to huff out that I'd been taking the preventative tea, provided by House, so I couldn't get pregnant.

He lifted one shoulder and held my gaze for long enough to say, "Fae men take precautions until they want to sire. Me included. No danger of children here." Then he was back to teasing my throat, finding every sensitive spot he could, setting my nerves on fire.

I'd only been locked in this house with him for a month, but it felt like I'd wanted this and denied myself it for a lifetime.

What an idiot.

But no more.

I arched into every touch, laughed when he grazed a particularly sensitive spot so lightly it tickled, and pulled him as close to me as it was possible to get. I was here, choosing this, choosing him, giving myself over to it entirely.

And, good gods, it was incredible.

"Rose," he murmured as he slid his rough palms up my calves, pushing the wet fabric of my gown out of his way. "I'm not a man of words. Certainly not pretty ones." He reached my thighs, and I leant back, hands in the water, body tight and aching with anticipation. "So let my actions show how I feel"—he kissed me, tongue flicking—"how proud I am of you for finding your wants"—his thumbs ran up my inner thighs, questing higher, higher, and I bit my lip—"how much I've been holding back these weeks."

The light silk clung to my skin where it was wet, but Faolán wasn't so easily defeated. He slid his hands beneath, gaze heavy upon me like he wanted to see the moment when—

I gave a breathy sigh, almost a moan, because finally he grazed my edges.

The corner of his mouth rose as he watched my lips, drinking up my reaction as he did it again. "So beautiful, Rose."

The next time that graze became a sweep up my centre, and my back arched as my legs bent under the fountain's bowl. My body was no longer under my control, it could only respond to his touch.

He bent closer, and I lifted my face, eager to feel his mouth on mine again. Truth be told, I didn't think I'd ever tire of it. And that was a terrifying tension in my belly. But somehow the fear only added to my desire, driving the flames from red to orange to hot, hot yellow that licked and leapt.

He nudged my nose with his. "So bright and sweet." Then he closed in, thumb plunging into me at the exact moment his tongue claimed my mouth, and I had no idea how I didn't fall apart into flecks of nothing at that alone.

I panted around his assault on my mouth, breasts pressing against the shifting, sheer fabric of my gown. Each little brush of that silk against my nipples doubled the effect of his thick digit inside me as his other thumb circled my clit, stoking the fire higher and higher until...

Every part of me exploded in white hot heat. There was nothing but his touch, nothing but searing obliteration, and I gave myself over to it entirely.

When the blaze abated, dying down to embers that he kept glowing red with that touch still on me, in me, I blinked up at him, at the wondering look he gave me like he'd just witnessed something miraculous.

"What?" I huffed, trying to catch my breath even as the glowing embers inside me grew hotter with each thrust and circle.

"Watching you"—he shook his head, throat bobbing —"incredible. I could never grow tired of it."

I shouldn't want that, the fearful tension in me said.

But I did.

So I smiled and kissed him and tore at the buttons on his trousers, body fighting me as every muscle drew tighter and tighter, ready to break on another overwhelming climax.

Not wanting to lose the perfect pressure of his thumbs, I shoved his trousers down, first with my hands, then, when they couldn't reach any further down, with my feet. The thick, hard length of his cock sprung free, glistening from the fountain's water. I closed my fingers around its width as best as I could and was rewarded with a low groan that bordered on a growl.

His eyelids fluttered shut as his eyebrows peaked together. "Fuck, Rose." He shuddered as he inhaled. "I've waited for this for so long. I've dreamt of it, but..." Eyes opening and snapping onto me, he shook his head. "I was *not* prepared."

I slid my thumb over the dark, flared head of his dick and savoured the way it twitched in my hold. The power of that, his responsiveness, it pulled my walls tight around his thumb, which had fallen still from my distraction.

As though realising that, he growled and resumed his thrust inside me, harder this time, pushing me further onto the fountain, making water splash up around us.

"Once more, Rose." His voice was low and gravelly as his gaze bored into me. "I'm making you come once more, and then I'm fucking you." His thumb on my tingling clit circled faster, a little harder, wringing a whimper from me as my body shuddered in response. "And I will not hold back. Do you understand?"

I could barely nod because the very thought of it had my body taut, so close to another peak. "I want it, Faolán. I want you. Unbridled. Untamed. Entirely yourself."

His cock strained in my hand at the words, as though in anticipation. "Hmm." It was a hum of approval this time, and the sound vibrated into me as he bent to my breast and closed his mouth over the tight bud of my nipple.

Crying out, I broke again. My pleasure overflowed, like the fountain's surge, sweeping me away.

"That's it, flower. That's it."

His voice brought me back from the nothing, as he laid me back in the bowl of the fountain, cradling my head. A few inches of blessed, cool water lapped at my body, making my gown stick to every curve and swell. The appreciative look he gave me, slow and consuming, told me the light silk had turned completely see-through.

"Stars a-fucking-bove, Rose, you're going to kill me, looking like that." He peppered kisses over my cheeks and lips as he palmed my thighs. It felt like ten years, though it was probably closer to ten seconds before he raised his eyebrows in question. Asking permission.

"Faolán," I sighed. "You said you weren't going to hold back. I hope you weren't lying."

He chuckled, a warm, rough sound that reminded me of the honeyed whisky he liked to drink. "Never." With a kiss, he set his blunt tip at my entrance and spread my legs wide, setting his hands at the backs of my knees.

He didn't thrust in sudden and hard, but he didn't slip in slowly, either. It was purposeful the way he entered me—determined and unyielding—and the hard certainty I'd seen in his face before came to the set of his jaw, the intensity of his eyes on mine as he filled me.

And the thick length of him stretching the very centre of me, just this side of pleasure and pain, was exquisite. I sighed at the bliss of it. At the feel of it, yes, but also the fact it made him mine and me his.

The tug at the corner of his mouth softened that hard expression on his face, but made him look no less certain. Just as I was sure I couldn't take any more, he squeezed my thighs and paused, and I realised he was fully seated.

We stopped there. Eyes locked together, bodies, too. Each breath heaved through me, through him. My skin was alight with his every touch, with the lapping water, the slick caress of my gown, and the cool brush of air.

And in my chest, my heart was alight with…

I swallowed, consumed by his hazel eyes with their molten gold flecks.

My heart was alight with *him*.

I shivered, and goosebumps bloomed over my flesh, but I had no time to think about the implications of that realisation, because he covered my mouth with his in that moment and all thought evaporated.

"Rose," he murmured between kisses as he took up a steady, hard thrust that would've pushed me further into the fountain if not for his unyielding grip on me.

Lights sparked at the edges of my sight, and I couldn't be sure if it was fae light or what he was doing to me. I didn't care. Not when it felt so much better than anything I'd ever experienced. Not when it made me arch to meet him at such a perfect angle.

"My Rose." His chest heaved but the words came out unwavering. "So many nights at your side, I wanted this." He drove into me as though to illustrate his point, forcing a cry from my lips that made him grin in feral delight, canines bright in the moonlight.

Something about that expression made my body, my pleasure coil all the tighter.

"I wanted *you*. My sunshine." His words unravelled now as his pace built and that wild brutality took over.

He released my legs long enough to tear apart the front of my gown, then devoured my breasts, my nipples, kissing, sucking, biting like he was starving and I was the food of the gods themselves. And it was the sight of it as much as the feel of it that ratcheted my pleasure higher and higher.

Not for one instant did he stop pounding into me.

Harder, faster, his grip on my thighs tighter as each unrelenting thrust drove the breath from my lungs until I couldn't cry out anymore, just give a strangled whimper. I clung to his huge shoulders, anchored myself to them, because it felt like I was about to slip away from the very world.

"That's it." His voice was jagged, laced with a growl as his mouth dipped to my ear. "Come for me, Rose. Come on my cock. Let me feel you fall apart." He nipped my earlobe, the sharp clip of his canine making me jerk, bringing me tighter around him.

It was enough... too much... it sent me spiralling past the point of no return, sent me far beyond the pull of this world to a place where there was only throbbing pleasure and a low voice saying my name.

I was his. Entirely. And I couldn't even summon the energy to care what that meant.

Because there was no way something that felt so good, so right could end in tragedy.

So as I surfaced from my decimating climax, I rolled my hips, meeting him thrust for thrust, and was rewarded with the sight of his neck cording, the feel of his fingers tightening around my legs, claws pricking my skin, the sound of his wordless shout.

The beautiful brutality of it consumed me. The wild perfection. The glorious abandon of his wild fucking, every part of his chiseled body coming together in a symphony of movement, right before he came apart with a bellow that contained my name.

The twitch of his cock inside me dragged me with him, and I lost myself in the primal pulse of my body, of his, of the lines between us blurring to nothingness.

After, his massive body draped over me, spent, though he still managed to keep much of his weight on his elbows, not quite crushing me. I wouldn't have minded if he had. Not when his body fit mine so perfectly.

In the still night air, there was just our panted breaths and the lapping water—the gentle aftermath of our frenzy.

"Rose?" His death grip on my knees loosened, and he shifted like he was about to pull away, but I looped my arms around his neck. "I didn't hurt you, did—?"

"No." I shook my head, nose brushing his before I pressed a sweet, long kiss against his lips, savouring the tickle of his beard. "That was…" I blinked up at him, losing myself in the green and golden-brown of his eyes for a moment. At last I breathed the word out: "Wonderful."

His chest swelled as he brought his arms around me and gave a wide grin. "It was, wasn't it?" He lifted me from the fountain, kissing the top of my head, and pulled the tattered edges of my gown closed. "It was even more than I'd dared dream. You are…" He shook his head as he carried me from the courtyard. "I…" The pulse in his throat leapt, and I brushed my finger over it, but he only shook his head again, not finishing those aborted sentences.

"What's wrong?"

"Not wrong." He smiled down at me, looking the happiest I'd ever seen my grumpy husband. "Just… I don't know how to say it. And I need to tell you something else first, but"—a frown shadowed his eyes, spoiling his moment of contentment—"the house won't let me." He squeezed me closer, like he feared losing me. "I promise I'll explain as soon as I can. But… I'm yours. I'm your husband. Your beast. *Yours*."

The way his eyebrows peaked together, I believed him.

BREAKFAST

I woke in our bed to birdsong and... my hand slid across the sheets—the cold, empty sheets. I bolted upright. Other than the wrinkled bedding there was no sign of him. My heart thudded, a dull ache that drove my gaze around the room.

His trousers from last night lay crumpled on the floor, discarded with my shredded dress. So I hadn't imagined all that. No, my body ached too sweetly for that to have been a dream or fantasy.

I followed the trail of my memories from last night, which were admittedly a little blurry after we'd made love in the courtyard. He'd carried me to bed as I drifted in and out of sleep. I'd been blanketed in a haze of bliss, and it had felt even better to be looked after. I could get used to that.

Back here, he'd peeled off the ruins of my gown, touch firm and lingering as he dried me off before carrying me to bed, where I fell asleep tucked against his chest.

That was another thing I could get used to.

Exhaling, I rubbed my face and forced out a short laugh at myself. All these years, I'd avoided complications with my lovers, all too often being the one who thanked them for a great night and slipped from bed. It had driven some of them to madness, waiting outside the house and other such nonsense.

But now I'd found someone I didn't want to say goodbye to, and it had made *me* irrational, albeit for a moment, thinking he'd left me.

I am yours.

No, he wasn't the leaving type.

Sure enough, a moment later, House swung the door open and in strode Faolán, huge hands clamped around a massive tray of food. He also carried in the scent of a cooked breakfast, making my mouth water.

"You're awake." He beamed, white teeth showing through his beard, which he hadn't shaven off yet.

I liked that he hadn't rushed to strip it away. Clean-shaven Faolán wasn't my favourite. This one, a little more relaxed, a lot more himself—this was my favourite version of him.

Tilting my head, I gave him a bashful smile. "For a moment I thought you'd left me."

He snorted and brought the tray over. "Never." He paused, sitting on the end of the bed, gaze on me.

It was a look that became heavier the longer I held it. He really meant never. Maybe what he felt for me wasn't something that would fade or get distracted or become divided between too many. My heart twisted, a crumpling pain in my chest.

Not like Ma and Pa's love and attention when my brothers and sisters had come along.

It was a stupid thing to be hurt by. An unfair fleck of resentment that clung to me, like flour in my hair. But there it was.

I loved all my family, dearly. I missed them. Much as House had given me space, it felt quiet without them. And although I wanted to stay with Faolán, I also wanted to at least visit home and introduce him to them all and laugh as Peony and Rory clambered all over him like he was a great tree for them to climb and conquer.

Of course my parents had split their time and attention between us all as our numbers had grown. I didn't begrudge them that, not seriously, but it left me... a little hollow, a little wanting—hells, a lot wanting.

And when I'd seen Ari and Ly and that look they shared. I understood now—*that* was what I'd spent those years wanting.

It wasn't a million miles away from the look Faolán was giving me now.

"What's wrong?" His voice was a soft rumble in the quiet.

Cheeks warm, I shook my head, and grabbed a slice of buttered toast from the tray. "You know you could've just asked House to bring this up."

He looked away, and I could've sworn I caught a pink flush above his beard. "I wanted to make it for you."

"You *made* all this?" I blinked and reevaluated the crispy bacon, the overflowing rack of toast, the herb-flecked mushrooms, the eggs scrambled and taken off the heat while they were still just a little gooey, and especially the sausages that were just the perfect shade of dark brown with crispy skin.

He shrugged, but I spotted the flicker of pleasure or pride that pulled on his lips. "On the road there isn't usually a house to cook for you."

I chuckled and finished my toast, but my gaze snagged on something else on the tray. Next to the round teapot and tall coffee pot sat a steaming mug, its herbal scent unmistakable. The preventative.

It was a job to swallow; the toast suddenly stuck in my throat. "I thought you took something that meant you couldn't get me pregnant." My cheeks had gone cold and tingly, my stomach hard. Was that the first sign of pregnancy?

I sucked in a deep breath. No. I'd been taking the preventative for years—House had even provided it since we'd arrived here. That tingle was just panic setting in. I wouldn't be landed with a baby. This wasn't the start of my own huge brood of children.

"I do." He canted his head as though he could see the emotions that chased through me, then held out the mug. "But you only have my word for it. I thought this might give you peace of mind. By the look of you, you need it."

My laugh was one of pure relief. Not just that I was doubly protected from an unwanted pregnancy, but also because of his thoughtfulness. I grabbed him for a long kiss before taking the mug and tucking in to breakfast.

IT WAS the best day perhaps of my entire life to date.

Once breakfast had gone down, we did some light training, since he was still concerned about the healing of my arm. It wasn't only skin the kelpie had damaged, he explained—there were muscles beneath that were still knitting together. So I tried not to grumble too much at the slow, steady movements he showed me or the lighter weights he had me lift.

Despite my quiet frustrations, I found myself grinning at him like a fool more than once, picturing the night before. Finding warmth in thoughts of the breakfast he'd taken the time to cook so expertly this morning. Enjoying the way his touch lingered on me a little longer than usual when he corrected my form.

And several times I caught him smoothing a similar grin from his own face as he looked away.

We had lunch with Granny, one of our last, as she pointed out. We would stay tonight and tomorrow night, then we'd be free to leave at dawn the next day.

As wonderful as this day was, a small part of me wondered what would happen after. He'd said he was mine, and we were still technically married. But would he really be happy to keep our vows in place? What would our life together be like once the rest of the world was in it?

But his hand was a firm, sure weight on my thigh, and I remembered. We had faced the worst in this House's memories and we'd faced it together. We'd get through whatever the outside world threw at us.

With a broad smile, Granny eyed us and nodded, no doubt seeing something had shifted. She clutched her hands together, the joints moving with an ease that made me smile in turn. "For your last day, I've planned something special."

I didn't see how it could be any more special than today, but I couldn't bring myself to tell her that.

That night, we dined in our room, just the two of us as usual. But tonight it dissolved into slow, sweet love-making on the rug in front of the fire. And it really did feel like we were making love—making it happen, promising it, proclaiming it, even if we didn't say it.

But, of course, warm and sated, we fell asleep...

IN A DINING ROOM

ouse threw more of its usual strange memories at us. Tonight, as though it knew it was about to lose us, they were particularly dark. More sacrifice overseen by the sapphire-eyed woman as Faolán kept me safe from her charm. These poor people she cut into parts and the dream dissolved into tides of blood.

But we didn't wake.

Instead, we blinked and found ourselves at a dinner party with her. She smiled at her guests, teeth too sharp, mouth a little too wide, and when she clicked her fingers, the doors rattled, then swung open. "Meet my new servants."

On unsteady feet came something twisted, something that had too many legs and too many arms, but it was...

I couldn't move. Couldn't breathe. Couldn't even think about screaming.

Because those many legs and many arms, they were *human* limbs. In a shambling, mismatched gait, the thing crossed the floor, trays of food in its hands. My stomach turned, and sitting beside me, Faolán gave a low growl.

The other guests murmured in surprise and admiration. One chuckled, pointing at the way its legs moved.

I couldn't stop staring. Amongst all those limbs, I finally spotted the head. It peeked out, eyes wide and swivelling from side to side, as its jaw twitched and flexed, but no sound came.

Something inside me broke when I saw why.

Its mouth had been sewn shut. Blood seeped around the dark cords that held it silent, and no matter how much it moved, they didn't break.

And I recognised that face. It had been at the sacrifice we'd just seen, one of the victims. There'd been so many that I'd lost count... but now they were here, at least some of them merged together into this "servant."

The twist in my stomach that had been mingled horror and disgust fell loose. This wasn't a monster or something to be feared. This had been a person—several people, and now they were broken and afraid. A creature without a voice. A figure of pity and suffering. An outrage that the sapphire-eyed woman had created.

The world around me blurred. My eyes burned.

And then I realised that she'd said servants. Plural.

Two more shambled in, one with drinks, the other with desserts, both with lips sealed and that same desperate look in their eyes.

"Oh, bravo," one of the guests cried. Another rose, clapping. Within moments, they were all on their feet, clapping and raising glasses to their host and what she'd created.

She sat at the head of the table, drinking it all up with a smug smirk.

Until a crash shattered the applause. I leapt to my feet, and Faolán was already upright, clawed fingers raised ready. Ever the defender.

But it was no attack. The first "servant" had dropped a tray of food. Our host's smirk soured as her lips pursed. The second creature, carrying drinks, tried to help the first, hunching over, clumsy in its mismatched body. Down went another tray with a tinkle of broken glass.

The sapphire-eyed woman's chair shrieked across the floor as she stood, all elegance gone. "No!" Dark eyebrows clashing together, she pulled her slender finger hing into the third, who had also approached. In a tangle of limbs, they crashed to the floor, and finally my own body remembered how to work. I hurried towards them, ready to help.

"No, no, no!" Her voice rattled the cutlery, the chandelier, the floor tiles... even my bones. "This wasn't how it was supposed to—"

She swept her plate from the table and shrieked, the sound so tight with rage, it made me shudder as I reached out to help the first of her poor creations.

"Enough." She slammed her fists into the table, and there was quiet.

When I opened my eyes from flinching, there was no dining room. No sapphire-eyed woman. No "servants" or guests. Just me, Faolán, and the hallway outside the ballroom.

He surveyed me, nostrils flaring. "Are you all right?"

I swallowed and nodded, not able to find my voice after what we'd just witnessed. My stomach churned, caught between nausea and, of all things, guilt. I hadn't done that to those people, but I also hadn't been able to stop it. My eyes burned all over again.

Faolán gathered me close and bent in, like he could shut out House's dream-world. "This all happened long ago. There was nothing we could do for them."

But I felt the tension thrumming in his muscles. He wanted to rip the sapphire-eyed woman apart just as he'd done to the kelpie. But every time we'd seen her, she'd been surrounded by fae who stared at her not with disgust or hate, but with admiration. They cheered at her sacrifices and applauded her every abomination, just as they had in that dining room.

It was only in that moment I realised the very specific pain these memories caused Faolán, the shield who could not be a shield.

"I'm sorry," I murmured against his chest, stroking his back.

He shrugged and squeezed me tighter. "You don't have to apologise for crying."

"Not for that." I pulled back and met his gaze. His eyes were dark and dim as though they mirrored the tired shadows that pooled beneath them. "For you having to endure this when you can't change it. When you can't do what comes naturally to you and stop it—stop *her*."

He gave a grim, flat smile, shoulders sinking as he exhaled. "She's already done all this. And lucky for her, she's no doubt already long dead"—his lip curled into a silent snarl—"otherwise I'd hunt her down and..." His gaze skittered away and his mouth clamped shut.

Was that shame on his face? Or worry? Maybe both.

I shook my head and cupped his cheek, turning him back to me. "What would you do to her, Faolán? I want to hear it. I want to be able to picture that bloody justice the next time her crimes come to mind." Any other day, the cold intensity of my voice might've scared me. But not today or tonight or whatever this was. Not after what I'd seen.

He searched my gaze, eyebrows slowly rising as he read what was in there and saw my own impotent rage and how it hungered for justice. "First, I would haunt her." His voice was low and hard, no sign of hesitation. "Sounds in the night. A shadow at the edge of her sight. Always there. Always gone when she turns. Just enough to have her wondering if there was ever anything there at all." He dragged in a long breath, nose wrinkling. Did his teeth just grow in length?

I blinked and shook off the thought. The dream-memories were getting to me. Thank the gods we only had one more night in this place.

"Then louder sounds, more, closer. Scratches at her bedroom door. Under her bed. Howls outside her window. More and more and more, so she couldn't sleep." His fangs gleamed as he smiled. "And when she finally cowered in a corner, clutching a weapon, weeping for fear and gibbering from lack of rest, *then* I would appear to her."

I nodded, seeing it all, seeing how afraid she'd be, rejoicing in how much she deserved it.

"I'd let her run, and I'd hound her. Through the house, through the grounds, snapping at her heels, always just this close to catching her. And when she could run no longer, I would close in. I wouldn't use iron. Too quick. Bit by bit, I'd rip her apart."

There was a hunger in his eyes, mirroring my own and I leant towards it, towards him, eager to share it.

"Slowly. Deliberately. And as I did it, I'd tell her why. Every crime she was paying for. Every innocent life I'd seen her take. Every bit of pain we'd witnessed her causing. I'd make sure she knew that was why and *they* were why and that her body would be scattered in the woods, anonymous and alone, uncelebrated with no one to speak her name."

I shivered and clutched his shirt, nodding. "That is the right way." When I blinked, more tears fell, and I dashed them away before smiling up at him. "My beast. My darling beast."

His throat bobbed and a great shuddering breath came from him. "You mean you're not—?"

A shout pierced our quiet.

Faolán spun towards the white doors that led into

the ballroom. They were open a crack, letting out the sounds of struggle and a snarl.

He flew at the doors, me on his heels, but when he slammed into them, he might as well have slammed into a wall for all they moved. He shoved again, shoulders straining at his shirt, but the doors didn't budge, just sat an inch open.

Breaths heaving, he set his eye to the crack. He stilled, and I eased in beside him.

At the centre of the ballroom, the man I'd become in the painting wrestled with the wolf.

A memory unfurled in my mind, one I'd been unable to speak of. Faolán. The wolf. They'd been one and the same in that painting. And the man had stabbed them, except...

I caught myself against the unwavering door, head spinning. "Elaina?"

Faolán's claws scored the door. "You remember?"

"I do now. You were... she was..." But the words slipped out of reach, and it was only when I turned back to the battle in the ballroom that I could even think it again. The wolf was Elaina and the man loved her but didn't realise what she was.

A dull gleam in his hand. The iron blade that he would use to stab her.

"Don't," I shouted. "It's Elaina."

But he didn't react. He just clutched the wolf's neck, trying to keep its snapping jaws from his throat.

"Elaina," Faolán bellowed, hammering on the doors, "remember yourself."

We shouted ourselves hoarse. I smashed my fists into the doors until they bled. Faolán ripped at them with his claws but didn't so much as scratch the pure white finish.

It made no difference. The scene in the ballroom played out the same.

UNWELCOME BEDFELLOW

The dream-world faded to blackness.

Blessed thick blackness.

Deeper than night. More enveloping than the oblivion of a climax. More silent than the grave.

I sank into it, luxuriated in the fact it was a respite from House's nightmares and cruelties. This place suited its sapphire-eyed mistress.

But the nothingness didn't last, and eventually I woke.

It didn't feel like I'd slept a wink as I opened my gritty eyes. But at least I wasn't locked in another dream-memory.

The only light was the fire's embers. The sun didn't filter through the curtains' edges yet—it was much earlier than we usually woke. Perhaps House had taken pity on us and decided to free us from its nightmares early.

I reached for Faolán… and found only rumpled sheets. Cold. Empty. Again.

Surely it was too early for him to be making breakfast. "Faolán?" I called towards the bathroom, but the door was open. And, now my eyes grew accustomed to the dim red glow from the fireplace, I could see our bedroom door was also open.

Although we'd never seen anything or anyone in the house—at least the present-day version of it—other than Granny, it had been an unspoken rule between us to keep the bedroom door shut and locked at night. But here it was, half open.

From the bed, the door blocked my view out into the hallway, and a deep and primal and foolish part of me didn't dare leave the warm "safety" of the blankets. So I held my breath and listened.

Tick. Tick. Tick. The clock in the hall.

There was no other sound. The fire was too low to snap and crack. The birds outside hadn't started their dawn chorus.

The door creaked, swinging wider.

I gasped, clutching the blankets, wishing, wishing, wishing I had my dagger or iron blade to hand.

I tried to say Faolán's name, but no sound came out. That would be the logical answer. He would appear around that door any second, sleepy-eyed with a snack, complaining that he'd woken hungry because he hadn't eaten enough at dinner due to getting distracted by me.

Any second.

Wider.

Wider.

Wider.

Dark fur. A muzzle. Glinting eyes.

It wasn't Faolán.

The great head led to a thick neck, which flowed into powerful shoulders and forelegs. It moved so silently, its large claws didn't even click against the stone floor in the doorway. The only sound was a faint snuffle as it sniffed the floor as though following a trail.

Where my mind held the image of its fur shiny in the moonlight, now it was shaggy and ragged. That wasn't enough to stop me recognising the creature as a memory whooshed back.

The wolf.

The one I'd seen the night I tried to escape. The one that had stopped me. The one that had kept me as House's prisoner.

I'd thought the vague images just a dream.

But this was no dream. It was a waking, living nightmare. Bigger than me. Bigger than any sabrecat I'd ever seen. It was as though seeing it in the context of the room allowed me to finally understand just how massive it was. It might even have been bigger than Faolán. But he wasn't here.

Something prickled at the back of my neck and between my shoulder blades.

The wolf was Granny's. Had it hurt him? Had it taken him?

But... he wasn't here the first time I saw the wolf, either.

Not taking my eyes off it, I edged towards my bag, which I'd left in the bottom of the wardrobe. My iron blade. I needed it. Badly.

Still not all the way through the door, still sniffing, it didn't react to me, even as I took a shaky step towards the wardrobe.

Barely breathing, I eased the wardrobe door open. Thank the Lords and Ladies, it didn't make a sound.

Finally, the wolf's tail came into view. If it hadn't been so ragged or huge or terrifying, the creature might've been beautiful with that dark fur, the long sweep of its tail, and its powerful body made for hunting.

Unblinking, I slid my hand into my bag, past the few items left inside, and at long blessed last, my grip closed on the iron knife. I let out a soft breath of relief.

The wolf's head snapped up.

Almost as quickly, I brought up the iron blade. It shook—*my hand* shook.

With a snarl, the beast coiled and leapt.

This was what the stories had always warned us of. Vicious creatures. Fae monsters. Danger and death.

Heart in my throat, I flung myself to one side and rolled, like Faolán had taught me. Where the hells *was* he?

I sprang to my feet, muscles fast and ready, thanks to our training. Eyes fixed on the door, I ran.

I made it two steps. In a flurry of teeth and fur, snarling and snapping, the wolf blocked my way. Its hot breath ruffled my hair for an instant before I managed to stumble back.

Gasping for air, because it was like someone had hold of my ribcage and was squeezing, I held my blade out to ward the thing off. "This is iron."

Its black nose twitched, scenting the air, and it watched me warily. The fire glinted red in its eyes. The monster didn't come closer, but it still stood between me and the door.

If I could just circle around and get a clear path...

I side stepped, and it mirrored, not once taking its gaze off me. I tried the other way, but it was the same.

Pausing, I slowed my breaths, forced them to ease so I could get rid of that terrible tightness that had me in its grip.

But the wolf must've taken that as a sign of weakness, because it darted closer, snapping at my hand. I leapt away, but its fur tickled my knuckles. A fraction of a second slower, and it would've taken a finger.

A moment later, it snapped again, then again. Each time, I barely dodged. When I caught its sharp eyes on me, I realised: it was testing me, how fast I was. Or how slow.

With a gleam of ivory white, it bared its teeth.

Then it came, harder, faster.

I could do nothing but dodge, dodge, dodge, backing away all the while. Between the thunderous beat of my heart in my ears, I just about heard the grunts I made as I flung my body out of the path of those sharp teeth.

Then my heel hit something hard. The wall. And to my left—also wall.

Cornered.

Despite my lightweight nightgown, cold sweat slithered down my back.

It was going to kill me.

I wasn't even ashamed at the whimper that escaped me.

Like it also knew, it paused, eyeing me.

Out in the hallway, the clock chimed. *Dong.*

The world slowed as the wolf crouched, lower and tighter, readying to spring.

Dong.

I fastened both hands around the knife's handle. I wouldn't be fast enough to stop the beast from sinking its teeth into my flesh, but I could at least take it down with me.

Dong.

Its sides expanded on a deep inhale.

But as the final shivering note of that third chime fell silent, the wolf blinked once, twice, and sank to the floor, eyes shut.

Frozen, I stared. My arm shook like it didn't understand that it could stay still now.

The wolf let out a long breath, body easing.

Asleep?

I shook my head. This had to be a trick. A trap. The thing was toying with me. Body pressed against the wall, I slid to the right.

It didn't stir.

Further, further, and it didn't move.

Maybe it really was asleep.

Still, I kept my eyes glued to it as I peeled myself from the wall and took a step towards the door.

Then it moved.

But it didn't stand or leap or snap, its body *shifted*. Fur receded. Muscle and bone moved in ways they shouldn't have been able to.

Understanding crept over my skin in a wave of goosebumps.

And a moment later, there lay Faolán.

He was... What had he called them when he'd told me about the werewolves? Shapechanging fae. He'd pretended he was separate from those beasts, but his kind had made them.

He wasn't just a beast, but a monster.

Like all fae were. Like I'd always known. Oh yes, I'd let good looks and an incredible body distract me, soothe away my fears, blind me to the truth.

But here it was, lying naked on the floor of the bedroom we'd shared for the past month. Every night, he'd slept inches away, hiding teeth that could rip out my throat.

With a grumble, he sat up, rubbing his head. He blinked at me, then his gaze slid to the knife in my hand. A little frown etched between his eyebrows as he must've registered that it was the iron blade.

It really was Faolán.

Some part of me had clung to the idea that maybe this was a trick and when he sat up I'd see it was a wolfman, not Faolán, not the man I'd shared so much of myself with.

"Rose?" His head tilted. "Why have you—?"

But he must've seen something in my face that told him why I'd dared to draw iron in Elfhame.

And that I was prepared to use it.

His gaze swept over me the same way it had after our more dangerous encounters in House's nightmarish memories. Checking me for injuries. Ones *he* might've inflicted.

"You're..." I couldn't say it, and the thought tried to wriggle away, but, *no*, I was not letting this knowledge escape me. The house would not take this memory like it had the first night I'd seen him—truly *seen* him.

He was the wolf. He'd attacked me. Twice now.

"What have I done?" He looked down at his hands as though expecting to find incriminating evidence. His clawed fingers clenched and loosened. "I... I don't remember. Why don't I remember?" he muttered, shaking his head. "I wasn't myself."

Not himself? Did that mean his vow didn't stand when he was that *thing*? Was that form his way of being slippery with the truth?

Good gods, what a fool I'd been. Of course he'd twisted the vows to suit him. That was what fae did.

And House had helped him keep his secret with its geas.

If House had taken the memory of facing him on the edge of the forest, what other things was it stopping me from remembering? What might he have done to me? Had he, as a wolf, attacked me other times? Was that what the scars on my arm were from? Had House manufactured the whole encounter with the kelpie as a false memory to explain the injuries?

When I opened my eyes, his shoulders had slumped, and he sat, legs splayed, arms resting on his knees, looking up at me.

My heart still pounded so hard it made my face tingle: for all he looked so broken in that pose, it was a reminder that he'd attacked me.

I brought the iron blade higher, shielding myself.

I'd been stupid to think *he* was a shield. He was a lie. All of this was.

"You're a monster."

He flinched at my words, eyes screwing shut, and for a moment—for the briefest, silliest moment, the thrumming mass of my heart hurt for him.

Because, fae couldn't lie, but damn could they deceive. The look on his face was such a convincing picture of pain, like it hurt him to hear me say that, it had the pressure at the back of my eyes building *for him*.

"You're right." He said it so softly, I barely heard. "I couldn't tell you because of the geas. But... you're right."

Of course I was.

The stories had always warned me.

Worst of all, though, he wasn't just a monster, he was *her monster*. Terrorising her *dear* guests so they couldn't leave.

Not mine. Never mine. Always someone else's. My chest caved in, crushing my heart.

My beast. What a joke. It wasn't a lie, no, but it was a twisting of the truth—a reference to the fact we were married, nothing more. They must've planned it together —what words he could say to win me over. The pretty ways he could gain my trust. How he could make me think...

I swallowed, vision blurring.

How he could make me think I was in love with him.

"I'm sorry, Rose. You're not—"

"Don't say my name." I pointed the knife at him.

I had to be like this blade. Cold and hard as iron. Unbleeding. Unfeeling.

I had spent so many years protecting Ariadne. Now I had to protect myself.

Iron cuts through flesh. Iron cuts through fae. Iron cuts through lies.

I said the words over and over in my head—a call to the gods for strength as I edged towards the door.

Other than slow breaths, he didn't move.

I made it to the door and some stupid soft part of myself paused, because, it reminded me, this was the last time I would ever look at him.

We were in the early hours of the morning. I just needed to hide and survive for the rest of today and tonight, then tomorrow at dawn, I would be free to leave.

That was if anything I'd been told in this place was true.

I clenched my jaw at his back, at the way he was bowed over, like I was hurting him.

But it was my heart that was broken. And *my* eyes where the ones burning with tears that finally spilled over as I slipped outside and slammed the door before telling House to lock it.

When I heard it click, I huffed a breath of relief that became a sob. To think I'd given myself to him. To think of all I'd told him, all I'd felt for him, all I'd *trusted* him.

Fae were dangerous, like the wolves outside Briarbridge, Faolán included, and I'd been a damn fool to ever think otherwise.

HIDDEN

In a corner of the house, below a secret staircase I'd discovered a week ago and hadn't thought to mention to *him*, I found a hidden cupboard and stayed there. Light crept under the door, so I knew the sun had risen.

A tall clock stood in the hallway outside, its case carved in the form of a ribcage, its pendulum shaped like a heart. The morning *tick tick tick*ed on, the sound echoing through the hall and into my hiding place. Eventually its dark, deep chime tolled eight times.

Less than twenty-four hours before dawn. I just had to survive this day and night, and then I'd be free.

Only me and an iron knife against Granny and her watchdog Faolán, and an entire house. Though… House had locked the door when I'd asked. Maybe it wasn't all bad—or maybe it was only cruel at night… Or something else I didn't understand affected its moods.

Many years ago Ari's pa had told us a story about a

kind, cultured gentleman who became a wicked, evil brute at night. His two halves were so separate, they had different names and never remembered what the other had done. If a house could be alive and move and provide wardrobes full of perfect clothing, maybe it could have two sides to itself like that.

I rubbed my aching head, my sore eyes. The tears had stopped a while ago, but they still threatened any time my thoughts strayed towards *him*.

The way he'd killed those werewolves so easily, I should've known. I'd thought it was part of protecting me, but... it was just an expression of what he was. Maybe he'd even ushered me towards that apple tree growing so temptingly over the estate's walls.

He was definitely not on my side. He'd deceived me.

House? I wasn't sure.

Then there was Granny... Aside from trapping me here, I hadn't actually seen her do anything wrong. She'd told us she was stuck here because of a curse, which couldn't be a lie.

Maybe I'd jumped to the wrong conclusions my whole time here.

Granny wasn't the one I should fear. Nor House.

I stared at the door, chest tight and painful, throat sore as if I'd screamed myself hoarse.

He was the only one I'd seen hurt anyone. He was the only one I'd witnessed violence from. He was the only one I knew for sure had deceived me.

What if he was the one holding Granny here, cursed? And the geas stopped her from telling me?

Except that didn't make sense either. I slumped and clutched my head with one hand. The other still held my blade. I wouldn't put it down until I was out of this place.

I couldn't put all these lies-but-not together. It was like I had ingredients from three different recipes and somehow had to make something delicious from them. Except the ingredients were honey, beetroot, and rotten fish.

I sighed and let my head fall back against the wall.

How could Faolán be the man who'd protected me from the werewolves, who'd married me to save me, who'd tucked bluebells behind my hair, who'd tended my wounds from the kelpie... *and* be the wolf who'd kept me here? Not to mention, also be the fae who'd deceived me about what he was.

The stupid, salty tears came back with a vengeance.

How had I been so foolish to think I could trust him? I'd shared my bed with that beast... my *body*.

And my stupid heart.

I should've known we were destined for disaster.

I *did* know.

Fae and humans always ended in tragedy.

But like a fool, I'd let Ari's happiness, her exception that proved the rule, persuade me that maybe Faolán and I might be different.

Hells, it wasn't just persuasion—I'd *lied* to myself.

How the fae would laugh at that.

I sank into my sorrow and self-pity, curled up in the cupboard. The clock tolled away the morning and the afternoon as I lay there and counted down the hours I needed to survive. The hours to freedom.

Eventually, the light under the door faded, and I gripped my knife tighter. If House dragged me into sleep and one of its dreams, my attempts to stay safe might all be for nothing.

But the darkness deepened, leaving just a sliver of moonlight at the base of the door, and the clock chimed nine times. Ten. Eleven. Midnight.

Sleep didn't come. Maybe it was because I wasn't in bed. And no one had found my hiding place—maybe House could be trusted, at least to some degree.

I lifted my head and whispered, "House?"

The small wooden box that was my lone companion in here slid away from the wall.

"Will I stay awake and out of your dreams if I'm in here?"

The box's lid lifted, tilting up and down as if in a nod.

I huffed a sigh. No supernatural sleep; I just had to fight my own body's tiredness. My head was heavy, my heart too, and my limbs ached. But I found an old boot scraper in the corner and positioned myself with it poking into my back. There, so uncomfortable it would be impossible to fall asleep.

No more of House's dreams. Even the good ones. And no more Faolán. Even the good I thought I'd seen in him.

I shoved the heels of my hands into my eyes, blocking any more tears. They were treacherous bastards. Faolán didn't deserve them.

"Oh, House, why did you show me all that?" I sighed

at the box. "The woman with her balls and rituals and failed servants…"

The box slid away, its lid rattling softly as it shook.

"And *not* him turning into a monster? What good was all that when you didn't show me the truth?"

The box fell still, and I thought maybe I'd upset House and sent it away, but then it slid close and brushed against my leg.

"You let me think he was good. You let me think he was… noble, even." I scoffed at myself, but I couldn't keep from stroking a hand over the box's lid, like it was a cat who'd just rubbed against my leg. "You let me think he would never hurt me."

Except… was it House that made me think those things?

Or was it that Faolán had sworn to protect me and never hurt me? He'd been true to both those promises up until tonight's attack.

He could've killed me a hundred times over the past month since grabbing me in that maze of rock. Hells, he could've cracked my neck the first instant we met, just as he had that werewolf's. Even tonight, he hadn't managed to hurt me—not physically at least. That might've been down to my speed, but he was faster than me and better trained—maybe it was the magic of his vow at work.

Besides, hadn't he told me to keep up my guard? Hadn't he tried to stand between me and Granny when she'd first appeared? Over an entire month, I'd convinced myself he wasn't a monster: had that really changed in a few minutes?

And last night—this morning, rather, I reminded myself, stifling a yawn—this morning as he'd sat on the floor, he'd looked so hurt... so *broken*. The man who was always so solid, so sure, with that hard look of certainty —he'd crumbled as I'd walked away.

Monsters didn't fall apart. They raved and ranted and broke the world. They didn't let it break them.

Perhaps he *was* awful and evil and everything I'd run away from. But what if he wasn't?

I didn't owe it to him to find out which of those was true, but I damn well owed it to myself.

He owed me an explanation.

I had iron, and House had tried to protect me when it had thought Faolán was hurting me. I wasn't entirely alone, though my stomach balled tight.

"You'll help me, won't you?" I patted the box, which capered around like an excited puppy.

What an odd entity House was. Even with the horrific things it showed me, I would miss how kind and thoughtful it could be, and the way its eagerness to please made me laugh. I suspected it couldn't help its dreams, or at least not all of them.

With a sigh, I unfolded myself from the floor. My heart tolled like the clock in the hall as I pushed open the door of my hiding place.

Seven chimes. Almost an hour to sunrise.

The hall was empty, just the vines in the carpet, the looming shadows, and the bone clock. Except the vines were twisting and pulsing, growing and writhing, all moving in the same direction down the corridor.

"House? Are you leading me—?"

A shriek pierced the night.

My hand twitched, bringing the blade up in a defensive stance, just like Faolán had shown me. "Granny?" Rather than tolling, now my heart sped, afraid but ready.

"Rose?" It was her voice, coming from the same direction the vines were leading me to. "Help!"

The Heart of the House

It could be a trap. Of course, it could be. But how could I *not* follow a call for help? It led me through the hallways until the white ballroom doors came into sight. My stomach tightened even more.

Bad things happened there. In all House's memory-dreams, the worst moments began in the ballroom.

And I knew that was where Granny's calls for help would lead me.

But, again, how could I not follow?

Iron blade held tight, I threw open the doors.

The ballroom wasn't as I'd seen it in those dreams. Vines didn't just decorate the floor, they grew out of it, thick and tangled, with thorns as long as my hand.

And in a clearing in the midst of those twisting vines, a great, hulking shape bent over a small one.

The steel-grey wolf—Faolán—stood over Granny, snarling. His ivory teeth snapped six inches from her face, but only because she clung to the fur on his cheeks, desperately trying to keep him away.

"Rose! Please! Help me." Granny's eyes were wide, staring up at him in a look of pure desperation as she wrestled to keep him from tearing her throat out.

My gut fell through the floor, maybe ending up in the terrible amphitheatre that stood somewhere beneath us.

Because Faolán was every bit the monstrous beast I'd tried to persuade myself he wasn't. Eyes half-wild. Muzzle wrinkled to reveal all those sharp, sharp teeth. Vicious ferocity in every movement as he fought to kill her.

His second attack in mere hours. What had happened in the bedroom was no longer an isolated incident.

"Help... me." Granny's voice grew strained, and Faolán reached an inch closer to her vulnerable flesh. "Kill... him."

My knees almost gave out as I approached through a path in the vines. Kill him? There had to be another option.

"Faolán?" I called. "Wake up. This isn't you." I wasn't sure if it was true, but it *felt* true even if it contradicted what my eyes told me.

He didn't so much as blink.

"Faolán, *please*." There was a desperate waver in my voice as I reached the clearing in the middle of the ball-room. "You need to wake up."

Nothing.

Upon the heart at the centre of the floor, Granny's form was tiny, her limbs thin, her body skinny with a dress pooled around it. And Faolán was this great mass of muscle and fur clad over thick, solid bone. I couldn't hope to wrestle him off her. He was too big, too strong.

I squeezed the leather-wrapped hilt of the knife.

"You need to do it, Rose." Granny's arms trembled as she took in little gasping breaths. Terror shone in her rheumy eyes. "He's a monster. Kill him. Save me."

My heart tolled in my ears, as final and heavy as the bone clock in the corridor.

She was right.

My eyes burned at the fact, but that didn't make it any less true.

Feet heavy, I took a step closer.

Even facing the kelpie, he hadn't shifted into a wolf or seemed quite so out of control. What had happened to turn him? Did it matter?

My shoulders sank as I took another step.

Except... if he was so beastly, he'd had a whole month full of chances to kill Granny. And even if he'd twisted his vow so it didn't apply in this form, he still hadn't hurt me the night I'd encountered him in the grounds. It had felt more like he was herding me back towards the house. Hadn't he said that if I'd tried to disobey the geas and leave, the best case scenario was broken bones and the worst was death? Had he been trying to protect me, even then?

Everything I knew about him didn't add up to the picture before me.

A picture where his fur was glossy and thick, not ragged and dull as it had been earlier.

And… if I couldn't fend him off in a fight, despite all the times I'd tried in our training sessions, how the hells was Granny with her skin-and-bone arms keeping him from tearing out her throat?

My gaze settled on the dark metallic grey of my knife in the air between us.

Iron cuts through flesh. Iron cuts through fae. Iron cuts through lies.

Maybe…

I slid my thumb from the leather-wrapped hilt, over the smooth brass of the guard, and onto the cold, pitted iron of the blade.

In a snap, everything changed.

Granny had hold of wolf-Faolán by the throat. He sagged in her grasp, eyes staring, glassy and unseeing, fur dull once more. A pale glowing stream flowed from his mouth into hers. Dim light surrounded him, growing dimmer by the second, while she glowed brighter and brighter.

Not only weren't her knuckles bent by arthritis anymore, but as I stared, frozen, and she took more of that glow from Faolán, I saw the wrinkles on the backs of her hands fading. The muscles of her arms filled out. The grey of her hair deepened to blue-black like someone coloured it in with a rich ink.

My heart lurched when I realised her face was no longer the elder lady's who'd invited us to her home, but smoother, younger, beautiful.

And one I recognised.

Because as the rheumy glaze over her eyes faded,

beaten back by the power she sucked from Faolán, it revealed the deepest, richest sapphire blue.

The woman from House's dreams.

I couldn't breathe. A low roar pressed upon my ears, as though away in the distance everyone else in the world was screaming.

It couldn't...

I lifted my thumb from the iron blade and everything snapped back into place.

Granny on her back, desperate and afraid. Faolán over her, vicious and monstrous.

Thumb on iron.

The sapphire eyed woman sucking the life out of him. Faolán powerless and wilting.

She smiled up at him, mouth too wide, teeth too sharp.

She had sacrificed humans, feasted on hearts, and made misshapen abominations to be her failed servants.

Faolán wasn't the monster here.

We'd been living with one all along, my wolf and I, like a twisted version of the story Ari's pa had told us.

"What big eyes you have." I didn't mean to say it out loud, but maybe some part of me needed those words to be able to take a step closer to that creature.

"All the better to hunt us with, Rose, dear." Her chest heaved as though she was afraid, and she glanced my way like she didn't dare take her eyes off him for too long. "Quickly now. He's going to kill me."

I took another step. "What big ears you have."

"All the better to find us with, even when we hide."

She shifted on the floor and with my thumb against cool iron, I could see the impatience seeping into her movements.

I lifted the blade in both hands, tip pointed down, right above his spine.

"What big teeth you have."

The sapphire-eyed woman smiled, revealing more and more of them as she saw victory was only a thrust away. "All the better to eat us with."

I clenched my jaw and lifted my chin. "I wasn't talking to him."

Feet planted, body centred low, like Faolán had shown me, I braced my shoulder and shoved into him. With my full weight ramming into him, he fell out of her grip and slumped to the side, leaving the sapphire-eyed woman staring up at me. Her sharp-toothed smile dropped as her mouth fell open.

With every bit of strength I possessed, I brought the blade down.

I knew the instant it touched her pale, pale skin, because even before my arms registered the resistance of flesh and bone, she shrieked.

Her body writhed and sizzled. "No, stop! It burns."

But it was too late—my blade was buried in her to the hilt and her blood spilled onto the ballroom floor. Thick and darkest red, it pooled and gathered around the heart design Faolán and I had danced across as though drawn to it irresistibly. With a groan, the heart turned crimson and twitched like it was alive.

Stomach turning, eyes ready to pop, I stumbled back.

I cursed myself for leaving the knife in her chest, because the way the heart pulsed to life, something worse had to be coming.

But a moment later, it shuddered and went black, leaving the sapphire-eyed woman's blood to trail along the cracks in the floor, following only gravity.

As I crawled to Faolán, who lay still, she grabbed at the hilt sticking out of her chest, but her movements were weak. The glow that surrounded her throbbed.

"You stupid girl." She gave up on the blade and reached for me instead, but I was out of her grasp, pulling Faolán's head into my lap. "You could've made this house great again—could've made me great again."

"Great? Do you mean young and pretty?" I scoffed and stroked Faolán's straggly fur. He was still warm, still breathing, but he didn't move.

"You... stupid... human..." Her back arched as she whimpered, the sound at odds with the vicious look on her face. "I had everything... was everything... more than you could ever..." She sagged, but those cold sapphire eyes glared at me. "Could ever have... could ever know." Then the breath left her and she fell still.

Along with the breath, the glow left her too, gushing back into Faolán. Beneath the fur, his body cracked and shifted, joints popping and reforming, muzzle retracting. I stared and stroked him as the fur retreated into his skin.

When he was somewhere between wolf and fae, the house cried out. I covered my ears but couldn't block out the inhuman shriek of timber, stone, and plaster, or that fact that somewhere beneath it all there was a flesh and blood voice. A woman's voice.

It made every hair on my body spring to attention. "Faolán?"

He was back to his hulking, tattooed self, albeit naked save for the braided leather bracelet. The wolves etched into his chest expanded and contracted with his deep, even breaths. Suddenly they made a lot of sense.

I didn't know the full story, why he'd attacked me, but after seeing Granny's lies, I would take my chances with him. I stroked his cheek. "Time to wake up, my love, my beast."

Nothing.

"Faolán?" I shook him. Nothing. I shouted for him, slapped his cheek hard enough to ring through the room.

He didn't wake.

The old stories were full of enchanted sleeps where the dreamer never woke.

Had I failed to save him after all?

My heart clenched as I stared at the rise and fall of his chest, eyes burning. True love's kiss. That was something else in the stories, wasn't it? I'd never put much stock in it, but right now I'd try anything. Cupping his cheek, I kissed his brow, his crooked nose, his mouth.

His eyelids didn't so much as flutter.

"Please?" I looked up at the cracked ceiling, like the gods might be listening to my cracked voice. "Please let him wake up. Bring him back to me. *Please*."

"Rose?"

It was the most wonderful sound I ever heard.

When I looked down, he blinked up at me, hand coming up to cover mine, to hold it against his stubbly cheek. He smiled.

Like I hadn't called him a monster, like he hadn't attacked me, he *smiled*.

"I'm so sorry, Faolán." There was so much to say, to ask, I didn't know where to start.

Maybe he was still dazed and didn't understand what I was saying, because he still smiled at me. But only for a beat longer before his gaze flicked over my shoulder, and he was on his feet between me and whatever he'd seen. "Who the fuck are you?"

When I whirled around, I found him crouched in a defensive stance, but past him, I knew the deep brown eyes looking back at me, the beautiful fae woman who was also a wolf. "Elaina."

She smiled and nodded. The movement rippled across her body and I could see the mirrored wall through her—she was insubstantial, like a ghost. "I know that's my name now. I remember. Not House." Her eyes were bright with tears though she grinned at me. "I remember. So many things I'd lost."

She was... "House?"

"I tried to warn you about who and what she was. But the geas affected me too. No speaking about changed forms." She reached for Faolán, who bared his teeth. With a chuckle, she stopped short and held out her hand for him to sniff, which he did with a frown. "You can't hurt me, Grey Wolf. I'm already dead. But I was like you, a fae, a shapechanger. And like you, I couldn't speak of it because of her geas."

His eyes widened, and he swallowed, turning to me. "I'm a shapechanger." His shoulders sagged as the corner of his mouth lifted. "I can tell you now. I'm sorry. I tried, but the words…" He shook his head.

Elaina inclined her head. "The geas died with her."

The blank spots from our experience in the painting came back to me. I stood, fingers closing around the fabric of my nightgown. I *wanted* to take his hand, to remind myself that he was alive, to reassure myself, but he was in a defensive stance and I wasn't sure how he'd react after all that had happened earlier. We needed to talk, and I had a feeling it would be a complicated conversation.

I frowned at her. "A shapechanger—like the fae who create werewolves?"

"Though most of us try not to."

"We saw"—I swallowed, throat thick at the memory —"you in the ballroom with a man. What happened?"

Her gaze sank to the floor. "She fed off me, draining my power. She fed off all her guests—their magic, their pleasure, their desires and cruelty. It gave her youth and power."

The way she whipped her guests into a frenzy with her rituals—yes, she knew how to stir their base impulses.

Faolán eased from his half crouch with a low "Hmm."

"She told me shapechangers tasted the sweetest and that our magic sustained her the longest." She gave

Faolán a long look. "When she fed off me, it left me confused, powerless, wild and vicious. I couldn't control myself or my form until the effect wore off."

My eyes flicked to him. That was exactly how he'd been this morning coming back to our room. Did that mean—?

"And that final night," she went on, "when she'd almost completely drained me, she tricked my beloved into killing the 'vicious wolf.'"

"Like we saw in the painting."

Elaina nodded, eyes closed. "I managed to sneak that one past her. I wasn't whispering my memories in your ear, so it didn't count as telling you. And some of the dreams were out of my control, like the kelpie. I'm sorry about that and even about the horrors I did choose to show you. I was trying to reveal her nature and what she planned to do to you—exactly what she'd done to us. I hoped you'd understand enough." She gave a rueful smile. "Evidently not, but... maybe enough got through, because you're here and she isn't."

Little pictures not of the house's past, but of Granny's. What she'd done. Who she really was. Elaina had been trying to warn us the whole time.

Faolán folded his arms, brows knotted in a deep frown. "Why, though?"

"Power, of course. It's why she did anything." Elaina gave a bitter smile. "To be killed by someone you love produces ripples across existence. Because of the geas, I hadn't been able to tell him what I was. I'd promised myself I would once we were out, but..."

She stayed quiet for so long, staring off into the distance and the past, I thought perhaps she might not tell us more, but eventually she stroked her upper arms and continued. "She used the power of that tragedy to fire the house into life." Nose wrinkled, she shot a glare at the shrivelled heart in the centre of the ballroom.

Its tiles were now outlined with rivulets of Granny's blood. Fitting that she died at the heart of the house she'd brought to life.

Elaina sighed. "And my trapped soul kept it that way. She had you on the same path, Grey Wolf. She fed off your strength most nights."

Faolán's gaze fixed on the tiled heart. "I felt so weak." It was barely more than a whisper. "Worse each day. I thought I was sick... *dying*."

My throat tightened, and I had to clasp my hands together to keep from reaching for him. The shadows had gone from under his eyes, and his cheeks were no longer gaunt. But to imagine Faolán had carried those fears in himself cracked my heart. He was strong and hearty. Weakness seemed his complete opposite.

"That was why you lost control of your shape and your actions."

I swallowed. He hadn't attacked me through choice, but wild, uncontrolled instinct. That wasn't Faolán in our room, not really.

"And you would've died if not for Rose seeing the truth," Elaina went on, voice low. "Over the long years, my strength has weakened."

I glanced at the cracked ceiling. "The shabby carpets

and damp patches."

"She wanted to trap Faolán's soul here with mine, so the house would be restored to its former glory. Her earlier attempts at creating unquestioning servants had failed—you saw that."

The sewn together bodies lurching around the dining room. "Those poor people. She wanted silent, obedient slaves... so she made you and the entire house into one."

"I had no choice, and my memories were fractured, blending with things the house remembered—her parties and sacrifices." She shook her head as if shaking those unpleasant images away. "Once she found what she could do with a soul locked in this place, she wasn't about to give that up. With Faolán's spirit in her house and his strength in her body, she would've been able to resume her terror. But you stopped her." She sighed, relief clear in the way her body eased and the soft smile that came to her face. "And now I'm free to join my beloved in the next place. *Thank you.* Both of you."

The house groaned. In the distance there was a rumble like thunder or something falling.

Her brown eyes widened. "You might want to run. I think I was the only thing holding this place together. It *is* rather old."

Beneath us the floor ground, then shook. My pulse lurched. Something was very, *very* wrong.

Faolán grabbed my hand and pulled me close. He curled around me, shielding me as dust rained upon us.

Even if it was only because he'd vowed to keep me safe in Elfhame, I pressed against him and covered his nose and mouth with the frill from my nightgown to keep the dust out.

With an ear-splitting *crack*, a fissure split the ceiling. I flinched, more than half expecting it to come crashing into us. He squeezed me tight, crouching, ready to dodge any danger, like he'd shown me in training.

No crash came.

"I'm trying to hold this place together." Elaina winced, fists clenching. "But I'm losing my grip. I'm already separating from this world, getting pulled to the next."

"Time to go." Faolán released me, and in the time it took to blink, he'd shifted into that huge wolf. His fur was no longer ragged and dull, but shiny and healthy, recovered from Granny's drain. Apart from his size, he wasn't frightening.

He was magnificent.

"Go," Elaina said between gritted teeth, her body rigid. "Get out of here. Have a long, happy life. Know that you have my gratitude forever."

"Thank you, Elaina. For everything." I touched the air where her shoulder should've been.

She gave a stiff smile and nodded, before waving us off. Her brown eyes stayed on the ceiling and that widening fissure.

Rose, Faolán's voice came through my mind, tearing my attention from the ceiling. He bent his front legs offering me his back. *I'm asking you to trust me.*

It wasn't something he needed to ask. I rested one hand on his shoulder and mounted. "I already do."

THROUGH CORRIDORS

He was as fast as the wind.

I clung to his neck, warm in his rich fur as we sped down corridors, turning left and right, dodging falling chunks of plaster and marble.

Dust choked the air. The ground opened up—a yawning black maw.

Still, he ran.

His muscles bunched and sprang under me, as incredible in this form as they were in his fae one. He coughed, and as I shielded my eyes from the debris falling from above, I spotted that his were streaming.

"Straight on," I shouted.

He eased under me and dipped his head. *Can't see shit in this.*

I coughed out a laugh. "Then I'll be your eyes." Maybe it was the years of working in our bakery with its air full of flour that had built my tolerance, but I only had to blink a few times to clear the dust.

I searched for falling timbers and cried warnings as they came down in our path. He dodged and leapt and followed my directions.

Until at last I spotted the doors that led out to the gravel drive.

"Left." I glanced back over my shoulder.

Two paces behind us, the walls tumbled. The ceiling caved in. Chaos and dust reigned. We wouldn't have time to stop and open the door. A moment's hesitation and we'd be crushed. Dying so close to our escape? No. That wasn't an option.

"You're going to have to knock the door down."

His scoff sounded in my mind. *Not a problem, little flower.*

"We're lined up perfectly." I patted his shoulder in reassurance—mine or his, I wasn't sure.

Head down, he picked up speed. I clung on, keeping close to his body so I wouldn't slow him down.

His breaths heaved, ribcage working like a bellows between my legs.

Come on, Faolán. I gritted my teeth and stared at the rapidly approaching doors like I could make them fall with nothing but my will.

His hind quarters bunched, then we were in the air. I held my breath. For long seconds we flew.

There was a hard jolt, and I screwed my eyes shut. The door was too strong. We weren't going to get through. Even in death, Granny was going to defeat us.

But then light pierced my eyelids and when I opened them, I saw the sky painted in peach and pink.

The dawn.

With a great huff from Faolán, we landed. The door was splinters around us. The house was dust at our heels.

And we were free.

At least, I was. And he was.

I wasn't sure if there was an "us."

HMM

P anting, Faolán crouched on the gravel driveway and returned to his fae shape. His *naked* fae shape.

I coughed and looked away. It didn't feel right to stare at his body when things between us were so unresolved.

"I'm sorry, Faolán."

He rose, a hard frown creased between his brows as he tapped the silver circle on his bracelet. "Come." He jerked his chin away from the house. "We need to get out of here. The untethered magic is interfering with this." He started off, though his stride wasn't that punishing one that I had to trot to keep up with.

"Didn't you hear me? I said I'm sorry."

"Hmm." He nodded, giving me a sidelong look.

"'Hmm.' Is that all you've got to say?" I stared up at him, keeping up as he led us towards the forest. "You almost died. I almost killed you! And you just reply with 'Hmm'? What does that even mean?"

"Right now, it means I'm listening."

I huffed and walked on in silence. At last, an explanation for one of his wordless sounds. I should've known they'd always meant something rather than just being a way to dismiss me.

He was listening. And I had much to say. I heaved a sigh and hugged myself.

"I'm so sorry I let you down." I could barely say it through the shame. I definitely couldn't look at him. "When I saw you as a wolf, I thought it had taken you and now was coming for me. I was afraid. And when I realised it was you..."

I shook my head, trying to swallow down the thickness in my throat. I must've made him feel awful. I hadn't scarred him like that mob had when they'd attacked, and my fear had been warranted, but I'd blamed him rather than searching for the truth or asking for an explanation. My words had hurt him all the same.

That had to be why he didn't reply.

So I went on. "I thought you were monstrous. I thought you'd lied to me about more than what you were. I thought you were somehow working against me, plotting... that all of this had been some sort of trick or lie." My voice came out thick and raw. "It was only for a while—I was coming to find you to hear what you had to say when Granny called for help. But I feel foolish for believing it for so long. I should've known it wasn't you

—that something had happened. I could've tried to help you, not hidden counting down the hours before I could escape."

Somehow, I found the courage to glance at him. He strode through the woods, eyes on the path ahead, expression hard and tight. His silence cut me.

"And I'm sorry"—my voice cracked—"so, so sorry for ever making you feel monstrous, less than. After all I said I wanted for you. But..." I didn't want to say the next part. Not when he'd given no sign he was interested. It felt more dangerous to admit than anything else I'd said so far.

With a shaky breath out, I straightened my back. "I'd like to spend the rest of our year and a day making that up to you."

His eyebrows shot up and his gaze flicked to me as he stopped mid-stride. "You... would?"

I couldn't form any words now he was watching me so intently, so I just dipped my head.

"You don't need to do that."

Meaning, he didn't want me to. My shoulders sank and it was like someone had pierced part of me inside and now I was deflating. I'd finally found something I wanted and I didn't get to have it. Maybe, deep down, that was why I'd spent so long avoiding want.

He canted his head. "You've finally gone quiet. Does that mean you've finished?"

"Mm-hmm."

He nodded slowly, thoughtfully, scratched his beard,

frowned at the dirt at his feet. "It must've been a shock seeing me like that, and I can't imagine how terrified you must've been when I attacked."

"That wasn't your fault. You weren't—"

"No, I wasn't in control. But I'm still sorry for it, and if I'd told you..." The wolves on his chest expanded as he took a long breath. "I know it seemed I lied—and I... I did, because of what I didn't say."

"The geas—"

"Fuck the geas. I could've told you before we came here, but... I saw how you looked at the pack and I didn't want you to look at me like that. So I was a coward, and I said nothing."

I couldn't help my soft gasp. He was as far from a coward as it was possible to get.

"For that, I'm sorry. Truly." He met my gaze, his eyes not hard or burning, but soft. "I don't want you to make anything up to me."

Just as I thought it wasn't possible for me to deflate further, there it was.

I clenched my jaw and nodded like I agreed—he was right to want what he wanted. How could he want me nearby after I'd made him feel like he was a dirty dog all over again?

But I wanted him.

Desperately, so desperately, I tried to hold in the tears that were building at the back of my eyes like water behind a dam. I wasn't going to use those as guilt to make him give in.

"But"—he took in the longest, deepest breath and his throat bobbed as he gave a slow swallow—"if you want to stick around for another reason, I'll gladly, greedily take you up on that offer."

I blinked up at him, lips parting on a wordless sound. My heart took up a slow, loud pounding in my ears. I must've heard him wrong. Misunderstood.

He took a step closer so we were toe-to-toe. His great hand cupped my cheek as he held me in his gaze. "I've wanted you since we got here, maybe since before. But..." He let out a soft breath, hand falling away. "I didn't think you wanted me."

The way he said it, the slight sink of his shoulders wrung me out. "But I *told* you I did. The night we... Didn't fucking you on a fountain give it away?"

His gaze lowered like he was suddenly shy, and his vulnerability was a tiny, fragile creature that I wanted to give a home at the centre of my heart.

I would kill for it. Destroy for it. I would face the kelpie and washerwoman myself just to keep it safe.

And this time *I'd* be the one tearing the monster limb from fucking limb.

He swallowed and lifted one shoulder. "I thought you just meant to fuck. I... I didn't think anyone would want me for me, beast and all. Not *really*." His face crumpled, just for the briefest instant, but I saw it and I ached for him. "When I realised I'd attacked you, it felt like those people were right all along... like my worst fears had come true. I was just a vicious beast no one wanted. And

I felt stupid for wanting anything more, for hoping that maybe…"

The tears I'd held in earlier came. Weeping in silence, I stared up at him and tried to gather my breath. "I *was* frightened. Not of you, but what she'd made you—mindless and out of control. When that faded, though, I realised I already knew exactly who and what you were."

He took my hand, his claws tickling my palm. "If I'd told you before we got here and became subject to her geas, it wouldn't have happened." He shook his head like he was still battling those mistakes. "I should have—"

"Oh hush." I placed my hand on his chest, revelling in the warmth of him, and used that to steady myself as I rose on tiptoes. "Has anyone ever told you you talk too much?"

He only had time to raise his eyebrows in what must've been surprise before I kissed him. A kiss to seal all we'd said. A kiss to prove he had nothing more to apologise for. A kiss to remind him we'd survived and that was what mattered most.

When I pulled away, he wore a grin that was part foolish, part dazed. "No one's ever told me that." He even gave a slight chuckle as he brought his arms around me.

I squeezed and shut my eyes and inhaled, taking in greedy breaths of bay and mint, musk and fur—of *him*.

I even grumbled when he pulled back, but he kept his arms around me and only pulled away enough to look me in the eye. "I love you, Rose. And in case it wasn't clear, I want you, too. I want you to be my wife, in reality, not just in a bargain."

His eyebrows clashed together and even as a thrill fluttered through me at his words, I tensed for the "but" I could feel coming.

"But I know us being together means leaving your home, your family, everything you know and want, all you—"

"Yes."

He blinked, twice. Quickly.

"Were any of those things on my list of wants?" I cocked my head at him. "Once I *thought* I wanted them, but I think I just told myself that, because they were the only options I thought I had. My family doesn't need me; they haven't for a long time." I gave a little shrug because that knowledge didn't hurt as much as it would've a month ago. "Ari said how well they've managed.

"And, yes, I love them, but it's a different kind of love." My heart thudded against my ribcage—he had to feel it where we were pressed together. "Different from what you give me or I feel for you. Visiting them—that will be enough. So. Yes, I will be your wife. I will have you as my husband—my *real* husband."

His lips parted but he said nothing, just stared back.

"There were some wants I didn't say the other night in the courtyard." My face grew warm. "*I* was the coward. But here they are now."

I held on to his shoulders, using their solid mass to anchor myself to him. "I want you, Faolán. In every way. I want to see your hard-earned smiles and hear that infernal *hmm* sound. I want you to be grumpy at me and pretend you don't find my jokes funny. I want to wake up with you even though we're no longer locked in that house. I want to be a shield, like you are."

If we hadn't been so close, I might've missed the slight widening of his eyes, the tiny flare of his nostrils. But I was close enough to catch every little detail as he absorbed my words.

Slowly, the corners of his mouth rose and he nodded like he was looking at a job well done. "Yes." He lifted me from the ground, still nodding. "That's my love. That's my little flower—my greedy little flower. Want, want, want." He clicked his tongue as though telling me off, but his canines flashed and gave away that he was fighting a grin. "We'll make sure you have it all."

He kissed me, gently, sweetly, deeply, which was exactly what I needed after all we'd been through in the past twenty-four hours.

We stayed there a long while, me wrapped around him, his attention tender but thorough.

Just as we crossed a line into heated rather than warm, he groaned, pulled me off him, and placed me on the floor at arm's length. He closed his eyes and exhaled. "Much as I could do this all day, we still need to get out of here. Now it isn't bound to the house, the residual magic is stopping me from contacting Bastian. I can *feel* it choking the air." He shuddered like a sabrecat shaking off flies, and when I looked closer, I spotted the hairs on his arms were on end.

I frowned and held still, but it was only once I closed my eyes and held my breath that I became aware of the faint hum in the air, too fast and too high pitched to be pleasant. I shuddered, too. "What if he doesn't come right away?"

"I'm tapping this thing until he does." He lifted his wrist. "I will irritate him into appearing and taking us home."

I laughed, and hand-in-hand, we walked through the forest. At last we found a strip of collapsed rubble that stretched away left and right into the distance—all that was left of the wall around the estate. Faolán stepped right over it, then lifted me across like I weighed less than a bag of flour. I couldn't help but smile at it. Back in Briarbridge I always felt too tall, too strong compared to women like Ari, but sometimes around him, I felt almost dainty. Almost.

When he placed my feet on the floor, he didn't let go, though, just held me close and smiled. "So, I get to keep you," he murmured and closed his eyes, touching his forehead to mine. "Even after everything you've seen of me, you're still here."

I threaded my fingers into his hair and basked in this closeness—not just the physicality, but the intimacy. "*Especially* after everything I've seen of you."

"Hmm." This one was a sound of pure contentment before he released me and tapped on the bracelet.

While we waited for a reply, him still tapping, I tore a wide strip of fabric off the hem of my nightgown. To his questioning look, I raised an eyebrow. "I know you aren't bothered about nudity, but I figure you probably don't want to return to your court in this state."

He looked down at his still very naked body as though only just realising. "Fair point."

I'd just finished tying the strip of baby blue fabric around his waist when the air shimmered and Bastian stepped through.

The coal-haired fae took in his surroundings with a casual glance, then his metallic eyes landed on Faolán and stayed there. A slow smirk eased across his face. "I have so many questions."

Faolán gave him a flat look. "You can ask once we're back in Tenebris."

Bastian's smirk widened. "Or I can ask now."

Faolán flat-out growled. "Hot bath, clean clothes, good food, and a warm bed—all of this for *both* of us, then I tell you everything."

Now *that* was how you made a bargain. Except…

I cleared my throat. "And tell Ariadne we're back and we're safe."

Shoulders sinking, Bastian sighed. "Fine. You have a deal." He inclined his head to me and opened the shadow door. "After you."

Faolán kept close, one hand on my shoulder, which was just as well because my stomach lurched at the thought of stepping into utter blackness. If he hadn't been there, I might've bolted.

"I must say, Faolán," Bastian drawled, "that really is a fetching colour on you."

"If you weren't my employer, I'd rip you to shreds."

Despite being around a foot shorter than my husband, Bastian didn't look the slightest bit afraid. He didn't even draw himself up to his full height or square his shoulders like he had anything to prove. He just scoffed. "You're welcome to try."

Faolán grumbled as we reached the shadow door.

Together, we walked through.

IN TENEBRIS

As soon as we were through the shadow door, Bastian showed us down a corridor, making for a set of double doors. The ceiling was richly decorated in shades of midnight that faded down the walls to the violets, pinks, and oranges of dusk. Gold stars and constellations spread across it all.

While I'd seen wealth at the house—I wasn't sure what to call the place we'd spent a month, now I knew it was Elaina—this felt different. The gold less ostentatious. The colours more subtle. It reminded me of Ariadne's embroidery—artful and elegant.

"Where are we?" I glanced at Bastian's straight back as he led the way. "Is this your house?"

His head turned a touch, so I glimpsed an amused twist to his mouth.

Faolán snorted. "This is the palace," he muttered.

"Welcome to Tenebris." Bastian gestured and the doors opened, revealing a large bedroom with similar starry decor. With a nod and the promise of food, he left us.

Faolán made a beeline to another door inside, which I'd have bet my life led to a bathroom. And I'd have won that bet.

Turned out, I knew my husband.

Just like at the house, the taps here ran with hot water that steamed the air, and I let Faolán choose the combination of scents. Honeysuckle and bay, with a touch of lemon.

We sat together, soaking away our exhaustion, my back to his chest, his chin resting on the top of my head. It was calm. It was quiet. And it was ours.

But one small thought dug into me, like a sharp stone underfoot. I traced a pale line where his tattoos faded down his arm and swallowed, not wanting to ruin the safety we'd finally found. "What do humans and fae do when they're together for longer than a year and a day? Because one day they don't have any longer—or at least the human doesn't."

That was the kernel of truth at the centre of my belief about humans and fae ending in tragedy. And it still stood.

He growled the softest growl I'd ever heard. It reverberated into me. "Not something I want to think about." He lowered his arms from the edge of the bath and squeezed them around me like someone was trying to take me away.

I pressed into him and pushed a smile on my face. "Well, I'm sure you won't need to for a long while. But…"

I turned my head to look up at him and nuzzled against his jaw.

He'd just shaved, but it was already rough and stubbly.

I bit back a giggle and instead covered his arms with mine. "*But* I want to stay alive as long as I can." I left out the *with you* that chimed in my thoughts.

The corner of his mouth rose as he touched a kiss to my brow. "Well, aren't you just *full* of wants now?"

I blinked up at him. "Was that a joke?"

He shrugged. "Almost."

Laughing, I turned in his hold, and planted my hands on his chest. "I'm counting it."

"Hmm." It was a stern sound this time and his eyebrows lowered as he made it, but he couldn't hide the glint in his eye. Amusement. I really was softening my gruff wolf.

"Just don't make too many"—I stretched out along his body, absorbing the silent rumble that came from him—"or I might think a changeling has taken your place."

His eyes hooded as he ran his hands down my back and pulled my hips against his. It seemed my wolf wasn't entirely exhausted from our adventure—in fact a sizeable part of him was just waking up. "I wouldn't let *anyone* take my place."

It was a delicious promise, which I sealed with a kiss that became slow, slippery lovemaking that sent water sloshing over the edge of the bath.

Eventually, we had to emerge—Faolán insisted that

topping up the hot water twice was enough, and his stomach growled its agreement. We dressed in clothes that had been left for us—me in an emerald silk gown with a low neckline and him in black shirt and trousers. Not as tight as the ones House had provided the night of the, uh, *fucking party*. Unfortunately.

In the bedroom, a table had appeared, covered in food. At its side, Bastian sat back in a chair, ankle resting on his knee, like this was *his* space. He speared a round, green thing that I didn't recognise and paused with it halfway to his mouth. "You took your sweet time."

Faolán's jaw rippled as he nodded at the platters of meats and fruit. "I also said bed."

Bastian shrugged, munching on the thing he'd speared before flicking the cocktail stick onto the table. It landed in an empty glass. "Yes, the bed is here. I have provided it along with your hot bath, the clothes you're wearing, and this delicious spread." He spread his hands and inclined his head to me. "And I sent a message to your threadwitch friend. I even arranged for guards at your door—a *bonus*. You can thank me later, Faolán. Now for your side of the bargain."

I didn't know whether to laugh or sigh at his reply and the answering scowl on Faolán's face. I patted my husband's shoulder as he slumped into a chair. "You didn't specify we had to sleep first."

"More fool me." He pulled the empty chair beside his even closer; when I sat, our thighs touched.

A month stuck in a house with me and my wolf still wasn't ready to be parted. No doubt, my smile was exceptionally smug as I selected a small spinach and cheese pastry.

Bastian and Faolán lifted their heads as one, turning to the door. A moment later, I heard the commotion outside.

"... said they weren't to be interrupted."

"I don't give a damn what that man said. Don't make me set my hellhound on you!"

My eyes widened. "Aria—?"

The door flew open and in she burst with a large white dog at her side. Lysander followed in her wake, looking a little sheepish.

I was still staring at the creature as I squeezed Ari close. The hound sat a few feet away, watching us with flaming red eyes. Her ears, paws, and tail were also wreathed in crimson fire, yet the carpet didn't singe.

Lysander cleared his throat and bent towards us. "Her name's Fluffy," he murmured.

"Oh, yes!" Ari pulled out of my arms, giving a bright smile. "She's our hellhound. And"—she ruffled the dog's head—"she's the best girl. Aren't you the best girl, hmm?"

Fluffy's tongue lolled as she closed her eyes and pushed into the affection.

Fluffy. The massive hellhound who came up to Ari's chest.

And Ari, the woman who was afraid of most *people*, had just threatened the guards with violence and was now cooing over a...

"Wait, *hellhound?*" I looked from her to Lysander and back again. "As in one of the Wild Hunt's hunting dogs?"

"She didn't get on with them." Ari shrugged, scratching the dog behind the ears before casting a look over me. "Are you all right? That place..." She shuddered. "The magic there smelled foul—like death and loss."

"The magic...?" I swapped a glance with Faolán who raised his eyebrows.

"Magic has a scent. Though usually only those with strong gifts—or sometimes the keen senses that come with shifting—can smell it." He gave Ari a long look as though reassessing her short stature and delicate hands.

He wasn't the only one. In a sense, Ari had shifted since coming to Elfhame. Rather than taking on another form, she had become more herself now she was free of Briarbridge with its stifling debts and closed minds.

My chest was full and warm as everyone sat and poured wine, and between Faolán and I, we explained what had happened since we'd last seen them. It turned out less time had passed than I'd thought—Bastian had a theory that repeatedly opening the shadow door to us created a tether that anchored the house to Tenebris, chronologically. Where our first two weeks had been six months in the outside world, our time since Ari and Lysander's visit had passed at a normal rate.

Bastian still sat in that relaxed pose, but his stillness suggested he took in every word. Lysander listened with a small frown. Ari was the most animated, mouth dropping open in shock, eyes widening in horror, then filling with tears as she heard about Elaina and her beloved. That was when Lysander pulled her closer.

It felt good to have Faolán touch my back at that point, too. A reassurance.

"It isn't clear who or what she was, really"—he shook his head—"but she isn't around any longer."

Lysander rubbed his chin, his other arm draping over Ari's shoulder. "The Serp—*Bastian* and I did some research in the palace archives. He managed to narrow down the location based on the moon and stars when he visited, so that helped our search."

The only movement from Bastian was his eyes turning in Lysander's direction. I guessed folk didn't call him "the Serpent" to his face. I would've paid to be a fly on the wall of the archives to see these two working *together*.

"It took some digging," Lysander went on. "We found one mention in a very old book hidden away in a corner —a woman with a palace in that general area. The exact location was lost, but the description fits with what you saw, so I think we can fill it in on the maps." Expression flat, he turned to Bastian. "It's probably worth warning people in the area."

Faolán wrinkled his nose and nodded. "It felt like a vile place as we were leaving. Evil things were done there." His hand curled around my waist, firm. "It'll attract all sorts." He raised his eyebrows at Bastian.

One elbow on the table, Bastian stroked his bottom lip. "What do you people think I spend my time doing? *Of course* I've already sent a patrol down there to take a look. Just like I checked the walls from the outside as soon as I was aware you two had been trapped." He rolled his eyes. "There was no way to get you out—at least not alive."

Faolán sucked in his lips and gave Bastian an apologetic look. "Of course you did."

Bastian waved him off. "Admittedly, I had to end my research stint early to attend to some business for Her Majesty. Lysander, did you find anything interesting after I left?" Again, that glance at Ari's husband. It was the first time I'd seen him address the man directly.

"The book pointed me to another document that was partially decayed." Lysander raised his hands and gave a soft sound of frustration. "The details are sparse, but the woman was from an offshoot of Dusk's royal family. It sounds like she was sore at not being from the ruling branch, so entertained herself by holding her own court at this palace of hers. Eventually, she did *something* that broke a law. I don't know what, but it was bad enough that she was sentenced to never leave her grounds for the rest of her days. That sentence"—he canted his head at me—"was sealed with a geas, so she couldn't ever escape."

"Hmm." Faolán's seat creaked as he shifted his weight. "Could've been any number of things we saw. What she did..." His jaw tightened and he pulled on my waist like he wanted me closer. The only way I could get any closer would be sitting in his lap.

I gave his knee a reassuring squeeze. "Well, she's gone now."

"Thanks to you." He covered my hand, that tension in his face easing to something that might've been pride.

Lysander shared a look with Ari, their mouths twisting like they were fighting smiles. "She's well and truly gone now," he said, a glint in his eye, "they scratched her name out of of all the records, even did it magically in one I found. I couldn't retrieve any part, not even what letter it began with."

Ari scowled, her little hands fisting. She looked all the smaller surrounded by these tall men. "Whatever she did, whoever she was, they thought her so evil that even her name wasn't allowed to survive."

"Good riddance," Faolán growled.

"Interesting, though"—I raised my eyebrows at Ari—"some of the things she did made it to Albion. After you... left, townsfolk were telling stories about how the Night Queen sacrificed humans and ate their hearts."

"If I were you"—Bastian swirled his glass of wine, eyes on it—"I wouldn't mention such stories again." Despite the apparent ease of his pose, his voice was low and carried a note of warning.

At my side, Faolán tensed.

"Calm yourself." Bastian gave him a sidelong look. "Consider it a friendly warning. Remember where you are and who you work for."

"Hmm." Faolán exhaled, but his jaw worked side to side.

"I understand." I smiled at Bastian. Ultimately, the Night Queen was Faolán's boss, and I didn't imagine most rulers wanted people in their realm telling stories about them eating hearts, even if they weren't true.

Lysander cleared his throat. "You're lucky you got out of there. That source suggested she had unseelie blood and you know what they say about—"

Ari elbowed him in the ribs.

At my back, Faolán's arm was hard, his claws lightly digging into me.

I would've sworn it impossible, but Bastian had gone even more still. "And what is it they say about those with unseelie blood, Lysander?" His voice was soft in that way distant thunder was soft.

Chest and throat suddenly tight, I swallowed.

Lysander watched Bastian for a long while, though he didn't return the look. The air was thick, and I swapped a look with Ari that asked if we should do something. What was the problem? I filed that question away to ask Faolán later.

Eventually Lysander replied, "That they can be dangerous. These two are lucky they survived the month if she truly was part unseelie."

"Really, Rose," Ari said, a strained laugh lacing her voice, "I can't believe you ate that apple. Didn't you listen to Papa's stories?"

Maybe it was the laugh, but something in her tone deflated the tension, and Faolán scoffed. "*Thank* you, Ariadne." He flashed me a rueful grin. "I could've murdered her when I saw it in her hand, a bite taken out."

Lysander gave a soft chuckle. Even Bastian wore a

slight smirk as he shook his head. "And this is what you get for taking a human bride."

Faolán rumbled, but the corner of his mouth twitched. "Watch what you say about human brides." Then he actually did pull me into his lap, arms fastening around my waist.

"Oh good gods," Bastian groaned, "not you too? I thought that was a matter of convenience—just a year and a day."

"The duration is up to my wife." Faolán looked at me, a question in his eyes that stilled my heart for a beat.

Nose wrinkling, Bastian stood. "I'm sure this is a conversation I don't need to be involved in." He bowed his head to me before making for the exit. "Glad you're both safe. Faolán, take tomorrow off. We'll debrief fully on Tuesday."

Ari cleared her throat and made an excuse about needing to take Fluffy for a walk. "You'll have to come see our home soon—meet everyone. Though"—her gaze slid to the large bed—"maybe not for a few days yet. I'm sure you'll be busy." She actually winked at me before taking her husband's hand. She paused at the door and promised they'd take us to see my family as soon as I wanted, then with a wide smile, she left.

TWO PROPOSALS

Once they were gone, Faolán nuzzled into my neck, his breath hot. "I know I asked you once before, but that was different." He turned me in his lap and met my gaze as my heart stuttered. "Rose, love, will you *stay* married to me? More than just a year and a day."

My cheeks were tight from smiling so hard as I touched my nose to his. It was the easiest answer in the world. "Yes. Of course, yes."

For a moment the widest smile I'd ever seen flashed on his face, then we were kissing. The pleasure of being held close by him hummed through my veins; the joy of knowing we'd stay together glowed in my nerves.

At last he pulled back and cupped my cheek. "I was thinking about what you said earlier." He frowned and a shadow passed over his hazel eyes. "We can ensure that's a long time, if you want to."

I cocked my head. Ari and Lysander had bonded,

which I understood tied their power together so she would live as long as he did. "But I don't have any magic."

He huffed through his nose. "Yes, but what is *my* magic?"

"You're a wolf… amongst other things."

"Right. And?"

He hadn't really told me the full extent of his abilities, only that he could shift forms. I'd witnessed how his abilities gave him greater strength and speed, allowing him to tear apart a kelpie and snap a werewolf's neck with one hand.

"Oh! The werewolves." I sat up straight. "You said they come from shapechanging fae. You mean, you could change me and it would extend my life?" Trust Faolán, the man of few words, to propose this by making *me* say it all.

"Exactly." His mouth curved, but it was tight. "Only if you want it, though. And there's no guarantee it will work, but we can try."

A longer life to spend with him. That sounded much better than the tragic ending where I aged and died, while he lived on alone. "But… won't it make me vicious, monstrous like them?"

"No," he said on a sigh. "They are… unfortunates. Lost boys. The ones who made them didn't also raise them. So they became werewolves alone, eventually finding each other, and learning from other broken boys how to marry the two sides of themselves." His gaze went distant, sadder. "You can see it in the way they can't control their forms—the fur and talons—just as they can't control their inner beasts. That's why my kind have such a bad reputation. Other fae consider us animals."

I frowned and glanced at the chair where Bastian had sat. He teased Faolán, sure, but I hadn't seen any disdain on his face. "But not Bastian?"

Faolán shook his head, a small smile beating back the sadness. "Never Bastian. He saved me from that attack. It's how we met. He didn't know me, only what I was, but he helped me all the same. He's had his share of being judged." He squeezed me. "We're not talking about Bastian, though. We're talking about you. If you wish to be made, I will teach you. I'll make sure you never end up like those lost ones. We'll work together."

The way he said together—my chest filled with it. He'd already shown himself to be a good teacher as we'd trained. And we made a good team. This would be the same.

"And"—he pushed the hair back from my face—"even if you don't wish to change, I will stay with you until the end of your time. And when that comes…" His voice grew thick. "I'll go with you."

I blinked, opened and closed my mouth, had to swallow past the blockage in my throat at what he'd just offered. "You'd…?"

He nodded. "I promised to protect you, Rose, and I will—in this life and the next."

I leant into him and traced the edge of his jaw. "If I change… what will that mean?"

"No more iron blades." His mouth twisted and he nipped at my finger. "You'll get a bit temperamental around the full moon. Everything will smell different. As you learn to control your shift, you'll be able to change individual parts of yourself." He held up his hand and the claws grew.

"Control each part of yourself? Like..." My gaze flicked to his mouth, my own suddenly dry. "Like your tongue?" In front of the fire, I'd thought it felt longer inside me.

"Exactly like my tongue." His grin was wolfish.

How hadn't I realised what he was from the start? Except... I had known—deep down, I'd known that he was both beast and shield.

A shield could protect, yes, but it could also cave a person's head in.

"You don't need to decide now. We have time." He kissed my brow, my cheeks, my lips, each touch binding me inextricably.

As much as I'd known he was a shield, I'd also known he was a danger to me. But I hadn't realised the danger was to my heart and to my whole outlook on the world.

I wasn't only made to help my parents raise my brothers and sisters. I wasn't just here to help others with what they wanted. I had needs and wants of my own, including plenty that I hadn't even discovered yet.

And now I'd unlocked that part of myself, I would discover every last one of them, with my beautiful beast at my side.

EPILOGUE

e didn't rush. We stayed in the strange, nightly-changing city of Tenebris-Luminis for several months and visited my family many times. My parents and elder siblings stared at Faolán with all the surprise his size and fae features warranted. My youngest brothers and sisters treated him like a climbing frame and traced the points of his claws with fascination, asking all sorts of questions. Eventually I had to tell them "Because."

The house and the bakery were managing fine. Although Ari had told me as much, it was only seeing them that let me finally exhale.

Truth be told, that was what let me decide at last.

So one quiet week when Bastian had no need of Faolán, we travelled deep into the wild forest outside the fae capital. The walk was easy, thanks to all the exercise. Apparently the fae had no stupid ideas about women not being capable, and I could apply to join the palace guard if I wanted or Faolán had suggested Bastian might find work for me. I kept up my training while I decided what I wanted to do.

It was a day's trek to a tiny cabin with lupins and lavender by the gate and honeysuckle scrambling over the front door. A strong bar secured the door from within, though I wasn't sure anyone would want to steal anything from the sparse room with a bed, a sink, a free-standing mirror, and large cushions scattered before the fire. Faolán showed me the separate shed out the back with a bathroom fed by hot springs.

That night he barred the door, lit the fae lights with a word, and touched the mantlepiece to start the pink-flamed fire. We sat on the thick rug, bathed in its glow. Despite the warmth, though, I shivered.

He ran a hand up and down my arm. "Are you sure?" His voice was soft as he held me in his gaze, the gold flecks of his eyes tinged copper by the magical fire.

"I am." I gave a rueful smile. "Just a little nervous, too. It's not every day you become a werewolf."

The corner of his mouth twitched. "I should hope not."

Another almost joke from my husband. It was enough to make me snort and ease into him. "Come on, then. Let's make our forever."

He squeezed me close, as warming as the fire, and kissed my brow. "Until the bite, you can change your mind any time."

I caught his cheek and his gaze and held them a long while. "I won't. I meant it when I said I'd choose beast over beauty. I meant it when I said I wanted you, and these past months have only made that more true. And I'm greedy, so I want as much time with you as I can get."

His grin was crooked and more than a little preening before he ducked his head and began the change to fur and fangs, to four legs instead of two—my wolf, instead of my fae. I loved him just as much.

He rested his head in my lap for as long as it took to get a scratch behind the ears, then he looked up at me, solemn. *Are you ready?*

"I am." I held out my arm and drew a deep breath.

He opened his mouth, massive canines revealed. I didn't flinch, but he still paused there and although he didn't voice it in my mind, I knew what he was thinking.

One last chance to change my mind. To stay fully human. To reject the beast. To have just one lifetime with him.

Screw that. Screw *all* of it. I wanted forever with him, but I'd settle for as close to that as I could get.

I raised my arm to his open maw and placed my other hand firmly on his shoulder. "I'm sure."

The tips of his canines dimpled my skin first, and I held my breath, watching, as they sank in and blood welled. The pain started a moment later, shrieking at me to pull away. It thundered in my nerves. I bit my lip and forced myself to hold still, despite the tears gathering in the corners of my eyes.

Then came the burning.

It began at the pricks of pain where his sharp teeth had pierced me, then it was fire spreading and licking up my arm, across my shoulders, down my chest and back, racing through my veins.

I cried out, hand fisting in his fur.

His hazel eyes watched me, soft and sorry, and they were the last thing I saw before the pain took over and there was only darkness.

I HAD no idea how much later it was when I woke up. The fire still burned in the unnatural fae pink I'd seen throughout palace; it didn't consume wood, so gave me no indication of how long I'd been unconscious. Faolán was a solid, warm shape that I lay half draped over. His comforting scent filled my breaths, and beneath that the wood and sap of the cabin tickled my nostrils.

But I didn't feel different. It hadn't worked. I was still only human.

My eyes stung and I sat up, head hanging low. Could we try again? Or did this mean it would never work and I could never be a werewolf?

Still in his wolf form, he watched me, waiting on my reaction to this failure.

I swallowed down my disappointment, or tried to. It was too big, too much to force back and when I tried to speak, it blocked my throat so I couldn't even hear myself say, "It didn't work."

He angled his head. *Didn't it?* His breaths steamed the mirror as he nosed it, tilting it down towards us.

Two wolves looked back at us, one massive and grey

with hazel eyes, the other large, with light reddish fur and golden eyes flecked with sky blue. I looked over my shoulder, but couldn't find the creature in the cabin. That had to be some mistake or magic or…

I frowned, and the red wolf's brows twitched.

Wait. No.

I opened my mouth to say as much, but the wolf's mouth opened, too.

When I leapt up, sucking in a sharp breath, the wolf mirrored me.

Because it *was* me.

It worked. I circled and yipped. *It worked!* It felt like my whole back half was waving side to side, but when I looked back, it was just the tail trailing after me, wagging.

My tail. Faolán, I have a tail! I licked and nipped at him, the voice in my head squealing as I yipped out loud.

He nudged my face away, laughing. Even in my mind, it was one of the most perfect sounds I'd ever heard. *Calm down.* He dodged another lick from me, face screwing up. *You're like an overeager cub.*

But I'm a wolf, Faolán! We did it! I capered around the room, bouncing into the bed and walls more than once.

Good gods, what have I created? He groaned, but I caught the way his chest expanded and his eyes gleamed and even in his wolf form, I recognised it as pride coupled with happiness. Those same feelings tinged his mental voice as he instructed me on how to return to my human form.

We'd spoken about this decision at length. No matter

how I changed as a werewolf, I would still always be human, too. Just like I'd changed from the little girl I once was over the years, but still carried her with me.

On my second attempt, I made muscle, bone, and fur shift back to two legs, two hands, and smooth skin. In the mirror, I stared at myself, naked, Faolán behind me, his hands on my shoulders.

"We did it." I turned and flung my arms around him, burying my face into his chest.

"*You* did."

We stayed there, wrapped up in each other and our shared happiness, for so long my face hurt from smiling so much.

Eventually Faolán huffed, blowing the top of my hair. "So much for a year and a day." He grinned at me—that rare, unrestrained grin with no sign of grumpiness, and I laughed as much with pleasure at that as with amusement at his sardonic joke. He kissed the top of my head, then produced a wine bottle of cobalt blue glass. "I brought this because I knew we'd have something to celebrate." He winked and poured.

"You never doubted?"

"You?" He raised his eyebrows, handing me a glass of rich red wine. "Never." One arm looping around my waist, he held me close, our naked skin pressed together. He raised his glass. "To my wife. My beloved. My pack-mate. The sunshine to my raincloud."

I didn't need the fire—the love and joy in my chest was enough to warm even my bare skin. Vision blurring a little, I clinked my glass to his. "To my husband. My beauty *and* my beast. My packmate. The raincloud that keeps my world growing."

We drank and kissed, and the wine was sweet on our lips, a promise of a long, sweet life together.

THE END

If you're not quite ready to say goodbye to Rose and Faolán, you can get your hands on a bonus epilogue where they get married properly as a thank you gift for joining my newsletter.

A Note from the Author
Caution – Spoilers Within

I hope you enjoyed reading Rose and Faolán's story as much as I did writing it!

I had a lot of fun delving into something a little darker and twisting around the elements of the Little Red Riding Hood fairytale. Instead of the wolf being "the bad guy", it's little old Granny.

The title, *These Gentle Wolves*, is taken from Charles Perrault's close to the fairytale, where he spells out the moral of the story:

Children, especially attractive, well bred young ladies, should never talk to strangers, for if they should do so, they may well provide dinner for a wolf. I say "wolf," but there are various kinds of wolves. There are also those who are charming, quiet, polite, unassuming, complacent, and sweet, who pursue young women at home and in the streets. And unfortunately, it is these gentle wolves who are the most dangerous ones of all.

As soon as I saw the quote, I loved the contradiction of gentle and wolves – or at least it's a contradiction in terms of the expectation we have and the way they're portrayed in the fairy stories. I knew I'd found the title for Rose and Faolán's story.

If you're not quite ready to say goodbye to these two, you can get your hands on a bonus epilogue (where they get married *properly*) as a thank you gift for joining my newsletter at https://claresager.com/tgwsignup/

I email a few times a month with peeks behind the scenes of the fantasy romance books I'm working on, as well as giveaways and freebies.

Rose and Faolán make an appearance in *A Kiss of Iron* and will influence later events in that series. Read on for a sneak peek.

If you'd like to know more about Ariadne and Lysander's story (and Fluffy!), their book, *Stolen Threadwitch Bride*, is available now if you haven't already picked it up.

Thanks again for reading, and if you enjoyed, please consider taking a couple of minutes to leave a short review on Amazon and/or Goodreads. You've probably heard authors go on about it, but reviews really are important as they help other readers decide whether or not to take a chance on a book. Plus more readers means more people for you to squee about stories with! ;)

Remember to keep reading for your sneak peek of *A Kiss of Iron* and sign up for your bonus epilogue.

As always, happy reading!

All the best,

Clare

x

A KISS OF IRON

SNEAK PEEK

$$I$$

The moon was a sliver in the sky, a few days from disappearing altogether—a few nights from the Wild Hunt riding.

It gave me enough light to see by as my sabrecat, Vespera, picked through the undergrowth in silence. I rolled my hips with her gait, keeping my thighs loose: I didn't need speed from her, yet. Her ears flicked and her black coat gleamed, a stark contrast to how dull my red hair had grown this past year.

Beyond the trees and their shadows, the road was grey in the moonlight. And empty. I scowled and touched the butt of my pistol, like that would bring the prey I hunted.

If we wanted something more than cabbage and courgette on our plates next week, it needed to. We were down to the last of the flour, and I hadn't tasted meat in weeks. If I were a decent hunter, I'd come out in the day with bow and arrow.

But that was a big *if*.

I was a great shot, but an abysmal hunter. The butler, Horwich, had been passable, bringing rabbits to the table on the regular, but a slip on the ice last winter had ended his hunting career.

So instead, I rode at night seeking a different kind of quarry, one that frequented balls... Like the one this evening.

Once upon a time, the Viscountess Lady Katherine Ferrers had been invited to *everything*, but not anymore. She'd stopped accepting invitations so many years ago, drawing rooms were no longer abuzz with speculation. It had been a long while since anyone had called me lady anything. It was just Kat now.

Still, I got to hear about these things. And although I couldn't attend parties—wearing the same tatty gown every time would win me nothing but sneers—I could make use of them. And this way was much more practical.

I cocked my head. Was that a sound? With a gloved hand to her shoulder, I stilled Vespera and held my breath, listening.

At first, I was sure I must've imagined it. Wishful thinking.

But a distant pounding thrummed through the air, felt more than heard, and beneath me Vespera coiled like a spring.

After all these years, the adrenaline still kicked through me, making my skin tingle and my heart hammer. This was the only time I broke the rules, even my own.

They were simple. Some places and actions were safe. Home. Tending our vegetables. Grooming Vespera. And other places and actions weren't safe: almost everywhere and everything else. I didn't go there or do those. Except for when I rode at night.

Because it was less dangerous than the alternative, which was losing my home.

Besides, I was clever about it. I crept through the night, and I knew all the best routes for escape. I hid behind a hood *and* mask. And I'd have wagered my sabrecat was faster than any other in Albion.

There were a lot of reasons I'd never been caught.

Thank the gods. After all, the sentence for highway robbery was death, especially for the infamous Wicked Lady, as the papers called her—called *me*.

Thirty seconds after the initial thrum of paws on the road, came the squeak and rumble of a carriage in movement.

Partygoers heading home. Drunk and tired. And with any luck, their coachman had entertained himself with a hip flask—that would make my job easier.

Squeezing my thighs, I eased Vespera to the very edge of the forest. We'd wait here until the last possible moment when I'd block their way, pistols drawn—

A shriek pierced the night. The air in my lungs stilled. Even Vespera, so well-trained for any situation or surprise, lifted her head.

It almost sounded like a person. *Almost.*

But I knew that sound. A fox.

I peered out along the road. My quarry was a coach pulled by four sabrecats—that meant money. Lots of money. They could afford to pay my toll.

Again, the screech raked through the forest's darkness.

Shit.

If the coachman thought it was a woman screaming, he'd turn back. And then there would be no toll.

This would all have been for nothing.

Yes, there would be other nights, but tonight? It was my best bet—the lords and ladies travelling from the ball would be dripping in jewels. Although I wouldn't get their full value from my fence, I'd get enough.

With a near empty larder, I'd settle for enough.

Another shriek.

The carriage slowed.

"Shit," I muttered, making Vespera shift her weight.

I needed to chase off that fox.

WE CHARGED THROUGH THE FOREST, far enough from the carriage that they wouldn't hear the slight rustle Vespera couldn't help making at this speed. Even if they did, they'd put it down to the damn fox screaming like a woman being disembowelled.

Leaves and branches whipped past, forcing me to duck close to Vespera's back as I peered ahead. She wound between thick oaks and leapt over fallen trunks, breaths steaming in the chill of night.

Then we were in a moonlit clearing, a gap in the canopy big enough to see that sliver of ghostly white slashing through the night sky. And ahead, a flash of red, as bright as autumn.

The fox that was trying to fuck up my entire evening.

Except it looked like the poor thing was having a worse night than me, because glinting in the dim light was the thin line of a snare's wire. One end fastened to a tree, the other was buried in the thick fur of the creature's neck.

It didn't snarl or shrink away from me.

Brown eyes wide but calm, it watched as though wondering what I'd do. Which was a stupid thing to imagine, because animals didn't think like that, but...

It watched. And it waited.

Even in this silvery light, its thick fur was the richest red I've ever seen, deeper than my auburn hair. Its tail was a magnificent sweep of the same red tipped with white, and my fingers clenched around the reins, aching to test how soft it felt, how thick.

When they weren't taking chickens from our now empty coops, I'd always liked foxes. Clever and quiet, not obviously dangerous like a wolf or sabrecat. They snuck in, took what they needed, and vanished into the night.

This one was the most beautiful creature I'd ever seen.

And beautiful wasn't useful, but...

Blood specked the white of its throat. It was in pain.

Despite myself, despite my quarry back on the road, it tugged on my heart.

Besides, if I left it here in the snare, it would only scare away the coach. This was a matter of practicality.

"This is just so I can do my job," I told it with a nod before dismounting.

My leather gloves should give me some protection if it tried to bite, but I'd do my best to grab it by the scruff of its neck like a sabrecat cub.

Hands held wide, head bowed, I approached. "It's all right." I kept my voice soft and low. "I'm going to help you." *Quickly, so I can get back to that carriage and its fat purses.*

Even as I closed in, an arm's length away now, the fox didn't strain away at the end of the snare. It didn't react at all, just sat and waited.

Everyone knew a wild animal, even a semi-tamed one, would lash out when cornered and injured. Not this fox. In fact, its calm had grown eerie now, making the back of my neck prickle.

My feet stilled, telling me to turn and run.

Just some irrational fear. Listening to it would cost me the night's hunt.

I forced myself to take another step. "That's it." I wasn't sure if that was for the fox or my own skittish self. I'd been doing this—haunting the roads at night—for more years than I cared to remember. I couldn't afford fear. I certainly couldn't afford to give in to it.

"That's it. Nice and quiet." My heart pounded, louder

than the sabrecats on the road, as I lunged in, grabbing it by the scruff.

But it didn't dart away or snap at my hands.

And my bones ached with the wrongness.

"Unsafe. *Unsafe*," they whispered.

It was too late, because I had a handful of its fur. It looked up at me with eyes full of pain and far too much understanding for a fox.

My throat closed as I slipped a finger under the wire looped around its neck and drew my dagger.

You could kill it. That would keep it quiet.

It would. And it would quiet the feeling of wrongness slithering under my skin.

But...

Other than making me uncomfortable, this fox had done nothing wrong. Chances were that feeling was my mind playing tricks on me—the pressure of tonight's hunt making me foolish enough to entertain the idea a fox trapped in a snare was something more than just that.

"Pull yourself together, Kat." I yanked my blade through the wire.

Despite everything I told myself, I took a long step back.

As the snare dropped to the ground, the creature turned its neck side-to-side, something eerily human about the gesture. Then it stood. It was much larger than any fox I'd heard of.

I swallowed and didn't sheath my dagger. "There," I said, voice firmer than I felt, "you're free."

It regarded me with those large brown eyes for a long while before bowing its head. Its tail was the last thing I saw as it disappeared into the forest in silence.

Goosebumps picking their way across my skin, I hurried back to Vespera and mounted.

When we returned to the road, the carriage was gone. Only its tracks remained, leading away into the distance.

I slumped in the saddle. "Shit."

2

The next day I woke feeling like crap. That probably had something to do with the home brewed elderberry wine I'd used to drown my sorrows at the night's failure.

Sickness lurking at the back of my tongue, I dug in the vegetable beds, sowing seeds, coating my hands in mud like no "lady" should. Across the path, old roses watched, their thorns pricking me with my failures even from this distance.

Last night, I'd lurked on the forest's fringes, holding out for another carriage taking partygoers home. When dawn's pallor touched the sky, I had to accept I'd missed my chance.

Damn fox. I drove my trowel into the soil, sending up a spray of crumbly dirt.

In the sunlight, it felt utterly stupid that I'd even entertained the idea of the creature being anything more than an animal trapped in a snare. Fae weren't so stupid to get themselves caught. And save for the retinue that had presented itself to the queen recently, they hadn't been seen in Albion since before I was born.

It was just a fox. And I'd let the waning moon and promise of the Wild Hunt whip my mind into a foolish frenzy that saw strangeness and danger where there were none.

"Idiot," I muttered as I dropped seeds into the loosened soil.

Cursing that fox and myself, I worked past noon sowing, weeding, thinning out seedlings, and hunting slugs and snails. Since we'd been forced to slaughter the ducks last winter, it was my job to find the slimy bastards beneath stones and behind plant pots and squash them.

If the choice was between a slug and my vegetables, I chose my vegetables every time.

Just like I should've chosen my prey last night instead of that fox.

With a sigh, I finally went inside the third time the cook, Morag, called me from the kitchen door.

My head was about ready to explode and the heat kicked out by the oven didn't help. I slid into a rickety chair with a groan, depositing the radishes and salad leaves I'd harvested between my slug-murdering.

"Suppose you haven't eaten yet."

I didn't need to look up to know Morag was giving me That Look. The one where her lips were flat and her brow low—all disapproval and hard love. I'd learned to read people long ago. It was a useful skill—a survival skill with a family like mine.

"Felt too sick first thing," I muttered, shoving hair from my face where it had fallen loose while I worked.

"And I wonder why that is." I could *hear* the arched eyebrow in her tone. "Get this down you." She plonked a chipped mug on the table, the fresh scent of peppermint rising in its steam.

The smell didn't turn my stomach; I chanced a sip. It beat away the sick taste on the back of my tongue, so I kept drinking while she waved her rolling pin at me, eyes glinting.

"Look at the state of your hair. When was the last time you brushed it?"

I couldn't even summon the energy to wince. Although I hadn't looked in a mirror in... Gods, how long had it been?

"My hair doesn't matter."

"You need to look after yourself." She shook her head, tutting. "Out all night." Her look was meaningful, and I knew she knew what I did when I disappeared on Vespera, even if I never told her outright. "Then drinking that rubbish past dawn."

"I will." I tilted the cup as I shrugged. "Just as soon as the cabbage is harvested, the beds all weeded, the courgettes planted out, the hen house repaired, the gate rehung, that hole in the back fence patched up... And I'm sure there's something else I'm forgetting. *Then* there'll be time to look after myself."

That Look made a return, but the lines between her

brows were deeper and the shadows cast on her eyes darker. "And what if it's too late?"

Too late? I snorted. "I'll survive."

With a huff, Morag turned and stomped to the oven. Steam billowed out, carrying a sweet scent that had my mouth watering at once, all queasiness forgotten.

I frowned at her, even as I smacked my lips. "You didn't."

"I did." The little cake tins clashed against the tray as it thudded into the cork mat on the table.

The floral notes of honey in the air pulled a soft sound from my throat, but I clenched my hands. "We're supposed to be selling the honey, not eating it." My stomach growled, though, and my fatal weakness for sweet treats had me leaning over the table, inhaling as deeply as I could. Good gods, they smelled amazing. It had been so many months since I'd eaten anything so tasty, I could've wept with longing.

"Aye, well, I only used a tablespoon. The rest is in jars for selling." Her mouth softened as she looked at me, hands on her hips. "Treating yourself isn't a sin, you know."

Maybe it was that softness, maybe it was my weakness for the scent of fresh honey cakes, but part of me cracked as I looked back at her. I had to hold my breath and wait for the stinging in my eyes to fade.

Because I was tired.

So. Fucking. Tired.

Maybe that had made me prickly, not to mention ungrateful. So I sat up and nodded at Morag as she tipped one of the cakes from its tin onto a cooling rack. "Thank you."

At last she smiled, the hard glint gone from her eyes. "That's my girl."

When I reached for a cake, she swatted my hand. "Let them cool down first!"

I scoffed, rising and darting for the cooling rack before she could swat me off again. The sponge was hot and moist, perhaps too hot, but… "No time for that. Work to do."

As I backed away, she folded her arms and shook her head, That Look firmly back in place.

Standing in the doorway, I took a bite of the honey cake and sighed. Morag had lived and worked here since she was a girl. It was the only home she knew. Lucky for me, because she was good enough to work in any stately home she wanted. Yet she remained here in this crumbling manor where I could barely afford to keep up her wages. Selfish as it may be, I was intensely grateful as the cake's sweetness bloomed across my tongue.

Floral honey and the rich caramel flavour of brown sugar consumed me.

I sank into it. Lost myself in it. Just for a moment. Just that one spark of pleasure that eased my shoulders for a handful of seconds. Glorious and brief and, most importantly, *mine*.

I opened my mouth to take a second bite when a pounding came from the front doors.

Morag tensed, head canted in a question, eyebrows

twitching together in something that was part-confusion and part-concern.

"Looks like you get your way and I have to let it cool down." I grinned and deposited the rest of my precious cake on the cooling rack as I left the room.

Who the hells came to Markyate Cell? The once great estate had hosted balls and parties before I'd lived here. But it was a long time since we'd been able to afford to feed anyone outside the household. Recently, it had been challenging enough to feed the three of us.

I was untying my apron when the hammering knock sounded again, echoing through the empty halls. Not only a visitor, an impatient one.

Oh no. A chill crept over me. Not that prick's secretary again.

Some called my husband Lord Robin Fanshawe, but I preferred other, more inventive names. I hadn't seen the man in years, which suited me very well. I only heard from him when he needed money, which took the form of an invoice sent directly to the house from a landlord or tailor. Or, when I was *really* unlucky, when his secretary came to help himself to the contents of the safe on behalf of his master.

Such a loyal dog.

Jaw ratcheting tighter and tighter, I opened the large front door. "Mr Smythe, you're going to have to tell—"

The words withered on my tongue.

Because it wasn't the gangly secretary at the door.

3

A man stood on the top step, his charcoal suit smart but not *too* smart. Some sort of professional—the kind who worked in an office. An attorney, perhaps. But there was something a little rougher about him. Beyond, half a dozen burly men waited on the gravel driveway, arms folded. From their size and casual shirts and brown trousers, I guessed they were labourers.

My throat constricted. Attorneys meant trouble. And burly men meant more trouble. Either the official kind or the kind that hoped to find a woman home alone. I'd sent Horwich on an errand, and Morag was hearty for her age, but I wouldn't duck behind her for protection.

Home was usually safe—away from society, somewhere I didn't have to play by its rules. But this? This was decidedly *not* safe.

I clasped my skirts, wishing my fingers were

fastening around the butt of my pistol, but that was upstairs in my bedroom. No way would I outrun these men to reach it.

Politeness was my only protection. My back straightened, and it was shocking how easily I slid back into that old mould—ladylike and poised. "How may I help you?"

"Morning, miss." The suited man nodded. "We've come to execute the warrant. Has Lady Fanshawe…? Sorry, it says Ferrers on here." He glanced down at a sheaf of papers in his hand. "Has Lady Ferrers left the keys for us?"

"*I'm* Lady Ferrers." Yet my brain clamoured with questions. *Warrant? Keys?*

His eyes went wide and his face grew maybe a shade paler. "Oh. I was…" He gripped the papers with both hands now. "I thought you would've vacated the estate by now, milady."

"Vacated the estate? Why would I do that?"

He shuffled uncomfortably and cleared his throat. "Well, because of the warrant." He paused and when I didn't reply, raised his eyebrows. "The one served on Lord Fanshawe three months ago?"

"A warrant for what?"

But I knew. Deep down in the ice creaking through my bones, I knew.

"To seize the estate."

My breaths were too loud, blocking my ears. *Seize the estate. Seize the estate. Seize the estate.*

The sentence went round and round in time with the

drumming of my heart, a jumble of sounds I couldn't make sense of.

The man's mouth was still moving, but I didn't hear a word.

Seizing. Warrants. No more estate. No more home. Not safe. Not safe *at all*.

I blinked and found myself clutching the doorframe, the world spinning slowly, sickeningly.

"Milady, are you—?"

"What has he done?"

The bailiff explained. I took in half of what he said; it was enough.

The foetid cesspit I'd been married off to had secured a five-thousand-pound debt against Markyate Cell—the estate I worked myself to the bone to keep afloat. The estate that hadn't made that much money in any of the years I'd been here.

And, being a useless bag of bones, he'd failed to pay the debt *or* respond to the warrant he'd been served three months ago.

"Three months." The words scoured my throat. He'd known all that time, and he hadn't even sent a letter to warn me.

The bailiff shifted his weight, lips tightening as his fingertips traced the edge of the warrant in his hands. "You knew nothing of this until I appeared on your doorstep, did you?"

I shook my head, though it took far more effort than it should've, as if my bones were suddenly heavier and my muscles had forgotten how to work.

He swallowed and glanced down the steps at the men waiting. As though coming to a decision, he leant in closer, shoulders blocking them out. "Look, madam... they don't like us telling anyone about this, and normally I wouldn't, but it seems unfair on this occasion. There's a clause on the final page of the warrant." He flicked through the papers and held one up, but I couldn't take in anything more than a jumble of ink. "If you pay one tenth within a week, we'll accept that as part payment, with another tenth due a month later, and so on, until the debt is cleared. As long as you keep up payments, the estate won't be seized."

Five hundred pounds. That was still a huge sum, ten times what I paid Horwich in an entire year.

"I'll do it." I heard my voice as if it was from very far away. As if someone else had spoken.

His shoulders sank a fraction of an inch as though *he* was relieved. Putting the papers back in his briefcase, he promised to return in seven days' time. He handed me a card with the address of his offices and bowed his head before leaving.

Face tingling, I slammed the door and fell against it.

How the hells was I going to raise that much money in a week?

"A week!" My hysteria-edged voice bounced around the hall.

There was only one way I stood a chance. Despite the danger of being on the road so often, I had to ride every night.

Even that might not be enough.

A whole set of gold jewellery—necklace, earrings, brooch, bracelets—would bring in perhaps two-hundred and fifty. That was without the taint of stolen goods. I'd be lucky to get two thirds of that from my fence if she was in a good mood... a really, *really* good mood.

My stomach churned as I walked through the halls, no particular destination in mind. There was no space in my brain for anything other than what had just happened.

Five thousand pounds. *Five thousand*! That was a year's income, even for a wealthy gentleman.

At last, I stumbled outside and threw up everything I could. The mouthful of honey cake wasn't sweet coming back up. I could only taste bitter, sour bile as I heaved and heaved, tears gathering at the corners of my eyes from the effort.

When I looked up, the roses still watched.

How I used to love tending them.

Once upon a time, I'd read every book I could on the subject. I bought every different variety and fertiliser I could get my hands on, testing them in different beds to see what gave the best results. I wrote notes on the outcomes. I even started breeding different varieties together, seeing if perhaps I could create something new. But my project ended before they had a chance to flower.

Because I found out the truth about my husband's debts and the floundering financials of the estate.

What a foolish girl. Such frivolous concerns. It had been an utterly pointless way to spend my time. Roses were pretty and they smelled divine, but they were useless.

Vegetables, though—they were entirely practical. They'd kept us going these past few years.

And with the bailiff breathing down my neck, we would need to grow and hunt all our food for the foreseeable future.

Before I even consciously thought about it, I was approaching the nearest rose bed. The soil crumbled under my feet, still clayish after all this time. The soft sensation made me want to sink to my knees and clip the tangled stems to ensure I'd get the fattest flowers. For a moment, I paused, weight on my toes, so close to succumbing.

But only for a moment.

I didn't bother to dig, I just grabbed close to the base. Dry bark cracked in my grip as I pulled. The stunted bush came out easily—too easily. Its roots had been half dead for a long while. I threw it to one side and started on the next.

Thorns tore at my palms. Pinpricks of beautiful, useless pain.

I didn't stop.

Their twisted branches tangled in my hair. They scratched my face.

Teeth gritted, I yanked out that one and the next and the next.

I needed food more than I needed this reminder of past beauty.

Maybe that hot liquid trickling down my cheeks was blood from the scratches. Perhaps it was tears.

I'd killed for the sake of survival. I'd fucked a husband I hated for the sake of *survival*. Tears were as useless as the roses I ripped up, but blood? Yes, I would bleed for survival.

Whatever it took.

4

The gods weren't on my side, judging by the rain pouring in a constant drizzle. But fuck them if they thought a bit of weather was enough to put me off.

I didn't love Markyate Cell the way some aristocrats might love their estates. It didn't belong to me; it was *his*.

Part of me would've been perfectly happy to watch it all burn—the angry, seething part that was all thorns and no flowers. But without it, I had no home. And Morag and Horwich needed it just as much. She refused to move away, and since his accident, he relied on a walking stick and would struggle to get another job.

So despite my stupid husband frittering everything away on his grand tours and terrible "investments," I'd spent ten years trying to clear up his financial mess. And I faced losing it all anyway.

Fuck him, too.

Selling a parcel of land from the estate's edges

would've helped when the debts were smaller. Every time I'd asked, he'd refused—that was back when he bothered to reply to my letters at all. Being a woman, by Albionic law, I didn't even own the land myself: I needed his permission to sell it.

Fuck the law, especially.

So I rode and peered through the drizzle.

And I found nothing.

No coaches. No riders. Not even a fox's screams on the breeze. Just the splatter of rain rippling through puddles and spiking Vespera's fur in black tufts. Her ears bent forward and she kept her head down, as fed up with the weather as I was.

But come winter, the weather would be far worse, and if the bailiff took the house, we wouldn't have a roof, never mind fuel or food. So I clicked my tongue and urged her on.

"I'm sorry." I stroked her powerful shoulder, every muscle in my body aching from the day's work. "I'll let you come in and lie in front of the fire—promise."

She huffed, breath misting in the cool air before it disappeared in the drizzle's constant grey.

I couldn't tell if the sun threatened on the horizon yet, because the clouds blocked out everything. It felt late enough for that to be a real possibility. My tired shoulders sank as I turned Vespera on the road home and fixed my gaze between her ears.

Another night, another failure.

I only had a week. I'd ride out every night if I had to. Yes, I could sell the last of the furniture, but that wouldn't come close to five hundred pounds. Robbery was my only chance.

The weather had kept people off the road tonight, but last night had been clear: there should've been more than just that one carriage. Maybe the Wicked Lady's reputation had scared people from travelling far after dark. If they stayed with the hosts of their parties or at nearby inns, they'd be indoors and safe before I had a chance to reach them.

If they kept that up...

"Shitting hells."

Despite the rain, Vespera's ears pricked. She lifted her head, and her nose twitched, steam puffing out.

My heartbeat sped. "What can you smell?" Urging her to the edge of the road, I peered ahead. It was long minutes before I spotted a figure in the drizzle-haze.

A lone rider.

My breath caught, and I steered into the forest's edge. Pickings wouldn't be as rich as with a carriage, but a lone rider was more vulnerable. I'd take whatever I could get.

Still, what would drive someone out in this weather? Desperation like me? Or something else?

We waited, and I chewed my lip. They had a sabrecat, so they probably weren't poor. But what if the cat was borrowed or stolen? The Wicked Lady's fearsome reputation came from preying on the rich—after all, they had the most to take, and they screamed loudest to the newspapers when it was taken. But most of all, they could afford the loss.

I wouldn't take from those who had too little.

I drew my pistol and cocked it, watching as the figure came closer, closer. Like me, he wore a hood. Broad shoulders and a sure seat despite his cat's swift canter. He knew how to ride, and he was large enough that I wouldn't want to face him in a toe-to-toe fight.

But that was what my pistols were for.

I drew the second one, eyes burning as I stared, waiting for details to resolve themselves and tell me whether he was a have or have not.

He was five sabrecat lengths from where I needed to step out if I was going to stop him, and I still didn't know.

I strained forward, holding Vespera still with the butt of my pistol on her shoulder. My heart thundered, and I couldn't hear anything except for that and the constant rain.

Please. Please, gods.

His sabrecat took another stride. Slate grey, powerful flanks, elongated canines gleaming. No decoration on the saddle, but its cut was so sleek it had to be made for his cat, not second hand. His hooded coat was plain, too, but dyed a rich, pure black. Darker than any simple farmer could afford... or was it just so sodden, it looked that dark?

I swallowed, caught between lifting my hand from Vespera's shoulder and letting the man pass.

What to do?

Then the dim light gleamed on something that wasn't just another puddle or the wet fur of his sabrecat.

A small metal sphere chained to his belt.

Not just metal, *gold*.

I didn't have time to work out if it was gold or brass.

Two more strides and he'd be beyond my ambush point.

I lifted my hand, and Vespera surged forward.

---

*Kat's adventure continues in **A Kiss of Iron**, book one in a steamy new fantasy series featuring a scorching enemies-to-lovers slow burn romance full of deceit, desire, and dark secrets.*

Acknowledgments

Thank you to all my readers – you are brilliant and I appreciate every review, message, and share! They really do mean the world and help more than you know. <3

Thanks to May Sage for inviting me to the Flirting With Darkness anthology where this story first appeared, and thus for giving me the excuse to write Rose's story!

Thank you to Dominique Wesson and Saint Jupit3r Graphics for the covers for this book – they're both stunning and I loved working with you!

Thanks, as always, to my author wives for all your support and advice. Carissa, Lasairiona, and Tracie – you are the best! <3

Thanks to my actual husband for all your support, patience, and for being the best partner in crime I could ask for.

ALSO BY CLARE SAGER – SET IN THE SABREVERSE

SHADOWS OF THE TENEBRIS COURT

Gut-wrenching romance full of deceit, desire, and dark secrets.

Book 1 – *A Kiss of Iron – Now in Audio*

Book 2 – *A Touch of Poison*

Book 3 – *A Promise of Lies*

BOUND BY A FAE BARGAIN

Steamy fantasy romances featuring unwitting humans who make bargains with clever fae. Each book features a different couple, though the characters are linked.

Stolen Threadwitch Bride (Ariadne & Lysander)

These Gentle Wolves (Rose & Faolán)

MORTAL ENEMIES TO MONSTER LOVERS

Five fantasy romances each by different authors, set in their own worlds. These enemies to lovers stories are united in their promise to deliver "I came to kill you" angst, scorching romances with inhuman, morally grey heroes, and happily ever afters.

Slaying the Shifter Prince, by Clare Sager (Featuring Zita and Sepher)

Discover the full series here:

www.mortalenemiestomonsterlovers.com

BENEATH BLACK SAILS

An enemies-to-lovers tale of piracy, magic, and betrayal.
Featuring Kat's sister Vice. Complete series.

Book 0 – *Across Dark Seas – Free Book*

Book 1 – *Beneath Black Sails*

Book 2 – *Against Dark Tides*

Book 3 – *Under Black Skies*

Book 4 – *Through Dark Storms*